WHEN SPARKS FLY

THE FALLOUT DUET BOOK ONE

AMANDA MARQUARDT

SILVER LANE PUBLISHING

Editing by Megan Carver

Proofreading by Hannah G. Scheffer-Wentz, English Proper Editing Services

Cover art and design by KBG Designs

Paperback ISBN 979-8-9915280-1-6

EBook ISBN 979-8-9915280-0-9

CONTENTS

Dedication

To me. For all the times you lied to yourself and said you never finish anything you say out loud. You did it.

INTRODUCTION

Dear Reader,

Thank you for taking the time to read When Sparks Fly! I can't wait for you to experience the start of Maci and Sutton's story. Their small-town romance includes city life, ranch life, and a motorcycle club. A glossary is available for some terms that may be unfamiliar.

If you are family, and have somehow stumbled upon this book, no you haven't. Put it down and back away. This book is intended for readers 18+. It contains on-page depictions of sexual situations and adult language.

This is not a dark romance, however, it does touch on sensitive subjects. Your mental health matters, so please consider before reading. If you prefer to read without spoilers, now is the time to skip ahead.

Content includes death (not on page) and grief, discussion of birth trauma (human and animal), animal hunting (no animals are harmed), discussion of assault, on page aggression/assault, weapons (knives, guns, crossbows). Addiction is also referenced in a joking manner.

If, considering all of this, you would like to continue, happy reading! Enjoy Bull Creek!

GLOSSARY

Ranch Life

Ag - Agricultural education

Caliche - A white soil made of mineral deposits used for farm and county road paving

Blind – a concealed area used for hunting

Bull - intact male

Cattle - ungendered plural

Cow - full grown female

Heifer - unbred female

Springing Heifer - pregnant heifer in final weeks of pregnancy

Steer - neutered male

Tack – equipment or accessories used on horses

Motorcycle Club Terms

Cut - leather or denim vest (leather in this book)

Member - official members who have been voted into the club

MC - motorcycle club

Patch - insignia applied to cut to denote personal identity within the club

President/Prez - Club leader

Prospect/Probate - probationary member until fully voted in

Rocker - a curved patch that carries the club name(top) and area or region (bottom)

Playlist

Humble and Kind – **Tim McGraw**

Me Too – **Meghan Trainor**

Lost Without You – **Freya Ridings**

Dancing in the Sky – **Sam Barber**

My Way – **Ava Max**

If You Go Down (I'm Going Down Too) – **Kelsea Ballerini**

Copperhead Road – **Steve Earle**

Everything There Is To Know About You – **Mark Wills**

The Red – **Chevelle**

Wildfire and Whiskey – **Tenille Arts**

Head Over Boots – **Jon Pardi**

Break Stuff – **Limp Bizkit**

Wildfire – **Miranda Lambert**

Taste – **Josh Abbott Band**

Made For – **Will Dempsey**

Till There's Nothing Left – **Cam**

Black – **Dierks Bentley**

Arsonist's Lullaby – **Hozier**

CHAPTER 1

SUTTON

The quiet of the still dark morning is broken when I push the front door open to The Big House. Together with the unmistakable sizzle of bacon frying in a pan, the aroma of strong coffee and baked goods beckon from down the hall. The door has barely closed behind me when Mama's head pokes into the hallway from the kitchen. She's made breakfast for our family and our small ranch staff every day of my life.

Except for when my sister, Sammi, was in the hospital.

"Hi, honey." Mama's welcoming smile and matching tone are always so full of love, never tired of seeing the same faces or completing the same tasks.

"Is Dad in here?" My dirty boots thud against the wood floor as I head up the hall, stopping to kiss Mama on her head.

"He's in his office." She flips the bacon and I nod at two of our three staff, seated in the dining room adjacent to the kitchen on my right. The ranch hands have a separate bunkhouse, but The Big House is always open for breakfast. Not all ranches do it our way, but it fits us.

I make my way through the cozy living room on the left and into the back hallway. Dad's office is the first door I come to. It's ajar and he sits behind the mahogany desk, in his leather chair. I double-tap the trim with a knuckle as I enter, drawing his eyes up.

1

"Mornin'." He's a quiet man, not often annoyed by interruptions. We've spent a great deal of time discussing the ranch in this space. Lost animals, sales, purchases, increasing prices, tack, the list goes on and on.

I take up my usual spot, sitting on the leather couch across from his desk, and throw one ankle onto the opposite knee. He gives me a knowing smile.

"How do the numbers look?" His reference to weighing and categorizing cattle last week is right on time. The last few weeks have been all about assessing our two herds. We weigh and examine each animal, and consider their overall health, productivity, and potential. Determining which cows to keep to maintain the integrity of the herd, along with which animals to sell for beef, and which to keep to continue cattle production is all based on these considerations. I dive into what our groupings looked like.

Occasionally we trade with other ranches, but this year has been good to us on bulls, so we won't need to.

"So it sounds like between the two herds, we have five solid bulls." Dad seems pleased with his confirmation.

He's equally happy with hitting our numbers for our clients in town expecting beef. With repeat, steady commercial and private customers, meeting that goal is our bread and butter. Thankfully, through the year we've also built strong ties with butchers in town, which helps everyone involved.

Once he's abreast of the details of the last few weeks, I continue. "I've been thinking. I have some ideas for the ranch."

Dad kicks back in his chair, the bulk of it leaning far enough back on the swivel to tease at falling over. "What do you have in mind?"

"My thoughts are two-fold. Diversify what Strickland Ranch is known for and find ways to generate increased stable income. If we had more acreage, then expanding the herds or adding a third, and expanding our clients, would be an option. But with what we've got, I'm not sure that's our best option."

He steeples his fingers in front of his chest as I continue. "If we break the resting pastures down differently we could offer one as a hunting lease. Maybe two. It would keep the land active with rotating crops and wildlife, without additional hardship on natural resources. Guided hunts and companion livestock could also be options to increase exposure and revenue."

For a few beats, he says nothing as his head bobs in thought. "I like where your head's at."

"Thank you." His praise catches me off guard.

"I already trust you to handle this place on your own. You did as much earlier this year when your sister was in the hospital. I know it's a bit of a formality that I'm still running things."

I squeeze my leg. This is not where I saw the conversation going. "I never considered it a formality. I assumed if and when you decided you were ready for things to change we would discuss it."

"I think we need to start discussing it."

My eyes widen and I make a point to tamp down my surprise.

"I'm not saying you need to take over tomorrow." He leans forward, resting his arms on the desk. "But you're right; we need to start looking to the future. The ranch needs that."

"Yes, sir." I hadn't realized he'd considered any of this. "Alright. I'll put together a more detailed plan and we can talk it over."

"Sounds good." His eyes twinkle. "One more thing. Have you picked a location to build on?"

A couple of months ago this came up, but the timing didn't feel right. Unlike some legacy cattle ranchers, my role was never assumed.

Rather than attend Ag school, a common track for those who want a role similar to mine, I worked up from a stable boy mucking stalls and grooming horses, until I had learned as much as I could and felt honest in my position as Ranch Manager. I cared more about being on the ranch. Ag school was too far away and I didn't just care about any business, any ranch, any livestock. I cared about the legacy of our family's ranch. Strickland Ranch.

I've saved my growing salary over the years for when I would ultimately build a house. Even with a private entrance to my quarters, more separation would be appreciated. I certainly never anticipated being thirty and living in my parents' house.

"Not quite. I'll get on it." I stand. "I'm headed into town. Need anything?"

He shakes his head.

On my way through the house, I stop in the kitchen to swipe a fresh muffin. The large baked good is still warm in my hand when I pluck it from a tray on the counter. Mama turns sharply, but her features are too soft to be scary.

"Those are for tomorrow." Her tone is matter-of-fact as her hand finds her hip.

I grin. "This one's for today." She opens her mouth, but I don't give her a chance before I bite into it, affixing a mischievous smirk to my face while I chew. Her jaw opens in a silent gasp.

"Banana nut," I observe, after swallowing. "I'm heading into town. Do you need anything while I'm out?"

She presses her lips together to hide her amusement and shakes her head. "No. I'll see you in a bit, son."

I make my way out to my truck. Daisy saunters by the porch steps as I reach the bottom. She bonks her big, red head into my chest affectionately and I give her a pat.

Daisy is an anomaly on the ranch and it's all Mama's fault. Her mom died shortly after delivering. Orphaned calves are typically paired with another cow, but Mama wouldn't hear of it. She bottle fed her in The Big House for entirely too long. When she finally gave in, Daisy's mind was made up that she belongs up here. She's a Houdini of cows, always escaping to say hi and wander around the area near the house.

"Mornin' to you, too, Daisy."

She heads down the drive as I climb into the truck.

My plans this afternoon could be handled electronically or through the mail, but meeting in person maintains our personal relationships with vendors and town residents.

Already a core value, our newly discussed transition makes this an even bigger priority for me. I've been the face of Strickland Ranch for a few years, so I'm optimistic it won't feel like much of a change to everyone else.

My last stop is always a restaurant where we frequently sell beef so I can return a bit of patronage to them. The bar fills one of the two rooms, surrounded by dark leather booths, and is a good place to have a quiet drink.

A few lunch patrons stop in while I savor a whiskey at a stool on the far end, glad no one talks to me today. People are fine in moderation; I'm a friendly enough guy, but even though I'm working on tasks for the ranch, I enjoy a peaceful break from the chaos when possible.

Three TVs line the wall above the liquor selection, all set with the volume on low, and I study the one closest to me. A show about Texas Game Wardens is running. They don't film in our area, and it's a good thing or my best friend, Nick, would blow up on social media overnight.

Not that he'd take advantage. Nick is the type you trust with your sister: even-tempered, respectful, and loyal. I don't have to worry about that since Sammi's married and they never had a thing for each other, which I'm grateful for. Despite trusting him, my sister and my best friend dating would be awkward as shit.

Nick doesn't need celebrity status. On the occasions when we're out, he draws enough attention with his charismatic personality. Being handsome helps, according to Sammi.

I set the empty tumbler and some cash on the bar, and wave to the bartender as I head out the door. I'm eager to get back to the ranch. I plan to sit down this afternoon and work on a proposal of what growth could look like over the next two years.

Strickland Ranch has been my parents' baby since they were first married. While Sammi showed no interest in the ranch—past horses—I've always wanted to carry on the business and lifestyle my parents built. As a teenager, I took on a bigger role to assist my dad, enabling my mom to step back. She can't help but take care of everyone, but it's given her more and more freedom over the years to explore other ways to be a part of the community.

My dad is different. He's friendly, but he doesn't necessarily care about socializing. I want him to be as involved as he wants for as long as he wants, but based on our conversation this morning, I suspect he may take a backseat sooner rather than later.

A handful of ranches dot the land on my drive home. Most are smaller than ours. These days, the area is predominantly single-family residential homes, hoping to maintain a bit of tranquil privacy away from the big city. Life in the hill country is such a mash-up. The same roads showcase custom homes on heavily treed properties, next to pasture land, next to rocky terrain full of shrubbery.

As I round the last bend to our property, a truck going the opposite way slows and I recognize our neighbor, Terrence, in the driver's seat. He shoves an arm out the open window and waves urgently at me. I wave back as he whips the truck around and follows me to the drive where we pull over on the side of the road. He parks behind me, jumping out in a hurry.

Neighbor is a loose term. Terrence is closer to my dad's age than mine and inherited the ranch next to us when his dad passed several years back. Our driveways are about two miles apart and we aren't popping over for a cup of sugar when it's out, but we have helped each other in a bind and our families have known each other all of my life.

"How are ya, sir?" I greet, exiting my truck.

"Good, good. How ya been?" Terrence has one of the strongest southern accents I've ever heard, and that's saying something. He shakes my hand, his rich umber skin glistening in the heat, then adjusts his deep green ball cap which bears their ranch name.

"Doing well. What brings you over today?" Terrence is welcome at our ranch, always has been, but his sudden need to speak to me is unusual.

His dark eyes scan me and the truck casually. "I don't wanna take up a bunch of your time. We can sit down and chat if we need to, but I wanted to tell ya about somethin', in case it matters."

Terrence's property butts up against ours on the west side, so any problems he has can spill over onto our property with no effort. I'm not interested in handling illness in the cattle, or any other catastrophe, with everything else going on. I do my best not to tell him to get on with it.

"Well," he pauses, peering into the uninterrupted horizon across the street from us, "I'm sellin'."

7

My jaw slackens, but I manage not to let it fall open. Of its own will, my mind begins running through various scenarios. Ultimately, I know gaining the property Terrence has could be a massive expansion for us. At the moment, I have no idea how we could make it happen. It would be a huge endeavor, financially and logistically. A kernel of desire sparks in my chest anyway and I don't extinguish it.

"Well, that's certainly something." I try to remain impassive.

He spits into the ditch. "I haven't gotten with a broker, yet. Wanted to give ya a heads-up first." He's throwing me a bone and he knows it. My head bobs up and down in affirmation.

"If ya wanna discuss it, let's set up a time to chat. I'm on my way into town, but thought I'd grab ya since I saw ya," he says.

"Appreciate it, sir. I'll let you know." He shakes my hand one last time and then heads back to his truck.

This could be the move I need to get us where I think we need to be. I wave as Terrence pulls past me onto the road and turns around. He gives me a two-finger wave through the passenger window.

I drive through the front gate and over the cattle guard, veering left at the fork in the road toward the stables and the barn. The stables house all of our supplies and equipment, plus stalls for our horses. The barn serves to hold excess food, calves who need bottle feeding, and animals needing vet care.

Our permanent ranch hands, Jason, Kelly, and Cody, happen to be near the stables when I pull up. I motion toward the trailer for them to start unloading.

We hire seasonal help on occasion and sometimes get a dumb shit or two, but these three are the bulk of our team. As we grow, one of them will need to step up to fill a role similar to mine. If this new endeavor comes to fruition, this party will get a whole lot bigger. I look over the three of them, already speculating at who can move up.

CHAPTER 2

MACI

I'm positive I will wither away and die if I don't get something to eat soon. My stomach grumbles in agreement.

The sun is lowering behind the tree line, casting the nature preserve where I'm set up in dusky light. Sweat trickles down my spine and my long, dark hair is like a blanket against my neck. The ebbing light is doing nothing to relieve the day's stifling heat. Texas refuses to admit it's autumn.

In contrast, I fully embraced October and all its glory for family photo sessions today. Halloween is my favorite.

The last family of the day is leaving with their witch-costumed toddler. "I'll send your proof package over as soon as it's ready. These are going to be adorable!"

"I can't wait to see how they turn out!" A huge smile splits the mom's face as she almost squeals at me. She squeezes me in a hug before they gather their things and head back to the parking lot.

A small would-be lemonade stand draped with black tulle sets the Halloween scene. Glass bottles of various shapes and sizes, painted in black matte, line the mantle. Their white lettering reads things like "Pick Your Poison" and "Tail of Newt". One showcases a Jolly Roger. A tiny, round folding table topped with black pumpkins, a glittery skull, and a plastic cauldron completes the whimsical look.

It takes two trips to load my Jeep with the backdrop and decor items before I can jump in and turn the AC on full blast. I beeline for the nearest drive-thru. A juicy bacon cheeseburger with all the veggies—except onion, because seriously, who eats that—is just what I need. My mouth waters and I shove a scalding parmesan fry into my mouth before clearing it with my vanilla shake. An appreciative groan escapes into the otherwise quiet Jeep. This simple pleasure is the cherry on top of a perfect day.

Rush hour traffic in Austin is always a nightmare, but it gives me a chance to finish my meal. A few minutes before I reach my apartment, I use the preset to call my grandmother.

"Hellooo?" Her silly greeting floats through the phone to me, lightening my heart. There's nothing she can't fix. Today was a high, but so many times I called during lows over the years and just hearing her comforting voice often gave me the strength I needed to persevere.

"Hi, Nana."

"Hi, baby. How are you?" Even through the phone, her love wraps me in a much needed hug.

"Good. I just got done with some mini-sessions and now I'm headed home."

"That sounds nice. How did the photos go?" The TV chatters in the background.

"Actually, really well. Most of the kids were comfortable. I'm sure it helped that most of them were in Halloween costumes. The last one was a witch and she was so cute!"

"Oh, good!" Nana's entire personality can be summed up as a sassy heart of gold. I know her care for these children having a good time during their photos is genuine. Talking to her only intensifies my need to see her. I miss her so much and long for the days we were under the same roof. Summers and holidays spent with Nana make up most of my favorite memories.

"What do you have going on tomorrow?"

"Oh, baby, you know I'm so busy." A giggle tumbles out before she's had time for the joke to land.

"You're so silly." I shake my head with a small laugh of my own. "I want to take you to lunch. Think you can pencil me in?"

"Oh, I'd like that. I want to see some of your recent work."

"I'll bring some things for you to keep this time," I promise.

The unmistakable sound of her hands clapping once in excitement bursts through the phone. "That'll be wonderful."

"Where do you want to eat?" I park in my usual spot and gather my trash.

"How about Aimee's?"

"The French bistro? Ok." I should have known she'd pick her favorite place. I'd be happy with sun tea and her cheesecake, but I want her to get out for a bit. "I'll be there around eleven. Is that ok?"

"Yes, baby. See you then. I love you so much." She makes a sweet kissing sound.

"Love you, too, Nana. See you tomorrow."

After a long shower, I settle on the couch dressed in my favorite comfort leggings and a thin, baggy sweater. The coffee table is hidden beneath my laptop and folders from today's clients. The scent of toasted marshmallow fills the living room, wafting from the lit candle on the side table. Faux pumpkins, similar to the ones I used in photos today, surround it.

My tiny one-bedroom apartment is minimally decorated, aside from my celebration of fall. I never spend much time, effort, or money on decor if it isn't photos.

Color prints of my favorite shoots from over the years hang above the thrifted, suede couch. The coffee and side table, also second-hand, don't match. None of the three pieces fit any one aesthetic, nor was I focused on one.

A giant spoon and fork are mounted over my bistro set in the blip of a dining room. I think every aesthetically hopeful dining room in America has the same set. In the hall are my favorite black and white photos. Five years I've been here and it's always seemed temporary.

Before getting started on editing the photos from today, I check the group chat with my best-friends, Izzy and Leah. No messages. I send a quick message wishing Izzy a safe arrival in Hawaii and reminding her to take a thousand and one photos so that I can live vicariously through her. Her obligatory "I got leid" picture fills my screen in response, eliciting a huge grin. She's all legs in a pale blue dress with a golden lei around her neck. Leah follows up with entirely too many middle finger emojis.

Our trio is akin to Neapolitan ice cream. Izzy is vanilla. Not because of her ice-blonde hair, but because she's subtle, reliable, and always put together. She fits well in every situation. Leah is strawberry. A little bit tart, a little bit sweet. The wild one that maybe you don't expect to enjoy, but thoroughly do because it's strawberry and how could you not? And I'm chocolate. Versatile in a similar way to vanilla, but packing a bigger punch and also not everyone's cup of tea.

I work until my eyes blur, managing to edit half of the photos from today's mini sessions, before padding into my bedroom with my phone. The stark white, thousand-thread-count, Egyptian cotton sheets call to me. Only the bed has received luxury attention in the years I've lived here. Otherwise, I splurged on photography equipment, backdrops, or session decor. Focused solely on building my business and honing my craft, everything else was an afterthought.

I set my phone on my secondhand nightstand, flip off my lamp, and shove myself deep in the covers, asleep instantly.

Sometime in the night, my phone vibrates across the nightstand, jarring me awake. Adrenaline surges through me. *Stephanie*, my mother's name, flashes on the screen, adding to the dread.

I put my phone to my ear, pushing my hair from my face and sitting upright. My mother's curt voice comes down the line before I can utter a greeting. Her clipped tone isn't a surprise, but the words she's throwing at me are crushing.

"Mother passed. The funeral will be this weekend."

"Nana?" My voice is a cross between a squeak and a croak. Obviously, she's referring to my grandmother, but my brain is frazzled.

People talk about pain being a knife to the heart, but this is a battering ram. A crushing force on my chest making it nearly impossible to breathe.

Stephanie's words remain composed. "Alan and I are driving down now." I'm only half listening to my mother's voice.

How did this happen?

"I don't understand. I just talked to her." My eyes land on the album and loose photographs I prepared to take to Nana.

Stephanie scoffs. "These things happen quickly, Maci."

Silent tears hit my cheeks. I know better than to count on her for emotional support.

While my relationship with my mother has been strained since I was a teen, my relationship with Nana only grew over the years. Despite my lack of proximity, I often called Nana daily through high school. The calls may have been less frequent in the six years since graduation, but our bond never diminished.

This loss is compounded by knowing how close I was to seeing her.

CHAPTER 3

MACI

I can't go back to sleep after we hang up. Instead, I prepare for a long weekend in Bull Creek, starting with emailing my recent clients about a delay due to a family emergency. While packing a suitcase, I make sure to pick the perfect dress for the service.

Lunch with Nana would've been a day trip, including the two-hour drive each way. Now, it makes more sense to stay in Bull Creek at Nana's for the weekend.

The sun chases my Jeep as it rises behind me when I eventually head for Bull Creek. Twisty roads, single-stoplight towns, and spotty reception greet me on my drive. This road has been calming in the past, offering a peaceful, often uninterrupted expanse of road, perfect for daydreaming. Today, each mile heightens my anxiety at dealing with Stephanie and Alan, my step-father, and facing this heartbreaking loss.

I choose soft music to fill the background of my thoughts, emotionally ill-equipped to deal with love songs or heartbreaking lyrics. When I lose signal on the back roads, I'm forced to switch over to the radio from my streaming app, adjusting the station as I drive in and out of coverage areas.

By the time I reach the east outskirts of town, I've been subjected to at least three self-indulgent radio hosts. Three too many for my liking. More coffee would help curb my building frustration, but my travel mug is empty.

Instead, silence reigns when I smash my finger on the radio power button, ceasing the incessant chatter.

There are three whole stoplights in Bull Creek. I turn left at the second, where River Road and Main Street meet, and head south. Then it's a right at the first to drive across town and back into the hill country to Nana's house.

Dread fills my insides the closer I get to my final turn. I have half a mind to turn around and head straight for a bar. At last check, there were only two to choose from. Stephanie's reproachful voice echoes in my head, speaking of obligations to be fulfilled.

Obligations.

As if this is nothing more than a task on a to-do list. For her, it likely is.

Still, the promise of an ass-chewing isn't what keeps me moving toward Nana's house. There is nowhere I'd rather be than honoring Nana's life, even if I would prefer to mourn her in relative peace. Something that will never be achieved with my mother and step-father around.

Mature oak trees line the driveway, greeting me at the entrance, and lead directly to Nana's farmhouse. Alan's Mercedes is parked next to Nana's older Toyota on the gravel near the house. My Jeep settles behind her sedan, but I don't get out.

I wait for the echo of the drive to vacate my ears and then take in my reflection. Swollen eyes stare back at me from the rearview mirror. Crying intensifies the vibrant green of my irises, an uninvited positive. Soft brown hair is falling from the loose bun I secured it in. I refresh it quickly, somewhat out of habit, in an effort to give Stephanie less to pick at. Ten months of no contact and her years of grooming still affect me.

The deep breath I take before exiting with my purse in hand does nothing to prepare me for what I'm about to endure. Nothing can.

This is gonna hurt like Hell.

As if they've been watching, Stephanie and Alan open the front door, not bothering to step out on the covered porch. Instead, they create a bottleneck where they want me to enter, but won't move unless I ask. I say nothing.

"Hi, honey," my mother greets me with emotionless words.

Alan and I eye each other, but neither of us speak. It's better that way. His usual look of contempt is frozen in place. Without further preamble, he walks into the kitchen.

I don't know why he bothered to come to the door except to give me another dirty look.

Stephanie backs up robotically for me to enter. Her programming right on time she asks, "How was the drive?"

She doesn't care and we both know it.

Pick your battles.

I swallow deeply. "It was fine."

It's my turn to look her over. Loose, blonde hair shines against her black outfit of mourning, a trend I've no doubt she'll maintain for her stay. Her cold mannerisms and polished appearance couldn't be further from Nana's warmth. I've never been to the house she and Alan share now, but I assume it's modern, sterile. Similar to the house we lived in when I was a teenager. Nothing like the cozy embrace here.

Voices drift in from the kitchen, but all the sounds of normal life in this house are gone. The TV isn't on with Nana's favorite reality shows. There's no giggle as she thinks of some random funny thing to share with me, something I grew used to during all of my school holidays and summer breaks spent here.

"Who's here?" My voice cuts through the tension as my mother continues to stare at me.

She lifts her chin. "Your Aunt Randi and your cousin Olivia." Liv's name sounds odd coming out in full, even though it doesn't surprise me when my mother uses her given name. She clears her throat. "I didn't mention it on the phone because it didn't seem pertinent at the time."

Her nails make a clicking noise as they flick against each other, drawing my eyes down. I've never seen her fidget. "Your Aunt Randi was the one to...find Mother."

My jaw drops before I can stop it. I snap it closed. She blinks, but her face is otherwise composed, her body still again.

"I'll let you put your things away. We can gather in the kitchen and discuss what comes next." In typical Stephanie fashion, she turns sharply, exiting to the kitchen before I've responded.

I inhale until my lungs are uncomfortably full. The distinct scent of Nana's house rushes through me and I'm hit with an aching wave of nostalgia. Home-cooked meals, paperback books, and her subtle perfume envelop me simultaneously in a blanket of comfort and longing.

Nana will never wrap me up in her arms again and the scent will fade with time.

Despite the bodies seen and unseen here, it feels empty. Terribly empty.

Turning toward my usual room, I decide to get my bag later. The small foyer and narrow staircase separate the living room on the left from the hallway on the right, where the downstairs bedrooms and bathroom are.

I set my purse inside the first doorway on the right. A tattered stuffed bear with a red shirt sits on the queen bed. The sunflower quilt beneath him was handmade by Nana. My chest aches.

Venturing deeper into the hallway toward my grandmother's room, I drag my fingers along the wall. A tiny part of me still hopes to find Nana reading on the bed atop her plush, coral duvet, but she doesn't look up and smile as I enter. That image will forever live in my heart.

Fixed in her doorway, I peer around the quiet room. It's entirely too still.

On the nightstand are a cup of water and two books. A bookmark peeks out of the one on top. A feeling of intruding tingles within as I step into the room, lifting them gently. Still, I clutch the books tightly to my chest. These are some of the last items touched by Nana's loving hands.

A crater threatens to burst open in my chest and I force it closed. "I miss you already, Nana," I whisper into the vacant room.

I grab the clear cup on my way out and set the books on the foot of my bed before continuing through the house to the kitchen, where everyone is congregating. Atop the stairs is a secondary living area, which Nana used as a small home office, as well as the main bedroom. I don't have to guess if Stephanie and Alan have already placed their things there. The only way to the kitchen is through a hidden hallway behind the staircase.

"Hi." My voice comes out weaker than anticipated as I set the glass by the sink and move to the dining table. I haven't seen my aunt or cousin since summer when we celebrated Nana's birthday. It makes me both wildly happy and desperately sad to see them now. Unlike Stephanie, Liv and Randi are warm, comforting people, much like my grandmother. Holidays and events were always easier with them around.

They stand and meet me halfway, the three of us squeezing each other in a smothering embrace. Randi brushes a few wispy hairs back from my face and looks me over and with an equal measure of love and sadness. Much the way one would expect a mother to act.

Alan is reading a newspaper, of all things, mostly oblivious to our presence. Stephanie stares silently out the dining room window into the backyard. She turns to us blankly as her sister's tears flow freely. I remind myself to keep my shit together for the sake of my grandmother's soul.

"I can't believe she's gone..." Randi recounts finding Nana without prompting as Liv strokes her mother's sandy hair. "I stopped by to make dinner with her. She naps frequently, so I wasn't surprised she was in her room." Her voice breaks with a sob and she shakes her head fervently. "I couldn't wake her."

Stephanie turns to look out the window again. Her voice is ice. "According to the coroner, it was a heart attack."

Silence falls in the room.

Except for the turning pages of the newspaper.

My medium is photographs. I'm shit with anything else, unlike Leah who has a gift for melding any scrap of metal into stunning jewelry by hand. Without a camera, I'd be lost. Still, my mind's eye creates a painted canvas image of this moment. Gold Baroque frame, muted hues, a woman in black staring out the window. A tiny metal label: *A Study of Mourning*.

Stephanie's voice breaks the silence before long. "Alan and I have hired a caterer for the lunch reception here, following the graveside service." *Well, that was fast.*

"Thank you. I think people will appreciate that." Randi sits again, wringing her hands together on the table. I seat myself next to her and lean my shoulder against hers, hoping to infuse some emotional support into her body. Her mouth softens into a hint of smile and she replicates the pressure against me.

"I think you should give the eulogy," Liv says, looking at me from Randi's other side. She twirls the end of her low ponytail after speaking. Stephanie pins her with a gaze, managing to appear perched on a throne. Ignoring the cold look, Liv adds, "And I'd like to write the memorial bulletin."

"That sounds nice. I can do that." I look at my mother and aunt. Both nod quietly in agreement. "Has anyone chosen an outfit for Nana?"

Randi opens her mouth to speak, but the words get caught. No one speaks as she swallows and tries again. "I know which one. Her navy dress with the white polka dots."

Stephanie's face softens. "She looked beautiful in that dress." For a moment, her eyes hold a hint of warmth. An inkling that this isn't just a production to her. Her mask returns and ice floods my heart again.

"What about a photo?" Liv looks around the table.

"I have one in mind," Stephanie offers. "I'll have it printed tomorrow. The funeral home has a set playlist they use. Will that be a problem?"

We exchange looks. "Nana would probably be happy with that," I say.

A minute passes and no one speaks. Stephanie stands. "It sounds like everything is settled then. By the way, Nana's lawyer will be coming by tomorrow morning to discuss the will."

Everything is far from settled, but she's steadily checking off her to-do list.

CHAPTER 4

MACI

Around noon, Randi and Liv leave, having been at Nana's since the night before without sleep.

"I'm going to try and rest. I'll be back in the morning. If you all need me, just call." Randi hugs me on her way out.

Liv squeezes my arm as she follows. "See you tomorrow."

Within moments, anxiety spirals through me. My skin feels tight and my eyes flit between Stephanie and Alan.

"I'm going to rest." I don't spare a backward glance.

I throw myself back on the bed, exhausted and angry. So fucking angry. I don't want to deal with Stephanie and her husband right now. I don't want to think about a will and what it means. I don't want to entertain the town when they hear the news; bless them for being so thoughtful. I just need to be alone.

Several messages wait in the group chat, responses to my middle of the night texts.

Leah:

> **OMG. I'm so sorry! Do you need me to come over?**

> **Are you in town?**

23

OMG. Are Stephanie and Alan in town? They have to be right? You definitely need me to come over. Text me when you get this.

I respond with the basics.

Me:

I'm getting by. It will be a miracle if I don't commit murder before this is all said and done. I'll hold back for Nana.

Maybe.

I close my eyes. Nana would've patted my leg and told me to pull myself up by my bootstraps and get on with it. My anger reignites, now directed at myself, for allowing my emotions to get the better of me.

Vibrations on the bed draw my attention to my phone.

Leah:

Let me know when the service is and I'll be there. Sooner if needed but I know how you are.

Izzy:

I'm so sorry honey! I hate that I'm so far away!

Me:

There's no reason for you to be sorry.

There's also no reason for you not to enjoy Hawaii. Take lots of photos!

I follow up with the memorial service details.

Needing to expend some mental energy, I swipe a pen and notepad from the drawer of the bedside table, leaving my phone behind and heading onto the front porch. The wooden swing creaks under my weight once I settle. At least I can move my legs while I sit.

I maintain a constant rhythm, lulling my heart into a false sense of peace. The squirrels scavenge around the trees, no idea of the heartbreak going on nearby. Do squirrels mourn the dead? My mind conjures a tiny squirrel memorial in the middle of an asphalt road, but it's immediately squashed—intentionally and unintentionally—when I realize that would result in more deaths.

A warm wind washes over my skin and I lean my head against the top rail of the swing, shutting my eyes. A long, heavy exhale follows the wind. One day, I won't feel shattered inside.

When the feeling of wanting to jump out of my own skin passes, I lift my head and stare down at the notepad. I have no idea what I'm doing. How do you express a lifetime of love in a few sentences? I don't know how to write a eulogy. I've never even been to a funeral.

I know why Liv suggested me. She and Randi would never be able to get through a speech. Stephanie would come across too cold. I'm the one who needs to pull it together.

I jot down a few notes to act as a guide. My emotions are all over right now and getting sidetracked isn't appropriate, so it will still feel authentic. I take the paper with scribbles to my room where the little yellow bear stares at me from the pillows. A small smile pulls at my lips and I'm suddenly inspired.

Feeling completely caged in after funeral prep, I decide to stop by the grocery store for a few staples. A short drive through town may help clear my head.

Everything looks exactly as it was a few months ago. The old library, which was turned into a cute café about thirty years ago, has its front entrance propped open, encouraging passersby to stop in. All of the best restaurants are hole-in-the-wall places owned by local families, with rickety ceiling fans, outdated fluorescent lighting, and not nearly enough parking on their caliche lots. The majority of which are Bar-B-Que or taco joints. Nostalgia alone makes the food better in those unassuming places.

Traffic slows to a crawl at the new high school, just inside the city limits. Only recently has Bull Creek been big enough for two. Now they can boast an in-city rivalry.

Football is an expected staple in any Texas town. The next best thing here is the annual Christmas festival. Every Christmas season, the town organizes a three-day event which hosts carolers in period attire, a Polar Express ride made of fifty gallon drums, and the largest hot chocolate bar ever. Everything is bigger in Texas, right?

Best of all, faux snow is pumped into the skies each night of the event. The irony being that in Texas, you are just as likely to be sweating to death in December as you are to be iced in.

The picturesque streets embody a quaint Christmas town and the residents fully embrace it. Halloween never had a chance here. Not that anyone asked for my opinion, but the architecture of the historic German buildings is also perfect for creepy decor. Their loss.

Nana has always loved living here and I've always wanted to be closer to her again. Yet, small town life feels so oppressive. Intrusive. Unlike Austin, I have a memory from some point or another in almost all of the buildings on the main roads. I just can't decide if that's comforting or not.

I've been to the grocery store here with and without Nana a countless number of times, but I'm still surprised by the memories the aisles hold. In the produce section, I recall being taught how to choose the best cantaloupe and avocado around age ten. My eyes well with tears and I attempt to blink them away, rubbing my cheeks furiously to catch the ones managing to escape. Thankfully, no one else is loitering around apples and bananas so my impromptu cry fest goes unnoticed.

Get your shit together. You're crying over fruits and vegetables.

Determined not to completely lose my shit, I hurry through the rest of the store, grabbing must-haves for a few days, and head back to Nana's house.

The lights are on when I return. I rush through unpacking my grocery haul to avoid dealing with Stephanie or Alan. In my room, I switch on the small bedside lamp. The books from Nana's room are on the bed, not far from my well-loved Pooh bear, who appears in need of some additional stuffing. I flop onto the bed and pull his faded body into one arm, playing with the hem of his shirt absently. "You look like you could use some additional honey, my friend," I tell him quietly.

Pooh has called these pillows home since Nana took Liv and me to the happiest place on Earth when we were six or seven years old. We rode every ride our tiny bodies were allowed on, ate way too much ice cream, stayed up well into the night to watch the famous fireworks show, and did it all again the very next day. On the second day, while we took refuge from the brutal Florida heat in a souvenir shop, I found Pooh and was not willing to negotiate on the matter.

A tear rolls down my cheek and drops into my ear. I shift onto my side and wipe more away, but it's no use. The dam has broken. I clutch Pooh as tightly as I can and let the waves of sorrow I've kept at bay consume me. My heart aches deeply for the most loving person I've ever known and the loss that has altered my entire make-up already.

CHAPTER 5

SUTTON

I've kept my conversation with Terrence under wraps since yesterday. Dad is going to have plenty of questions and I'd rather have as many answers as I can before going to him. This is the perfect opportunity for me to prove he's making the right decision in choosing me to carry on his legacy.

This morning, I check in with Jason, Kelly, and Cody, making sure they can handle the usual, then head back into my office to work. With assessments out of the way, the focus will be on property clean up and prepping for all the cows that will be delivering in the coming weeks.

Dad and I remodeled the area of the house Sammi and I shared after she headed off to Baylor. She was pretty clear, come Hell or high water, that she wasn't coming back to the ranch. At least not to stay. Our Jack and Jill suite and adjacent hallway became their own entity, accessible only through a new exterior door on the back of the house.

Sammi's old room transitioned into an office. It's not a place I spend much time in, but it comes in handy when I need to work things out without baying cows, hollering ranch hands, or my dad's critical thinking skills. It's the same reason my dad has an office in the house versus using the one in the stable.

Seated at the desk my grandfather built, with maps of the property and surrounding areas spread before me, I have a bird's eye view of what adding Terrence's ten-thousand acres would look like. A few years ago, we completed an extremely detailed survey that identifies every important aspect of the property, including water access, permanent blinds, pasture lines and numbers, buildings and names, and several other key pieces of information.

Terrence's property line runs along our west. I imagine he has something similar completed for his, much more extensive, land. At twenty-five hundred acres, we've always been small fries compared to them.

For this to work in our favor, not only do I need to attempt to get this land at a steal, while also posing that as a win for Terrence, but I need to have a rock-solid plan in place for monetizing the land. From past discussions, I know Terrence leads guided hunts, which is something I had planned to begin on a much smaller scale for Strickland Ranch.

I think about his offer to discuss and wonder how forthcoming he would be about what's worked and what hasn't through the years. All of the information is set on a very large variable, which is that they raise quarter horses and we raise cattle.

I spend the next couple of hours finding comparable properties, looking at the current average cost of land, and taking into account what's already established next door as well as what I hope to gain. Once I have the best computations I can, without having an appraisal yet or talking numbers, it's time to bring it to my dad.

Mama is hanging up the house phone when I walk in the front door of The Big House. Her face is damp and she sniffles as I reach the kitchen.

"What the hell's going on?" My eyes pinball around the room, searching for the cause of her distress. Dad's heavy footsteps head our way from his office.

"Ms. Ruthie passed away, honey." She struggles to get the words out and additional tears threaten to escape her bright eyes. I wasn't extremely close to Ruthie, but she's been a staple in the community since before I was born. She and Mama hosted gatherings through the years and she was comforting to Mama when Sammi was sick.

"I'm sorry, Mama." I open my arms for her and she falls into my chest as I wrap her up. I've been taller than her since I was eleven, but her sweet annoyance over that dissipated the first time I swooped her up in comfort, the same way she always had me.

She doesn't stay long, pulling back and bouncing around the kitchen again. "I'm stopping by there shortly. I'm sure Randi is just devastated."

"Was she sick?"

Dad moves past me into the kitchen and kisses Mama on the head. She doesn't linger long.

"I don't think so, but I'm not sure," she admits, pulling an insulated bag from a basket in the pantry. I take the bag from her and load an array of food she's put together already. "I'm sure I'll find out more when I get over there, but she wasn't a young woman." She pauses briefly. "Us old ladies aren't what we used to be."

I drop my chin in disapproval at the same time my dad counters with, "Now, Andi." We exchange an exasperated look and turn our eyes on her. She grins sheepishly.

Mama and Dad had me young, so they're hardly getting up in age in their mid-fifties. Ranch life is hard on bodies, though. Long hours, hard labor in the elements, and more often than not, a lot of stress. I'm glad Mama's been able to take a step back in recent years, but that doesn't mean she's over the hill. There's at least a twenty year difference between her and Ruthie.

"You're not going anywhere anytime soon," I tell her, kissing her cheek. "Except to Ruthie's to deliver this food. Let me know when you're ready and I'll take you over there."

"I can drive myself. I know you're busy," she says with a pointed look. I hold her gaze until her features soften and she beams at me. "Fine."

CHAPTER 6

MACI

My eyes are heavy and swollen from crying in the morning. Stephanie will happily reprimand me if tears fall at the service. Though, that's the least of my concerns over the coming days.

Only coffee can make this morning better. I drag myself to the kitchen to start a pot, but find Alan already seated at the table, further souring my mood. Nana loathed him and she loved everyone. She never said why, but he has that effect on people. He nurses his black coffee while he reads. How anyone can drink it plain is beyond me. If I were on death row, I would give up my last meal for a perfect cup of coffee with caramel creamer. If they brought it to me black—or Heaven forbid, with sugar only—I would gladly go without in my final minutes.

I open the fridge for the creamer I made sure to pick up at the store. A whole cheesecake stares back at me.

Well, shit.

How did I miss that yesterday?

New York style cheesecake is my absolute favorite. Finding a whole one in Nana's refrigerator right now is no coincidence. The ache in my chest flares, causing each inhale to become painful. I close my eyes and focus on controlling my breathing.

Eventually, I'm able to fill Nana's favorite snowman mug and the mixture turns a familiar mocha color. I lean against the butcher block countertop, drinking deeply. The brew is strong, the way Alan's always made it. It's about the only thing he's good for.

Eyes closed, I conjure memories of past mornings in this kitchen. The comforting aroma of Nana cooking biscuits and gravy is just beyond my reach. Unshed tears burn the backs of my eyelids.

Alan clears his throat, drawing my attention. Anger replaces my grief, igniting a tingling current in my veins. A response to years of dealing with moments when Alan gaslit, belittled, or criticized me. Determined not to allow him to overshadow my focus this weekend, I force down my rising anger and turn to leave.

Alan speaks. "I think a 'thank you' is in order."

I whip around. "Excuse me?" His eyes remain buried in his book.

"For the coffee."

He can't be serious.

Something inside me snaps. I burst into laughter. A pair of shit-brown eyes finally rise, widening in an uncharacteristically shocked expression. It adds to my amusement and my laughing intensifies. My stomach aches and I rest a hand on the counter for balance. Hysterical tears rain from my eyes.

My mind must be protecting itself, creating a flawed emotional response to avoid dealing with the grief and other long-held emotions that threaten to wreak havoc on my psyche.

Sharp footsteps announce my mother's arrival. She stops at the threshold. With effort, I peel my eyes open, trying to curb my mania. Stephanie's mouth falls open as she assesses me with her crystal blue eyes. "Are you alright?"

Her uncanny ability to douse emotion in cold water prevails. She looks at Alan perplexed. His eyes are fixed on me as he seethes, so still I wonder if he's breathing.

"Your husband is really funny."

Alan slams the book closed on the table as he stands. My mother sucks in a small breath, either at his reaction or my apparent mental breakdown.

Something awakens in my mind. The area of my brain responsible for anticipating a threat. Self-preservation. It's not naturally occurring in everyone. My own was built over a series of moments. My posture morphs into something challenging as I hold my head high and look between them.

My senses hone-in on Alan. From across the room, I hold his stare. "Thanks for the laugh, Alan. I needed that."

I brush past my mother, still stationed in the doorway, knowing Alan is one step away from blowing his top. I wonder briefly if she's ever seen it.

The scalding shower eases some of the tension in my muscles and settles my nerves. Covering my swollen eyes beneath a bit of makeup gives me an excuse to spend more time locked in solitude. Finally, I dress, prepared to deal with the day, including our meeting with Nana's lawyer.

A knock lands on the front door as I enter the hall. Bright blue eyes twinkle beneath the jet black hair of the man giving a friendly wave through the window in the door. He has a very pretty face. Sharp jawline, cleft in his chin, and a killer smile.

For some reason, I anticipated Nana's lawyer would be older. And grayer. Not that we ever discussed her legal counsel.

I open the door wide and make an effort to sound welcoming. "Come in."

"Hank Campbell." His voice is kind and he offers a warm handshake. He's tall and well-built, even in his impeccably tailored suit. A little buttoned up for my taste, but perfectly within Izzy's wheelhouse.

"Maci McCullough." I gesture over my shoulder to the kitchen around the corner. "We should all fit around the dining table, if you're okay talking in there."

"Lead the way." A wave of ease passes over me at his charming, down-to-Earth demeanor.

Randi and Liv are seated on the back side of the dining table. My mother and Alan are seated on the left, both dressed in all black and looking camera ready.

Stephanie stands, followed by Alan, and extends a hand to Hank. "Mr. Campbell, thank you for coming," she beams. I make an effort not to roll my eyes.

He gives her a returned, short smile. "Nice to see you, Mrs. Young."

She turns to Alan. "This is my husband, Alan."

Alan shakes Hank's hand a little more aggressively than necessary. Hank doesn't indicate he notices. Alan presses his lips together tightly and sits.

"Randi, Liv." Hank greets them with a brief nod, causing Stephanie's eyes to narrow. "I appreciate you all gathering so that we can discuss Ruthie's will." He sets his briefcase in the chair closest to him.

Stephanie returns to her seat next to Alan and I lean against the countertop.

"Ruthie has been a client for several years," Hank explains. "She assigned me as the Executor of her will three years ago." Tension at the table is palpable, but Hank continues comfortably.

"As the Executor, I will oversee the probate process for the will. Every will is required to go through the same process. This can take quite a while in many cases." Stephanie's frame shifts forward and I anticipate the start of an interrogation. Hank gives her a warm smile and gestures softly for her to wait. "Luckily, in Texas, the process can be much faster, and Ruthie's will and assets are such that you should be at an advantage with time."

"What should we expect for a timeline?" Alan asks and I clench my teeth. "Weeks? Months?"

"I feel confident we can close the estate in eight weeks. "

Alan bobs his head as if this is an acceptable time frame.

"Now, I'm not sure if any of you have ever been through this process before, but it may look a little different than you've seen in the movies." Hank's lips lift in a hint of amusement. No one so much as blinks.

I smirk when his eyes land on me. "Tough crowd." This is not his first rodeo and he seems to be trying to lighten the mood some. Whether the others do or not, I appreciate his efforts.

His grin extends into a full smile with teeth. Beautifully straight, white teeth. I'm dying to send a photo to Izzy. She would be all over him like white on rice, as Nana used to say. The memory brings a smile to my face.

"I won't be reading the will today. It's not actually a legal formality." Hank opens his briefcase and removes a manilla envelope. "However, I am providing each of you a copy."

He pulls several stapled documents from the manilla folder and passes them around to each of us.

"As soon as the death certificate is received, I will file a petition with the county clerk to start the probate. Getting the certificate can take a few weeks."

Liv's eyes widen after she looks hers over and she gapes at Hank.

"In Texas, when probate begins the will is public. Anyone can access it. I've provided copies to you for ease and because some of you here are listed in the will. While we won't read it together, I encourage you to take the time to look it over.

"Once probate has begun, I'll post a public notice regarding the will. Anyone who may potentially have a claim to Ruthie's estate has to be notified, and this is how we achieve that. However, I assisted Ruthie in the creation of the will and know with certainty you all are the only individuals listed. Unless there are any secret family members I'm unaware of, you make up the remaining kin, as well, so the notice is a formality."

He pauses and looks around the room. "If there is something you want to contest or you don't understand, please reach out to me. Two weeks after the notice is public we'll begin settling the estate."

"What does that mean?" Randi's voice is quiet, her eyes curious.

"Essentially, dividing up any property and funds as Ruthie wanted. She didn't leave any debts and the assets are limited to the house, car, and a couple bank accounts. And you all lucked out because Texas has no inheritance tax. Legal costs have already been covered, so there shouldn't be anything to worry about before everything is divided as she requested."

She nods and whispers a thank you, going back to staring at the document in her hands.

"The last step is a hearing to close out the probate process, which I will attend." He leaves another moment of quiet. "Any questions?"

"We'll be sure to go through this in detail." Alan doesn't look up from the paperwork in his hands as he addresses Hank. If there is going to be any argument to what's contained in the will, it will be from him. I couldn't care less if I've been left anything or what it is. I'd rather have my grandmother, or at the very least, be free from all of the tension within my family.

Stephanie doesn't wait for anyone else to respond before standing and reaching out to shake Hank's hand again. "Thank you for coming, Mr. Campbell. We look forward to your updates."

"My pleasure." His formal tone doesn't go unnoticed. I press my lips together, hiding the rush of glee that races through me at his ability to see through Stephanie.

Randi and Liv murmur gratitude and I stand upright from my place at the countertop. "I'll walk you out."

He nods and closes his briefcase, before heading toward the door as I follow with Nana's will in hand.

At the door, I stop him. "One sec." I hurry to my room, swapping the will for a business card.

"Shouldn't I be giving you *my* card?" he asks pleasantly when I hand it over.

"You can do that, too." I gesture to his hand. "For updates. I'll handle Stephanie and Alan."

Understanding fills his eyes. "You got it." He puts the card in the pocket of his suit jacket. "Nice to meet you, Maci. Ruthie spoke so highly of you and Liv." He presses his lips together in a tight smile and I assume in a way, he's experienced her loss as well.

"Thanks." I swallow and open the door for him. "Bye, Hank."

Stephanie and Randi depart to finalize details at the funeral home while Alan retreats upstairs. Liv and I curl onto the living room couches, reminiscing over vacations and sleepovers at Nana's, and catching up on the past few months.

"Oh my God, do you remember when Nana let us camp in the backyard?" Liv's eyes are huge and excited.

"Yes!" We were ecstatic. "We thought we were so independent at ten."

"And then it rained."

"She was so mad we tracked water in!" We laugh hysterically. Nana was so angry. She made us clean the floors and take down the tent by ourselves. Thinking back, I don't think we minded. We were just happy to have some dedicated time with our only cousin.

Before long, people start showing up with food, flowers, and way too many hugs. I'm relieved by Liv's presence and her ability to welcome townspeople when they arrive. Through the years, I've had the opportunity to meet some of Nana's friends during my visits, but my ties to the community are loose. Liv has deep roots here. She's grown up here, teaches here, and is familiar with many of the guests coming by.

The constant talking and well-wishes bring on a headache, so I busy myself in the kitchen. After cleaning up from breakfast, I decide to start on the refrigerator and the copious amount of food we've received.

Frenetic energy has me pulling all the food onto the counters, ignoring the still whole cheesecake, and deep cleaning the fridge. I don't stop until it's sparkling clean. As sparkling clean as a ten-year-old fridge can be. Casseroles, bagged salads, meat and cheese trays, and fresh fruit all get reorganized into the refrigerator.

The elbow grease I pour into the cleaning eases little of the buzzing within me. Guilt at leaving Liv alone to greet everyone intensifies my muddled emotions. I make my way back into the living room as overzealous springs cause the storm door to slam closed as someone leaves.

Liv stands uncomfortably in the entryway. "I need a minute." It's a request, but she waits for me to confirm before turning for the kitchen.

"Of course. Go." She squeezes me in a hug before disappearing into the kitchen. Car doors close in the driveway, whoever inadvertently slammed the screen door leaving, and silence rests in the entryway. I drink it in.

Cool October air breezes through the screen door. Nana always enjoyed an open house and in some way it keeps her around. I close my eyes and inhale deeply. I love fall.

Footsteps on the porch startle me and my eyes pop open as someone taps on the wooden door frame.

"Hi, come in." I try to affix a pleasant smile to my face, but I know it isn't genuine and I'm convinced they know it, too.

It's not like you owe everyone a smile. Your grandmother just died.

I cringe at myself.

A woman and man, I presume to be mother and son, enter. She's holding several containers and his arms are full of insulated bags.

We're going to need another refrigerator.

"Hi." The woman's eyes twinkle and her smile is sunny. She reminds me of a summer day. It makes smiling back at her easier. "I'm Andi Strickland. This is my son, Sutton."

My eyes flit to the man behind her, also sun-kissed. He evidently works outdoors, and judging by the amount of food he's holding easily, he does hard labor. His expression isn't unkind, just blank.

"Thank you for coming. I'm Maci, Ruthie's granddaughter."

Liv approaches from behind me. "Here, let me take that." She extends her arms to the stack of dishes Andi holds.

"I'll come with you." Andi follows Liv into the kitchen with Sutton still carrying the bags behind her. If he minds, he doesn't show it.

The only thing people bring more of than food is flowers. I don't understand why. Logically, I will accept the tradition has some historical connection to scent. Past that, they only die. A reminder of death and of what's just been lost.

Unfortunately, the overwhelming combination of floral notes is giving me a headache. The few side tables where they've all been placed are overflowing and with nothing to expend my nervous energy, I begin rearranging the vases chock-full of freesia, roses, tulips, and wildflowers.

"I'm not gonna watch you die," I mutter to a vase of mixed wildflowers. "First sign of drooping and I'm tossing you." Beside it is a tiny basket of pink buds. As if the fact that they haven't bloomed yet will grant them eternity in this house. My eyes roll. "Rather have a cactus."

Turning from the vase, I startle at Sutton standing in the entryway again. Studying me.

Good job, you lunatic.

Liv and Andi return from the kitchen chatting quietly, the insulated bags tucked under Andi's arm. Liv has more color to her face than I've seen the last few days. "I've been craving your jam."

I slip past them onto the front porch, taking a deep breath to flush out the flower shop from my sinuses. When the door doesn't bump against the frame like normal, I snap my head back and find Sutton has followed me out.

"I'm just headed out to the truck," he offers, showing me the insulated bags he now holds as proof. His voice is deep and smooth. It seeps into my body, warming me. From his straw hat and tan button-up to his jeans and dirty boots, he looks like he stepped out of a *Texas Ranchers* magazine. It doesn't even matter that his sandy hair is somewhat long, not quite brushing his shoulders.

"It's fine." I wave him off, moving to the porch railing which wraps around the entire house. Sutton dips his chin in my peripheral, a typical southern departure.

My eyes tingle. Of its own volition, my mouth opens and words tumble out. "We were supposed to have lunch."

Sutton halts at the top of the steps, but doesn't speak. His eyes are trained on me.

One of my arms flails wildly at the porch swing before coming back to drag two fingers along my eyebrow. "She made cheesecake. It's my favorite." The last part comes out in a whisper, but catapults me into a frenzy of words. "She knew I was coming. It was planned. She did it for me."

I throw my head back studying the roof of the porch. "She was perfectly fine. Her normal self. We were going to Aimee's. It's her favorite." I right my head, letting my eyes fall to the floor. I can't bring myself to look at him. "Was...It was her favorite."

Tears pool in the corners of my eyes and I will them away, swallowing thickly. It doesn't help. "She was my favorite person in the whole world."

Sutton's boots thump against the wooden planks, approaching slowly. He remains silent, likely thinking I could lash out at any second.

Wild energy bounces around inside of me. I exhale heavily, hoping to rid myself of some of it. What possessed me to share so openly? "Sorry."

"You don't need to apologize." He takes another step, his boots coming fully into my downward gaze. Finally, I meet his steel-gray eyes. He studies me, tipping his chin down. "Grief isn't a sign of weakness. It's a sign that you loved deeply."

My mouth parts slowly. The tears threaten to spill over again and I blink. I wasn't expecting him to say something so insightful.

The screen door creaks open and Andi steps onto the porch. Her eyes zero in on Sutton and I near the porch swing. She gives me another sunny smile, behind which I feel a measure of her own loss. I wonder briefly what it would be like to have a mother who looked at me similarly.

"We don't want to overstay our welcome." Her eyes swipe to Sutton then back to me. "But we'll be around if we can help with anything. I'm so sorry for your loss, Maci."

"Thank you," I manage hoarsely.

Andi looks at Sutton once more then heads down the stairs. My eyes trail her movements absently, dropping to the wood planks. Sutton shifts forward again, causing my gaze to slide up his body. He has a soothing nature, like beautifully still waters.

His mouth opens to say something, but fresh tires coming over the drive catch my attention. I welcome the interruption. I don't have the bandwidth for all this emotion and support.

"Nice to meet you." My voice comes out a little harsher than intended.

Sutton straightens and takes a step back, and I walk past him into the house.

Stupid small town.

CHAPTER 7

SUTTON

The trip to Ruthie's was my first time there. She visited our home several times over the years thanks to a friendship with Mama that spanned my entire life. Any conversation I had with her was in passing, though. Truthfully, I'm not sure I ever discussed Ruthie's family with her. Maci was a surprise.

She wasn't openly grieving, but the hurt was evident, even if she tried to hide it. It's not really my style to deal with emotional stuff. I've never been great at reading people to help them unless it's my family. Wanting to comfort her shouldn't have been a natural instinct. But it was.

Maybe my being a stranger is why she slammed up her walls. Then again, what do I know? This is exactly why I don't fuck with emotions.

Once we're back home, it's time to go over my proposal with my dad.

"Hey, son, how'd it go at Ruthie's? Mama doing ok?" He's behind the desk again, but I get the impression he recently entered because the top is empty.

I settle on the couch with my notepad next to me. "She's ok. Think it made her feel better to be there." I spare him my thoughts on Ruthie's granddaughter.

He gives a curt nod. "So, let's hear the big plan." His fingers tap softly on the desk and there's a tiny glimmer in his eye.

I pick up the notepad for something to do with my hands, having already decided the best course of action is to start by sharing my conversation with Terrence and build up. For a man of few words, when my dad is working something out he is filled with questions, so I'm not entirely sure how far I'm going to get before he interrupts me. It doesn't matter. If it takes all afternoon and into the night, we'll hash out this plan and see where it leads us.

"Based on our last talk, I prepared a potential game plan. My plan took a bit of a detour when Terrence stopped by."

Dad's eyebrows raise and I grin at him, knowing good and well he's as curious as I was when the conversation was dropped on me. "He's selling."

The eyebrows go higher, but he says nothing so I continue. "He hasn't been in touch with a broker, yet."

"Really?" His tone is skeptical as he leans back in his chair and hums. His fingers come up to steeple together in that thoughtful way he does. The office chair squeaks in a quiet rhythm as he gently rocks back and forth. The state map on the wall seems to draw his attention. His wheels are already turning. Like father, like son.

"We didn't get too deep into it, but I get the impression he's giving us the first opportunity to jump on the property." He presses his lips together, nodding at me blankly. "I don't think he plans to wait long. He asked me to set up a time to discuss if we're interested."

"How long have you known this?" My father's eyes narrow while the corner of his mouth tips up. The desk chair eases down into the neutral position as he turns to face me head-on again.

"Since yesterday." I tap the notepad with my pen and hurry on. "That's not the point."

"No?" His teasing tone isn't lost on me.

"I've considered this extensively. The truth is, we need a rock-solid plan if we're going to take on the additional note for ten thousand acres."

"And you have a plan." His cheek twitches.

"I have what I think is a pretty good start." I pull out the two most detailed maps and stand, placing them on his desk. Together, we go through all the areas of the two properties, similarities and differences, and what we stand to gain. We discuss what's working well for our land, what I believe could work well there, and how I hope to expand both by adding additional revenue sources. I also touch on staffing.

My dad listens to everything. His questions are minimal as he takes everything in. By the end, his head is supported by one hand, the fingers of which cover his mouth as his mind blazes. I don't push. I sit back down on the couch and wait.

"This is all well and good, son," he says after a long minute. "You've put a lot into this. What about the numbers? Your mom and I are about to make our last mortgage payment this year. I'll be honest, I don't love the idea of starting something like that over. And like you said, it's a much grander scale."

"Dad, I don't see a way into this without some sort of note, but I thought you'd say as much. I have another option in mind. It's a gamble and I don't know how you and Mama are going to feel about it." Honesty is the best policy here and he needs to understand the decisions ahead of us and the implications. "I think this has grown past making decisions without professional advice. A financial planner and a lawyer, for example."

My dad's eyes fix on me. "What's the gamble?" I imagine he's replaying the last thirty plus years of his life with us on this property.

"It centers around me getting the loan and using the ranch as collateral. There may be other options, but this way you and Mama don't have to be responsible for everything. You can take a step back if you want."

His mouth moves as he chews his cheek.

"We don't have to make a decision today. It's a big one no matter what and I really think we need to get some professional input." I stretch my legs out and cross them at the ankle. "And I'm sure you want to discuss with Mama."

He leans forward in his chair studying the maps again.

As if summoned, Mama pokes her head into the office. "You boys hungry?"

Dad looks up at her and his expression softens. She steps into the room cheerfully, waiting for a response. Dad waves her over, pushing his desk chair back and patting his leg. She blushes, but sits.

Thirty-two years of love slaps me in the face. They're just as smitten with each other as they were in high school. One day, I hope to have a love half as joyful as theirs.

"You must've read my mind." Dad gives Mama a chaste kiss, and when she heads for the kitchen, he gives her bottom a gentle tap.

"Michael!" she squeals. We both laugh at her retreating down the hallway.

He turns back to me, looking lighter than a few minutes ago. "I like it. Let me discuss with your mother. No matter what, I think we need to find a way to move forward with it."

CHAPTER 8

MACI

The morning of the funeral, I wake up prepared for battle. I remind myself to keep my temper in check before climbing out of bed.

No redness or swelling indicates that I've been crying. My hair does exactly as prompted. I've left it loose and miraculously not a hair is out of place. Everything about getting ready is easy.

It's misleading and an annoyance.

Stephanie would say that even through your grief you should be presentable. But I don't give a shit what Stephanie says.

I stare out the window above the kitchen sink, sipping a colder than preferred cup of coffee, and taking in the view of the backyard. The grass is uncharacteristically green, considering the drought and lack of a sprinkler system. Trees fan out from the back porch accentuating the hidden feel and providing intermittent shade.

Nana wanted to add a pergola with a bed swing further into the yard. I smile at the thought of it paired with string lights and a fire pit surrounded by casual seating.

Stephanie comes tapping in, her steps halting abruptly. "Is that what you're wearing?"

I don't respond. My knee-length navy dress is complete with a lace embellishment over the top half and finished with cap sleeves. Aside from being tasteful and one of Nana's favorites on me, it has pockets. There is no doubt, I chose the perfect dress for today.

The silver necklace I've paired it with was a gift from my grandmother. I reach up to the tiny gemstone dangling from the silver chain, tugging it side-to-side.

"Maci." My mother's tone is a warning.

Adirondack chairs surrounding the fire pit would be a nice addition.

"Maci!"

Or maybe rocking benches.

Her mouth is opening to speak again, something I feel rather than see, when I interrupt her. "I am aware of your thoughts on my attire, Stephanie. You are welcome to wear black if you desire. I do not. Nor did I ask for your opinion on the matter." I sip my coffee.

She huffs.

Alan's footsteps approach.

When I turn, they're standing side-by-side, taking up the majority of the cased entrance to the kitchen. My eyes narrow on Alan in a look of warning before rinsing my mug and placing it in the dishwasher.

"I'll see you at the funeral home." I brush past them, exiting the kitchen before either can respond, hiding the anxiety that races down my spine as I half-expect Alan to reach for me.

Randi and Liv meet us at the funeral home. We hug in turn. Randi struggles to let go of me and I don't pull away until she's ready.

"I miss her already," she whispers when she finally pulls back, tears threatening to spill from her deep, green eyes. Her hair hangs loose and she wears a simple, black dress coupled with plain, black flats. Meanwhile, Stephanie's blonde hair has been hairsprayed into submission after donning her own black dress—a long sleeved, form fitting number with a neckline at her collarbone. Up close, the black on black geometric embellishment can be seen in all its muted, sparkly decadence. She wears black suede stilettos with a triangular cutout at the heel to match.

"Are you coming?" Liv's voice is soft as she gestures to the giant wooden doors of the funeral home. They appear as twin mouths opening to swallow us up. Maybe that's just my grief threatening to break through. Normally, this space would be lovely for a family photo session, with its lush lawn and trees that flower in springtime.

I shake my head. "I'll stay out here a bit longer. You two go ahead." Truthfully, being inside is stifling, like the weight of finality pressing heavily on my chest.

Liv squeezes my hand sweetly and Randi pats my shoulder as they pass me to enter. I'm amazed at how many others follow them. Many—too many—offer condolences and well wishes, prayers and heartfelt memories, hugs and pats on the arm. My cheeks and jaw hurt from forcing a grateful smile for so long. I'm well past overstimulated.

Leah arrives shortly before the service and wraps me in her arms, holding tight without saying a word. Her familiar loving arms threaten to bring down the dam I've built and I desperately bury all the emotion deep within, squeezing Leah tightly in return.

"Thank you," I whisper into my best friend's mahogany hair. It's wrapped into a gorgeous braid instead of her usual wild and free style. Her light makeup and rosy cheeks give her a demure look. It's both captivating and wholly out of character. "You look gorgeous."

She brushes my cheek with a gentle kiss as she pulls back, all the thanks she can muster for my genuine compliment. "The end of the world couldn't have kept me away today." Her hands grasp my own with a reassuring squeeze. "I'll see you inside."

I give her a half-smile. "Find Liv. She'll be up front." She nods as she passes through the grand doors.

The arrival of guests begins to slow. Heading inside, I contemplate situating myself between Randi and Stephanie, but I determine we all need to be big girls and push between my cousin and best friend instead. I wouldn't wish for Izzy to be here instead of Hawaii, but I miss her immensely.

Liv has written a beautiful obituary for the program, which the minister reads, including the list of loved ones Nana has left behind. I'm thankful that the list is short. It doesn't change how hard I have to work to keep myself together when Liv and I are mentioned.

When the minister invites me up, I remove my notes and a travel-sized pack of tissues from my dress pocket, setting both on the podium. The silence is deafening.

Bull Creek boasts a population under ten thousand, but the turnout today is awe-inspiring. Nana's reach was wide. Pride fills me at the product of my grandmother's life, at the number of lives she touched.

"Queen Elizabeth II said 'Grief is the price we pay for love.' Our grief today is proof of the love we knew for Olivia Ruth Wagner. Many of you knew her as Ruthie. I called her Nana." Liv catches my eyes, silent tears streaming down her face at the loss and mention of her namesake. Leah wraps an arm around her from one side, Randi's arm snaking in from the other side.

"To you she was a friend, a colleague, a damn good cook." My mother inhales sharply, while many in the crowd nod. "She made *the best* chicken noodle soup when I was sick. She mastered Bridge and Rummy, the art of a pick-me-up when you needed comfort, and coincidentally a stern talking-to when you needed to get your ass in gear." A few soft chuckles fill the space, drowning out Stephanie's huff.

"But to me...to me, she was home. Summers filled with endless sleepovers, lessons in cooking, and countless hours watching trashy TV. Her doing, not mine." Liv and Randi laugh knowingly from the front and Leah is grinning, sharing in my memories of sleepovers in the past.

"She was the teller of so many amazing stories. I always thought she had the most fascinating childhood...I wish I could hear her tell just one more." My breaths are labored. I look around the room, filled with people who knew and loved my grandmother. The pews are full and many are standing along the back wall. A few dab their eyes with tissues and my focus lands on my pack on the podium.

Inhaling deeply, I draw my eyes up, preparing to go on, when I lock eyes with Sutton. He's positioned toward the back of the room, a chocolate felt Stetson in hand and his sandy hair in gentle disarray. There's something kind in his eyes, supportive.

"And she was the reader of bedtime stories, too. Her voice was the perfect instrument for sharing a myriad of tales. I'd like to share an excerpt from one of our favorites now." The excerpt from Nana's favorite story, *Winnie the Pooh*, rolls easily off my tongue, having heard it so many times as a child. The sentiment that she will always be in my heart, though not near, causes a fat tear to escape as I reach the final line. I bat it away.

I step down from the podium, blowing a kiss at Nana's photo perched nearby. Liv and Leah make room for me to sit again and Randi reaches around

Liv to squeeze my knee. It reminds me of Nana and I can't hold back the tears anymore. I lean my head onto Leah's shoulder as she wraps an arm around me. Liv leans into me from the other side.

The minister offers a few more heartfelt words and closes the service with an invitation to the graveside, then to Nana's house for a farewell lunch. I blow out a huge breath trying to compose myself.

Following the graveside service, I send Leah home. I'm secretly hopeful that the less people who join us for lunch, the less time we'll have to spend with those that do. Maybe they'll be bored of our faces and leave quickly. My internal levee is crumbling bit by bit.

Having foregone the graveside service to meet the catering team, Alan is the only one at the house when we arrive. Everything is executed flawlessly, and though the mood is somber, the setup is beautiful and inviting.

Somewhat cloudy skies and a moderate temperature leave us without the need for jackets and give us a reprieve from sweating. The expansive front lawn is interrupted by tables covered in the palest yellow tablecloths, surrounded by metal folding chairs. Stephanie somehow manages not to have a complete nuclear reaction to them. The breeze lifts the skirts of the tables periodically and the leaves whisper in response.

Despite the gourmet food present, I can't bring myself to eat. Any hunger I may experience is overshadowed by the feeling of being in a fish bowl. There isn't a moment when someone doesn't want to talk to me, anyway. I'm ecstatic when I can slip away to the restroom alone.

After washing my hands, I soak in a few silent moments, splashing water on my tired face. My blank reflection stares at me from the mirror.

Someone tries the handle of the door. "One moment."

I take one more steadying breath, dry my hands, and open the bathroom door. Andi stands on the other side, her sandy hair falling past her shoulders. Her eyes brighten when she sees me. "Maci." Everything about her is warm.

"Hi." My pleased greeting comes naturally thanks to her welcomed presence. I maneuver into the hallway to allow her to pass, but she doesn't move toward the bathroom. I resist heading toward the chatter in the living room.

"How are you?" Her words are genuine, infused with care. She's not asking because it's the right thing to do, but because she wants to know. At least, that's how she makes me feel. For once, I'm tempted to answer truthfully.

"It's been hard. But that's expected." I don't force a smile like I have with everyone else. There's no pressure to be okay.

"You two were close." Her observation hits close and I bite my lip. I summed up our relationship as best as I could today. I can't afford to go into more detail.

Andi gives me a moment of quiet. As if thinking of something, her eyes trace along the photos hanging on the wall. "I think it's been about fifteen years or more. Ruthie brought you over to my house once or twice to play Bunco. You may have even played with my little girl."

Her hands clasp in front of her, hinting that she probably wants to reach out to me, but doesn't. This restraint gives me more comfort than she knows.

"I doubt you know this, but your grandmother was at my house the night I got the call about my daughter being in the hospital." Her bright eyes slip to the floor in memory. "My daughter, Samantha, was pregnant with our first grandbaby. A little girl." Her mouth tips up wistfully and she draws her eyes back up to mine. My heart clenches and I expect the worst.

"Everyone was on their way out. I hosted Bunco that month." Her story isn't hurried, but her words pick up. "My son-in-law called—which was odd because, although we have a wonderful relationship, he didn't usually call. Sammi did."

She digs in her purse for a moment before removing a thin, black wallet. After unlatching it, she turns it to show me a photo without explanation.

A gorgeous young woman, looking close in age to me, beams widely back at the camera. Her dark hair is tucked into a black graduation cap and falls over the matching gown, with a deep green sash over her shoulder. The resemblance between the two is obvious, despite the dark hair color, which must come from her dad.

"She's beautiful." I meet Andi's eyes and hope for a pleasant end to this story. Whether she knows it or not, she's allowed me to focus on someone else's heartache instead of my own. To lean in, instead of pulling back.

"That was her graduation day. Baylor." She beams in opposition to her watery eyes, then closes the wallet and places it back into her purse. "Justin, my son-in-law, let me know Sammi had been admitted to the hospital. She'd had a stroke as a complication of undiagnosed pre-eclampsia."

My mouth threatens to drop open, but I catch it and reach forward without thinking to squeeze her hand. She gives me an appreciative squeeze back. "The baby, Viviane, was okay. It was an emergency c-section."

She's quiet for long enough that I'm not sure if she plans to, or can, go on. "I'm so sorry your family had to go through that. Is your daughter okay?" I'm terrified to ask, but also hopeful she wouldn't have brought up something she isn't ready to discuss.

"She's home now. Justin was amazing, taking care of Viviane and caring for Sammi. He's such a wonderful dad. We go up as often as we can."

She smiles at me. "I don't know what I would have done without Ruthie that day. I was determined to get in my car and drive right to Dallas, but she talked me into waiting until my husband, Michael, could get home and we could go together. She was right, too. I was in no condition to drive."

"I'm so glad she was there for you. Thank you for sharing with me." For a moment, I'm frustrated at my lack of words. Why is it that 'thank you' and 'I'm sorry' can't always convey what they need to, and yet they are so often all that can be offered?

"I'll let you get back to everyone else. It was good to see you again. I can see why Ruthie was so incredibly proud of you."

My heart swells. My grief is momentarily overshadowed by pride.

"Thanks for coming," I say with a smile and gesture awkwardly to the bathroom as if Andi needs my permission to enter. If she notices, she doesn't let on.

The living room has cleared out, though I notice more bouquets throughout the space as I head outside.

"Fabulous." I backtrack into the living room. "More fucking flowers."

It smells like a floral shop again and the mix of flowers invades my sinuses.

Rearranging vases, I catch a glimpse of Stephanie's head swiveling back and forth on the front lawn through the front window. No doubt looking for me.

The screen door thumps closed. I sigh heavily and turn from the window braced to head into the crowd. I've reached my quota of somber words.

Sutton stands in the entry, eyes on me.

"Sutton, hi." Surprise fills my words. *What a greeting.*

He removes his hat, holding it before him like he did at the funeral home.

"Maci." He greets me in that cordial, southern way, giving nothing away as to what he could be thinking. Though, I suspect it's that I need professional help.

Coming into the foyer, I gesture to the hall. "Your mom is in the bathroom."

His eyes follow the motion briefly before coming back to me. "I wasn't looking for her." He assesses the living room. "Giving the flowers hell again?"

My cheeks heat and a rush of adrenaline floods my chest. "I—"

He chuckles and raises his hands in supplication. "No judgment here."

I manage a small smile as he studies my face, like he's contemplating saying something. His eyes flit back and forth between mine and the necklace from Nana. Instinctively, I grab it and drag the stone along the chain.

"I was on the front porch." He jerks his chin over his shoulder and my eyes follow. Through the window, the tired swing glides back and forth, empty. "I thought I heard you in here talking to yourself."

My cheeks flame again and one side of his mouth quirks up as he breaks eye contact briefly. I'm unsure if it's for his benefit or mine.

"I just wanted to check on you." His interest seems different than Andi's. Though no less authentic.

"Thank you." My heart beats erratically in my chest. "Yes, I do tend to talk to myself. No need to worry. It's only a problem if I answer."

This time, I'm rewarded with a grin and my stupid heart does a somersault. "I'll keep that in mind."

Andi rounds the corner then and stops abruptly to avoid running into us. "Oh! Sutton." She looks between us. "Are you ready?"

"Whenever you are." His deep voice and the way he treats his mom does things to my insides. Things my insides have no business thinking about on a day like today.

My pocket vibrates.

Andi offers a small wave. Sutton gestures for her to pass him and lead down the steps before he tips his head in a silent farewell. I press my lips into a tight smile.

When they're both in Sutton's truck, I check my messages.

Izzy:

I love you so much. You have all my strength today.

Brunch next week when I'm back?

Leah:

Yes, please.

Me:

Perfect.

When the final guest departs, Stephanie and Alan ensure the catering team is clearing everything to their liking. Randi, Liv, and I ignore the clattering of dishes and rolling of carts out to the small refrigerated truck hidden by the garage as we say goodbye in the front yard.

"What time would you like us to come over tomorrow?" Randi calls lightly to her sister. Tension builds inside me. I discovered while looking over the will that Nana excluded Stephanie from any inheritance, so long as she's married to Alan. Not only was I thoroughly surprised, but I don't see Stephanie leaving him. This threatens to be a massive sore spot.

The task outlined for tomorrow is daunting at best, especially after the emotional struggles today, but we have limited time to discuss the items within Nana's house. According to the will, Randi has final say over the house and anything in it, while Stephanie and Alan are married. Although probate hasn't started and nothing should leave the house, the sisters have agreed to sort through sentimental items.

Stephanie's face gives away no hint of emotion. "As soon as you're ready. We'll sort through what's needed and leave the rest for the professionals. Alan spoke with a company this morning who will come by and pack whatever is left and disperse it where needed."

My eyes snap to the ground and I shake my head in disbelief. What could make a daughter so apathetic to the loss of their mother? Sadly, I have an idea. But that's never been the nature of Nana.

When I look up, Liv is staring at me with wide eyes and a sick look on her face. Her thoughts must mimic my own.

Randi manages to maintain her composure—how, I can't be sure, because my sweet aunt is on the precipice of an emotional breakdown. "We'll be over by eight. You and I can discuss what you want to take, but I'm not getting rid of anything at this point." Randi and Liv depart without another word, climbing into Randi's SUV.

"Mother would've been pleased at the turnout," Stephanie declares and I draw my gaze from the driveway, settling my stare on my mother and step-father again.

I force a dip of my chin in response. The entire town has bolstered her ego this afternoon with comments on how beautiful the reception turned out. I will be damned before I add fuel to that inferno. In truth, it was a well-executed event. Unfortunately, I can't say so because while Stephanie doesn't need to have anyone on her side to believe in the validity of her thoughts and statements; if even one person favors her position, then it will be a cold day in Hell before she'll back down. So I keep my thoughts to myself, knowing none of it was done for the right reason, anyway.

"It's been a long day, I'm going to rest." I don't pause for a response as I head into the house.

CHAPTER 9

SUTTON

After the funeral, I head to Terrence's to let him know we plan to move forward. During the drive, my mind drifts to the events of the day. And more than I care to admit, to Maci.

The service went as expected, until the minister invited Maci up from the front pew. She was wearing a blue dress, unlike the rest of the family, and she blew a kiss to the photo of Ms. Ruthie on display after speaking. I couldn't take my eyes off of her.

She has a girl-next-door aura to her. The one with grit underneath the beauty. Without question, she was heartbroken—is heartbroken—but she stood surveying the turnout with pride.

Her words were affectionate and she described Ruthie more as a mother than a grandmother. It caused an ache in my chest that I found myself rubbing with my fist. Not just because of her grief, but because I know beneath her pleasant, gracious facade she's also fiery and full of life.

You can learn as much about people by what they do as what they don't. Not once did Maci interact with her mom. Their bone structure is so similar, there's no denying the lineage, and yet they didn't comfort each other or even acknowledge each other at any point that I saw. It hints at a crater between them.

I've only seen her toss her anger towards flowers. It leaves me wanting to know what she's like when she lets loose.

Terrence is standing outside his truck near the first training ring I come to. He waves amicably as I park behind him.

"Afternoon." He smiles widely, extending a hand to me.

"Hey, there."

"What brings you over?" He eyes my sport coat as if to say it's overdressed.

"I wanted to let you know that we'd love to discuss the property with you further. Think you can check your calendar and call me with a good time?"

He dips his head in a nod. "You bet. Glad to hear it, son."

It doesn't bother me how he speaks to me, having grown up in the South. As long as it's not rude, I'm good.

We exchange a few more pleasantries and I confirm he has the house number before I head home.

CHAPTER 10

MACI

Sunday morning, I move quietly into the kitchen, brewing coffee before the sun comes up. Squirrels rustle the leaves near the back porch, interrupting the whir of the coffee maker.

The wooden blinds in the common rooms were left open, allowing the early light in. Gripping my scalding mug of coffee like an anchor, I move into the living room and peer into the front yard. A tornado of emotions swirls inside me. I'm already exhausted at anxiously awaiting what the day holds.

Over the years, I've become good at meeting Stephanie's self-serving tendencies head-on. Her ability to find advantageous loopholes in conversation is uncanny. It's what woke me earlier than necessary, expecting her to be pilfering around like a squirrel. My stomach tightens.

Stephanie travels in a hushed manner down the stairs and directly into the living room a short time later. Her dark, wide-leg trousers are exaggerated in the shadowed light of the room opposite her light-colored top. Tall heels regularly grace her feet, but today her steps fall silent on the hardwood, feet clad in soft flats. An intentional change, no doubt. She makes a beeline for the hutch situated on the back wall. Some of Nana's oldest pieces of serving ware are housed within it.

I sip my coffee silently. Stephanie registers that someone occupies the room with her as she passes me midway through the space.

"Jesus Christ!" She startles and clutches her chest, scolding me in an uncharacteristic loss of composure. "You should have said something Maci. I could have had a heart attack."

"Two in one week. Wouldn't that be a tale?" Riling her brings such satisfaction. I smother a smirk.

"It's rude to skulk about in the dark." Her tone is laced with venom.

I shrug. "I didn't want to disturb anyone." We both know I'm lying.

"Well, since you're up already, you can help me pull out the china from the hutch." She continues on her path.

The antique cabinet is somewhat misplaced. It sits on a wall in the living room instead of the dining room. The dining set, which has seating for six, is too large for the space. It really should be called a breakfast room, but there's no other dining space. Thus, the hutch had to be housed elsewhere.

"It's just after seven. You told Randi and Liv eight."

"No, I did not. Randi said they would be here by eight. "

And, there it is.

My grip on my mug tightens and I cock my head. "Do you hear yourself talk?"

"There's entirely too much to go through in a few hours, Maci Grace. I didn't see the value in arguing with her in a heightened emotional state."

"The items in this house have been accumulating for half a century. You knew what you were doing. Not to mention, probate hasn't even begun. This is why people have wills."

Her mask slips for a millisecond, perturbed, before she secures it in place again. "I was only trying to help." Finished addressing me, she turns to the hutch.

"What are you planning to do with it all? There's nowhere to sort it here." Stephanie doesn't respond. She hasn't thought of that part. I sigh and set my mug on a side table, pretending not to notice a small vase of already wilting flowers.

The coffee table in the living room is the easiest thing to move. I promptly push it across the floor toward the hutch.

"Thank you," she says stiffly. Her face betrays no emotion.

The light coming through the wooden blinds is brightening quickly.

Stephanie turns to the hutch. "Despite what you might think, I'm not trying to steal from my sister. I may not be as sentimental as the rest of you," she waves a hand behind her head dismissively, "but I do have a heart."

There isn't a time in my life when my mother hasn't consumed herself with appearances and emotional control. Anything of emotional value has been diminished at every turn for as long as I can remember. Still, I'd be lying if I said I wasn't a little surprised at the requirement of the will.

Stephanie eyes the contents of the cabinet. A set of white appetizer plates fills the space front and center. She reaches behind them, gingerly removing two small rabbit figurines. Her fingers trace over the knickknacks. The silence is heavy with tension.

It's as if we've taken a collective breath that neither of us is ready to relinquish. Her lips are pursed. A sixth sense whispers that she is on the verge of speaking, of sharing in a way I'm unfamiliar with.

"There was a time when you trusted me." Her voice is soft, careful. "When you talked to me."

My eyes set on the rabbits, rolling back and forth between Stephanie's fingers.

She continues, as transfixed by the rabbits as I am. "I wasn't surprised when Alan started coming around that you were slow to warm up."

"The word you're looking for is permafrost." I can't help myself. Stephanie shoots a warning look over her shoulder, but I don't cower.

"Alan was never meant to replace your father. He may not have been the father he should have been, but that was never the goal."

I hardly remember my father, and not in the way she's hinting at, either. The vague memories I have of him include a tall, well-built man with dark hair and a scruffy beard. Though Stephanie always said he was dangerous, she hasn't been an open book about him. I was too young to pick up anything when he was around. My memories are halted in that foggy, preschool haze.

She finally sets the two rabbits onto the coffee table behind her before reaching back into the hutch and slowly removing items.

It's an effort not to move from where I stand, but Stephanie's movements hint at being tied to her words so I plant my feet intent to listen. The Thanksgiving platter is unloaded near the rabbits with a gravy boat on either side.

"I wasn't surprised at Mother's instructions in the will. She never liked him." I can't tell if she's suppressing a scoff. "Alan liked to play cards. He would go to these men's club events once or twice a week. It was never a concern of mine. We needed time apart."

Her methodical movements continue. She avoids eye contact. An ominous tingle starts at the base of my skull.

"The second year we were together, he got into some trouble." She swallows and is quiet for a long minute, the silence encouraging me to calculate the timeline. Why is she telling me this?

"He had borrowed from the house—that's what they call the club—but he had a bad spell and wasn't able to pay it back. The interest was stacking up." Another long pause.

"He started to get threats from the club." Stephanie removes a butter dish and two ceramic pie plates, then begins pulling plates out of the hutch one-by-one. "We thought it might be a good idea to move."

The morning light fills the room now. Stephanie finally looks at me.

"Alan came up with the money." The words come faster now. "He paid the club. They stopped allowing him to play cards, but even if they hadn't, he had decided to quit. He was done." She shakes her head at the memories.

"They wanted an extra fee. Like some sort of exit deal. It was so absurd!" Her usual condescending tone returns briefly. "He got it, though. Alan got it all. We didn't think there was a reason to move. But then..."

Goosebumps break out over my skin.

She doesn't need to go on. We both know what she's alluding to.

I can almost feel the scalding heat of that August day again. Almost recall the gloved hand squeezing my chin when we were accosted in broad daylight in a grocery store parking lot. My jaw locks.

A tall man in a ski mask shouting at us. Gripping my face and calling me a "spoiled princess" who "needed to learn a lesson". Though it was never clear what he wanted, his overwhelming presence as he basically shoved me into the back of our open SUV, and the way he seemed disgusted with me, is forever etched into my memory.

It never occurred to me the aggressive interaction had anything to do with Stephanie or Alan.

Her eyes linger on mine. I say nothing.

Stephanie's words break through the memory. "So we moved. You were so angry with me."

I remember the feeling well. A week before I was supposed to start high school, my entire world flipped upside down. Almost overnight, we moved from thirty minutes away from my family, to two hours away. No one would explain anything.

She returns to her task and her voice smoothes over. "I was doing my best to keep you safe. Alan was obviously frustrated and you wouldn't speak to us.

Mother was furious. She never agreed with our decision to move somewhere safer."

As usual, her demeanor lacks any sense of empathy. She always seems upset with everyone *but* Alan.

"But you wouldn't let your walls down for Alan. You couldn't see what had been sacrificed to protect us."

My brows furrow. Beneath the composed surface, something she drilled into me over the years, my blood is raging. I'm about to snap.

"It was a weird custody agreement with his son, and once we moved, he basically never saw him. They communicated through letters and email for a while, but every time I asked about him, Alan got more agitated so I stopped asking." Stephanie presses her fingertips to her cheek bone for the tiniest of seconds.

I zero in on the movement, my rage quieting. Has Alan hit her? Have I been so self-consumed that I missed it? He was always cold and calculated, but never aggressive.

Except for the one time. But that was directed at me.

Before I can ask, Stephanie continues.

"More than once, he told me he just wanted a thank you. An acknowledgment of all we had done to keep you safe." She looks pointedly at me, halting her efforts to remove the contents of the hutch.

A thank you.

"You're both delusional if you think you're going to get gratitude from me." Taking after Stephanie, my words come out icy. Her stare doesn't waver. "You and your gambling-addicted husband put me in danger. Put *you* in danger. Paying them back was his own dues. Moving was responsible."

All the hatred and anger I've kept bottled inside pressurizes. "You just said the entire situation was caused by him. I owe him nothing. Nothing. The very least of which is a thank you."

My mother gives me her bored look again. "I thought you'd say as much." She sets the trifle dish she's holding onto the coffee table among the other items. "I did what I could to protect you."

"Protect me? I *told* you what happened the night he kicked me out. Did you know he was aggressive?"

He'd been brewing for days. I never knew why. He snapped during a disagreement about what time I should be home. At which point I told him that having turned eighteen, I was no longer bound by his ridiculous rules.

Fury coats her face. "You were a teenager! A spoiled teenager! You had massive attitude problems and all my mother did was coddle you. A thank you wouldn't have hurt. An apology every now and then."

"An apology? For what?" I'm positive my voice is echoing through the house now and red spills into the edges of my vision.

"For your attitude."

"My attitude?" I deadpan. "For being upset that you moved me away from my family, my friends, *a week* before I started high school? That at every opportunity that asshole—"

"Watch your mouth." In an instant, she's like a rabid dog, baring her teeth at me.

"That *asshole*," I repeat louder, leaning forward, "attempted to belittle me and make me feel inferior. That after everything, he put his *hands* on me, trying to strong-arm me into submission and you sided with him.

"At *best*, you stood idly by while I was verbally abused and insulted about clothing and normal teenage activities among so much more. At worst, you kept me in a situation where I was in physical danger, that you were aware of, by the hands of a man you were married to. You didn't protect me. You were a willing accomplice."

She's unaffected by the venom in my words. "You pulled a knife on him, Maci!"

"Yes! To protect myself! At the end, I did pull a knife on him. And he's lucky I didn't gut him like a fish!"

Alan had backed me into the kitchen wall, snatching my chin in his hand and telling me what a princess I was. How I would follow his rules or leave. His fingers dug into my jaw so hard they left bruises.

Following the incident at the grocery store, I carried a pocket knife with me. It came from Nana's shed and provided me with a semblance of protection. His actions mimicked that August day and the knife basically pulled itself out and greeted his hip in a whisper.

"You would've gone to jail. I made sure he didn't press charges." Condescension floods her words.

I stare at her in silence. "I can't imagine he listens to you. What did you do?"

She feigns aggravation and doesn't respond.

After all this time, she continues to protect him. She's chosen him over me at every opportunity. My hand lifts in her direction, willing her to see what's gone on. "We could've gotten help. For any of it. The gambling. The money. Him. We could've gotten away."

"You're always so dramatic." Dismissed again.

Where is the bastard anyway? The house isn't that big. He's heard enough of what's going on. I half-wish he'd come downstairs so he can see what else I carry on me these days.

Randi's tires crunch over the gravel drive. She's early, but after dealing with Stephanie's antics as long as I have, I'm not surprised.

I turn on my heel. Rather than opening the front door to greet my aunt and cousin, I walk out and slam the solid door firmly behind me. The glass rattles.

What a fucking joke.

CHAPTER 11

MACI

With Randi and Liv around, I take a backseat to discussions over purging the house. My cousin and I each pick out pieces important to us as we trail through the living room, dining room, and kitchen. Overall, conversation is amicable, albeit tense. I credit my aunt's forgiving nature.

By the time we've finished the three common rooms, it's lunchtime. "I don't know about you guys, but my stomach is growling," Randi says playfully. She rubs her belly to drive the point home. All morning, she's been attempting to draw Stephanie and me into conversation.

Alan has been scarce throughout the day, showing his face briefly to grab a mug of coffee and then head back upstairs, where he stays locked in their bedroom. I haven't a clue what's so important that he's working on up there, but it's for the best that we don't interact for the time being.

Stephanie checks her watch. "I'm not very hungry myself." She adjusts a few pieces of perfectly positioned hair.

I need a break. "I'm sure you could use a rest. We can grab something to eat and get back into things when we return."

Stephanie locks eyes with me for the first time since her sister and niece's arrival, the cogs of her brain visibly turning. "There are only a few things I'm really concerned about from what's left." Her gaze moves to Randi. "Why

73

don't I pull those together, and you and I can discuss once you've eaten." For once, her tone is genuine, though not really a question, and laced with fatigue.

Randi nods. "That sounds fine."

She doesn't ask before sweeping my mother into an all-consuming hug. At first, Stephanie is stiff at the gesture, but after a moment, she relaxes. Liv and I exchange surprised glances before forcing our eyes back to our mothers holding each other in Nana's kitchen. The hug seems to last a lifetime.

Stephanie's face is flushed, her eyes glossy, when they pull apart. She brushes at something invisible on her shirt and when she looks between the three of us again, they're clear.

We decide to grab take-out for lunch and regroup at Nana's where Liv and I sprawl on the couches in the living room.

"It was so lonely once you moved away. It was like losing a best friend," Liv tells me, her bottom lip jutting out in a soft pout. "I was surprised you didn't move closer after graduation."

I consider her words. As two only-children, when Liv and I were little we were very close. The years had an easy way of creating distance between us and moving to Austin right before high school only added to that. "I think up until then, it seemed I would." I never gave Liv the details of leaving my mother and step-father's house. "I had started working my senior year of school and there was a photographer who was letting me assist her to get more experience. It was my fastest way up. At least, it seemed that way to me at the time."

Photography, and my work during high school, saved me from being on the street when Alan kicked me out that night. I had a piece-of-shit car, a boss who let me crash at her house for two nights, and enough money to put into getting my first apartment.

Looking back, it seems like I would've come back to stay with Nana after finishing high school, but I craved independence so deeply that I took the forced opportunity to prove to myself what I could do. And to stick it to them.

"I get it. I wasn't here, anyway." She wipes her hands on a napkin, gathering her trash. A year older than me, Liv left for college before I finished high school, getting her degree in education. She's a third-year Kindergarten teacher, a path which always seemed so authentically 'Liv'. Her way with children is innate.

Randi and Stephanie return from another room where they've been discussing items Stephanie pulled aside. Randi carries a small box in her arms. She looks at Liv in question, a silent request to leave. Liv nods and stands. I stand as well, hugging them both.

"I've taken everything of sentimental value to me," Stephanie chimes. "If you three decide to keep more, that's up to you. As I said, Alan and I have a team on standby to move things out when we're ready."

Somehow, I manage to keep my face blank. I wonder if at some point she'll break over the loss of her mother. Maybe in the quiet comfort of her husband. I nearly snort.

They've always seemed like two peas in a pod. I'm skeptical Alan ever grieved the absence of his son. I don't even know his name or what he looks like, just that he's a few years older than me. Family photos weren't a frequent display in our house, an aspect that added to the iciness.

I never thought to analyze that until now. Is that why my focus is family photography?

"We have time," Randi says softly. "Liv and I can come over again on the weekend and give the rooms another once over." She wraps an arm around me in a side hug before addressing her sister. "Bye, Steph. Drive safe."

Stephanie drops her chin in a silent acknowledgment of departure. Her eyes flit to Liv for a split second, but that's all the attention she gives. Despite what she said earlier, I know more than the situation with Alan led to this chasm between her and the rest of the family. A part of me longs to have the type of relationship where she would open up to me. That's never been our way.

After Randi and Liv leave, I lock myself in my bedroom. I don't trust myself to be around Stephanie or Alan anymore. I had planned to leave in the morning, but with everything finished earlier than anticipated, I could head home now.

Sitting on the edge of the bed, I breathe deeply, preparing to pack when my copy of the will catches my attention.

Aside from the stipulation on the house, Nana requested to have her older Toyota sedan donated to charity. Her bank accounts are to be divided evenly between Liv and myself.

Nana was living on a fixed income for a while. I doubt there's much money to speak of, nor do I care how much it is. I'd be just as happy not to have it and have her instead.

I set the document on the bedside table and flop back on the bed, busying myself with checking work emails from my phone.

Sprawled on my back when my phone rings, I nearly drop it onto my face. It lands in the quilt instead.

"Ooof." I scramble to find it in the folds and answer out of breath. "Hey!"

"Uh...did I catch you at a bad time?" Leah's voice is half-serious.

I roll my eyes even though she can't see me. "No, silly. I dropped my phone."

"Right." She drags out the vowel with an auditory grin. "What are you doing? How was your day? Are your parents still there?"

"Which question would you like me to answer first?" After pushing off the bed to stand, I tuck the phone between my shoulder and ear as I make the bed. "And you would think by now you would remember that asshole isn't my dad."

Leah's laugh spills through the phone. "Touchy, touchy. Start with whatever put you in this stellar mood."

A heavy sigh precedes my pacing. "I don't even know where to start. The usual, I guess."

"What are you doing right now?"

"Talking to you." My steps halt and I give the wall a *duh* look.

"Oh my goodness, you are in such a mood! I know you're talking to me. Do you have plans tonight?"

"Yes. I *plan* to keep myself in this room until Satan and the Devil have left this house, otherwise I may end up in jail, or just pack up and go home."

She ignores my reference to illegal activities. "Come out with me. There's an okay bar in town. We can have some drinks, dance, maybe find a tall, dark, and handsome cowboy..."

A cowboy is the last thing on my mind, a truth Leah is fully aware of, but the idea of having no pressure for a night is enticing. "It's Sunday night." My argument is lackluster.

"Sex happens every day of the week, sweetheart." She doesn't give me a chance to respond. "And who cares? I miss you."

I ignore the initial comment. "Ok."

"Ok?" Rustling against the phone hints at Leah bouncing excitedly.

"Don't get carried away. A few drinks. Some dancing. No cowboys." The last two words come out forcefully, like a parent setting a teenager's curfew. She ignores it.

"Fine. We'll see. Do you need to raid my closet?" A purring starts.

"I think we both know your style and mine are two different worlds. And are you purring?"

She breathes a laugh. "It's Smokey," she says, referencing her Siamese cat.

"Sure, it is. I'm sure I can wrangle something up here. If not, I'll text you."

"Oooh, yes! Ok, meet me at seven. We'll drink our dinner tonight." Her plan is right up my alley.

"Ok." I grin. "Be a good girl and I'll bring you a treat."

Leah meows playfully back. "I'll catch you later." An air-kiss follows loudly.

CHAPTER 12

MACI

When I show up with caffeine in tow, Leah all but throws herself into the Jeep. I give her a once-over under the dome light. Sunday night or not, she's dressed to party from her black western boots to her wild and free hair, exactly how I always picture her. She swipes the coffee I hold out to her and takes a deep drink, smiling.

It's a cool evening so I'm a little surprised she chose cut-off shorts and a tank top. A black lace kimono completes the outfit. It looks more like one of Nana's doily runners with all its holes, but somehow she pulls it off.

I haven't been to the bar Leah directs me to in about three years. Back when we had all just turned twenty-one, any bar was a good bar. Though, Leah and Izzy have never taken me to the other one in town.

The establishment is split into two rooms. The entrance dumps patrons into a large rectangular space, featuring a dance floor surrounded by a wooden railing on the left. A long bar takes up the better part of the right wall. Pool tables fill a cutout space on the right side of the room that's not occupied by the bar. The area between the two attractions is filled with high-top tables and stools.

The back wall provides access to the bathrooms, the kitchen, and a smaller room. A few pool tables in the back room are visible through the open door.

Tonight, there's no bouncer and Leah picks a table near the entrance to the second room, giving us a fabulous vantage point of the main room. Members of the local motorcycle club claim tables near the dance floor—which has exactly zero occupants. Despite growing up around bikes and seeing a few of the members around town, I haven't interacted with any of them. I don't even know if they're a gang or simply local guys who ride together. Only a few other patrons inhabit the bar tonight.

While we drink, I tell her all about the day and the revelations Stephanie threw at me. She meets my story with enthusiastic anger, promising to provide my alibi if I decide to sic my wrath on Alan. Some of my angry energy is expended through the tale and I turn the talking over to Leah, content to listen and enjoy a slight buzz.

I kick my boot lazily against the leg of the bar stool I'm sitting on as Leah tells a story about saving Smokey from a raccoon. When I bring my straw to my lips, I discover the glass is empty. My lips purse in annoyance.

"Want another?" Leah stands, slipping her arm through mine and transitioning into a story about work as we head to the bar. She manages the western store in town and I know she wants more, like something with jewelry, but she hasn't convinced herself to take the plunge yet.

A single bartender handles an order from one of the MC members whose cut has a 'Prospect' rocker on the back. Despite the low headcount, the music is loud enough that we can't hear his order or much of anything else. He glances absently our way as he grabs the few bottles set before him.

His face is familiar. Maybe it's his eyes.

I smile when he makes eye contact, a result of my Southern upbringing. It always frustrates me when people don't return the gesture, a compulsion I can't ignore. He doesn't.

He turns momentarily back to the bartender before heading to his friends. The bartender strolls over. She appears sweet. And young. I estimate her to be barely old enough to serve beer, but not drink it. Which makes some of the looks she gets from older customers repulsive.

A battered name tag attached to the pocket of her plaid shirt, which is tied up between her minimal breasts, says her name is Tawny. I refrain from asking if it's a stage name.

"What can I getcha?" She leans on the bar casually. We place a repeat order and when she slides the drinks across the bar to us, I produce my debit card from my back pocket.

She pauses before walking away, saying, "The guy over there paid for your drinks," and jerking her chin behind us.

Leah and I follow the direction of Tawny's gesture to where the MC members are seated. The biker in question, who moments ago stood before us, looks our way as if summoned. We lift our glasses in thanks. His eyes bore into me and he winks in response. I blame it on the three drinks under my belt when I bravely ask Leah, "Ready to make some new friends?"

Her mischievous grin is answer enough and she motions with one hand for me to lead. "It's usually me pulling this kind of stunt."

Our drink buyer hasn't stopped watching us as we approach. His companion looks over, taking us in and grinning at Leah, who purses her lips playfully. When we reach the table, she jerks her chin for him to move over. Without hesitating, he empties his seat for her, taking the one next to him and greeting her with a, "Hey there," as she plops down.

My eyes sweep back to the purchaser of our drinks. "Wasn't sure if you'd come," he says by way of greeting.

I don't believe him.

Even seated, I can tell he's tall with dark hair and eyes, complimented by a casual smile. Tattoos cover both arms and disappear under his white t-shirt and black MC cut. At one point or another, every straight woman I've known has had a "bad boy phase". He's close, but no cigar.

"I'm Colt. That's Pete." His eyes don't shift to Leah and her new boy toy. I hold his gaze. The intensity isn't unnerving, but I suspect he's testing me.

"Maci. And Leah." I keep it short and sweet in return.

He gestures to the stool to his left, across from Pete. Sliding onto it requires me to nearly press my body against Colt as I climb up, due to the MC member sitting on the opposite side, and effectively boxes me in.

Leah and Pete slip easily into conversation and I envy the ease with which Leah is able to fit a scene. She's like a chameleon.

A single couple begins to make their way around the dance floor.

"You're not from here." Colt takes a swig of his beer, idly watching the dancers.

"Maybe not." With a coy sideways glance, I sip my drink.

"You move recently?"

"Visiting. I live in Austin." Leah convinced me to come out for some fun tonight, but I don't want to get into heartbreak and family drama.

One of his hands comes up to brush back and forth over his mouth. He sets his empty beer bottle on the table and rests his hand, drawing my attention. Completed in black and gray, a scorpion tattoo fills a large portion of his left hand. The tail is situated in the middle with the head facing the space between his thumb and pointer fingers. Large pinchers stretch out to the first knuckle of each.

I'm close enough to reach out and trace the pinchers of the creature. Which I do, because I'm four drinks deep. His eyes land on his hand and then move up to my face. I purse my lips playfully without looking, willing myself to relax some. Colt leans forward with his elbows on the table, shifting his body in my direction. His warmth permeates my favorite black Henley with lace sleeves. He takes another long drink from his beer, his dark brown eyes flowing over me. "You need a drink."

My eyes fall to my glass. *That one didn't last long.* "You like stating the obvious." His eyes flash and he grins.

Like she was summoned, Tawny approaches the table. Colt's eyes roam over me again while Pete and Leah make a few requests. The corner of his mouth curves at me in a half-smirk and he orders us another round.

Leah leans forward, looking directly at me. "How do you think we get table-side service?"

"Well, for starters, I'm confident her attire isn't for the benefit of you and me. Probably thinks she'll have better luck here." I hike a thumb toward Colt and raise my eyebrows toward Pete.

"Not a chance," Pete gripes. Maybe I'm not the only one put off by the pedo-feel of some of the other patrons and their treatment of Tawny. It's not her fault; she's cute, but I can't help but feel a little icky about it.

An older member walks up to the table and sits on the stool next to Pete. "What's up, James?" Pete asks.

"Petey." James' voice is warm and low, with a hint of something foreign I can't place due to his limited response. Leah leans back on her stool to look around Pete and take in the newcomer. Her eyes widen at me playfully and she mouths something like "hot".

James nods at Colt who hasn't addressed him, before his eyes slide over me and he tries to hide a double-take. His keen, green eyes are set in a distinguished face. Salt and pepper hair is styled impeccably, along with a well-groomed full mustache and short-trimmed beard. Not what one would usually think of for a motorcycle club member.

His broad shoulders give him a formidable build, though he exudes power, but not aggression. Beneath the taut black button-up and cut, it's easy to see how well-built he is, even if he's old enough to be my father. I scan his cut for a clue, trying to determine if we've met before, instead spotting the President patch on his left breast. Not entirely a surprise.

I will my face to remain impassive and make eye contact with Leah, wondering if she noticed. She's already resumed talking with Pete, though, and the newcomer swivels on his stool to start a conversation with someone at the next table.

Tawny arrives with our drinks and I take a long pull from my straw with Colt's eyes trained on me. "Like what you see?" he asks, his voice lower and closer than it had been.

Shrugging, I continue to sip my drink. He seems to be testing me. I'm aware he's referring to James and not himself, and I refuse to indulge him with a real answer, even if my attention is more about determining what James knows that I don't.

"Here!" Leah shouts over the music. She pushes two shot glasses our way, matching the ones near Pete and herself, then runs a hand through her untamed hair, throwing it over her head in Pete's direction.

"What is it?" My eyes survey the red drink suspiciously and I contemplate not partaking.

"Red hots!" She confirms my worst fear. Tequila. Leah's eyes sparkle at me and she bounces with excitement next to Pete. He smirks at her and reaches for the glass. "It's only one!"

I press my eyes closed momentarily then swipe the shot glass off the table, looking at Leah expectantly before I can change my mind. Leah grabs hers eagerly, and in my peripheral, Colt lifts the one in front of him.

Leah opens her mouth to toast, but Pete beats her to it. "To Hell! May the stay there be as fun as the way there!"

That eases some of my tension and Leah and I grin wildly at each other before throwing back our shots, the spicy cinnamon effect lingering in my mouth.

"Whoo!" Leah cheers. "This tequila tastes like I'm not going to work tomorrow!"

"Oh, fabulous," I tease, still grinning.

Out of habit, I scan the room and accidentally discover James with his eyes on Colt. He tips his chin down, acknowledging he's been caught, though he doesn't seem embarrassed, and then walks away from the table, joining a few MC members who are standing nearby.

Colt lays a hand on my thigh and squeezes firmly, drawing my eyes down to the literal pinchers wrapped around my leg, before they track taut muscles up his arm. Anticipation builds and I expect to find him watching me when our eyes meet. Instead, he's tracking James from the table with a less than pleased expression. Again, the tension between us is dimmed, while my curiosity is piqued at the exchange.

This whole scenario is not what I would anticipate club politics to look like. Not that I know all that much about motorcycle clubs.

No sooner do I set my glass back on the table when Colt grabs my seat and pulls the barstool several inches closer to him, causing it to scrape in protest on the concrete floor. My heart jumps and Leah and I lock gazes. She gives Colt a once over, but not seeing anything concerning, picks up her conversation with Pete. The right side of my body warms, my stool nearly tucked between Colt's legs. He leans toward me, his mouth right at my ear, all but whispering, "Don't worry about him," causing a chill to run down my spine.

A hip hop song comes on and Pete pulls Leah off her stool toward the dance floor, flipping the bill of his black ball cap to the back with his free hand. She shoots me a wink over her shoulder. They're grinding on each other in no time.

"You dance?" Colt's breath tickles my ear.

Before turning to face him, I shift back on the barstool, trying to create more space between us. "I do." Not for a second do I think he's going to ask me and he doesn't.

A silent moment passes and then Colt grunts as if responding to someone. My brows furrow. "What's that?"

"Nothing." His response is quick and holds a hint of agitation, which he quickly morphs as he continues. "You're quiet. You shy or do I make you nervous?"

I laugh. "I'm not usually quiet, or shy, for that matter, and you don't make me nervous. It's been a long few days and the drinks are catching up with me, I think." I immediately regret admitting the latter part.

"Mm." Colt finishes his beer. "That explains why you're tense." The fingers of his free hand tickle along the outside of my thigh.

I set my jaw and stare into his eyes. "Maybe I'm just bored."

He laughs. It's a gritty sound with a measure of darkness to it. "You need some entertainment or something then?" He draws his bottom lip between his teeth and rakes his eyes over me.

"Something." I'm going for bold banter, but it feels awkward coming out of my mouth. He doesn't seem to notice.

Pete and Leah rejoin us. Colt turns to me with a wicked grin. "Come with me."

I hardly have a chance to query, "Where to?" as he reaches for my hand and pulls me off the bar stool.

"You'll see." His tone is teasing. He gives Pete a glance. "We'll be back."

Leah winks as Colt leads me away. He doesn't head for the dance floor, instead making his way through the back room and toward an exterior door.

"Where are we going?" I'm laughing as I take two steps for every one of his. My legs are heavy and my feet are less coordinated. He doesn't respond as he pushes open the metal door and leads us into the dark of night.

Outside the air is cool and I rub my arms, mostly exposed by the lacy detail of my long sleeves. Colt turns sharply, kicking a piece of concrete at the door as it closes sideways. The corner of the door skids the rock along with it until they butt up against the frame, leaving a small gap rather than latching closed.

He cages me against the brick wall with an arm on either side of my head, his body mere inches from mine. His hot breath skates over my lips. "You wanted entertainment, so I'm about to show you how I can play your body."

Colt's composed demeanor from inside is a thing of the past. He uses his hips to pin me against the wall which scrapes my back through my thin shirt. His hands travel from my hips up my sides with a firm grip and he leans in, kissing me hungrily.

He tastes of beer and cigarette smoke and the scent of motor oil overwhelms me. The combination is threatening to make my drinks reappear.

When he releases my lips, I lean my head back against the brick wall and suck in a deep breath, willing my stomach to settle. The sky glitters with stars, void of any clouds.

A sliver of light from the cracked door penetrates the blackness of night. The warmth of the back room escapes through the gap, dancing over my skin, a complete contrast to the cool night air. Goosebumps rise on my arms and neck.

The possibility of someone coming upon us from the exit, or either side of the building, is equally terrifying and exciting. I lean into it, and my current blood alcohol content, in hopes of enjoying what's happening.

I discover that Colt's leather cut has soaked up the cold surprisingly fast when my fingers brush it, slipping under his shirt. I'm met with a firm build. His stomach muscles tense beneath my fingertips as he startles.

"Your hands are freezing," he grumbles between sloppy kisses up my neck.

"Sorry." It's a blatant lie.

He immediately releases his grip on my sides to grab both wrists, pinning them between our bodies. "I'm happy to warm them."

With one wrist locked in place between us, he thrusts the other hand toward his groin where I squeeze when he presses my hand against his erection. "Feel what I've been dealing with all night because of you?"

An inkling of doubt nudges me from within as my mind takes this opportunity to remind me one-night-stands are not something I've had experience with. Colt pinning me against a public wall for his gratification proves he isn't concerned with the speed at which I jump into bed with someone, and the short-term nature of my time in town means I don't care what he thinks of me since I don't plan to see him ever again. So I push the nerves away.

"Oh, is that all?" I give an extra squeeze for good measure.

Without warning, he releases both hands and flips me around. I throw my hands out to brace myself on the brick wall.

One hand slides around my hip and down between my legs, cupping my core through my jeans. "Don't worry, baby, I'm gonna take good care of you," he promises, biting and licking my neck.

His attentions are getting wetter, though it's taking me a bit longer. Something feels off. I attribute it to a little fear at doing something wildly out of my comfort zone.

"You're so fucking hot, baby," he whispers as he slides his hand up to pop open the button of my jeans and dip his hand inside.

When Colt's hand grazes my clit I jolt, but I'm shortly convinced it was accidental as he pushes further.

He slips out of me, brushing my clit again and another startled sound escapes me. He chuckles. "I told you not to worry, baby."

If he says baby one more time.

I'm not opposed to teaching. I did with my last two boyfriends. Either way, I don't get the impression Colt thinks he has anything to learn, and since I don't intend on this being a repeat experience, I let it go.

His hands work my jeans and underwear down my legs. The jingling of his belt and his zipper going down break through the quiet.

He grips my hips firmly with both hands and his exposed erection brushes my thigh. "I got you."

In a moment of clarity, I freeze. "Wait!" His fingers dig into my hips but he doesn't move. "Do you have a condom?"

Tension fills his silence. "I'm clean," he says after a long moment.

"I don't care." I'm on birth control, but letting him finish inside me feels entirely too intimate for what's happening here.

A hand leaves my hip, followed by a bit of movement. I dart my eyes over my shoulder to confirm he's tearing open a condom. Once covered, he thrusts into me fully without warning and I curse loudly. A low *"fuuuck,"* rumbles behind me.

My head drops forward against the brick, the thump softened by my hand. Colt pulls back and thrusts in again. I reach one hand between my legs to continue what he started. If anyone's going to get me there, it's going to be me.

His intensity increases quickly and he drives into me over and over. If he cared a little more, we could probably get this whole thing together.

I try to clear my mind and lean into the buzz I'm losing. My fingers pick up their pace between my legs, sensing he won't be lasting much longer.

His hands clench harder. "I can feel you squeezing my cock. You're close."

Sadly, he is mistaken.

"Shit." His voice comes as a warning. Thrusting twice more, he finds his release.

I don't give him time to come down before pulling away from him and redressing. "I'm going to stop by the bathroom."

A couple of MC members are using a pool table in the back room and heat rushes through my neck and face. If they hadn't figured out what was happening by the sounds, my embarrassment makes it clear.

That shit was not good and now I know one-night-stands are not my thing. I need more connection and someone who wants to please me, too. Just because it's one night doesn't mean it should be shit.

As I'm washing up, I notice minor abrasions on both palms from the brick. I roll my eyes. What a letdown.

Colt is seated at the table taking a long pull from a fresh beer. My hand rests on Leah's shoulder as I look down at her. "I'm headed out. You hanging around?"

Pete's eyes travel back and forth between the two of us before giving Colt some hardcore side-eye. I wonder which of us he thinks is the real cock block tonight.

For a split second, Leah meets my eyes and it's clear she knows something is up. "I should head out, too. I'm beat."

Pete looks at her with what can only be described as puppy dog eyes. He readjusts his hat needlessly.

"Give me your phone," Leah orders and he does. With her number entered, she hands it back and jumps off her stool, grabbing her phone from the table as it lights up with the message she's sent herself.

"See you around?" Colt asks.

"If you're lucky." I shoot him a wink for good measure, but some one-in-a-million shit would have to happen for me to ever consider him again.

Chapter 13

Maci

Monday morning the air is crisp and carries a light fog. The back porch swing squeaks softly each time I rock it backward while I sip my coffee.

A squirrel launches from the tree nearest me and lands on the sad wooden railing around the porch. It halts movements, aside from the occasional swift flick of its tail, as two beady eyes take me in. I bite my lip to stifle a laugh. If I say *boo* the poor thing is liable to fall off the railing backward.

Instead, deeming me a non-threat, it hops from the railing and runs along the edge of the house's facade. My eyes follow suit, taking in a few broken boards of the porch and the exterior which yearns for a good pressure washing.

The squirrel finds a gap between the porch and the house, and jumps below the platform. My attention returns to the backyard. It's a perfect space for entertaining. The tire swing in the front yard would agree if it still hung.

My cell phone shouting out a Katy Perry song pierces the still of the morning air as Leah's name flashes on the screen. "Good morning, Sleeping Beauty," I sing-song through the phone.

"Ha. Ha." Leah's voice isn't amused. "You forget, I wake up early every day I have to be at the store."

"You're going to make it in after all?" Coffee almost spills over the rim of my cup when I push the swing back too forcefully, making me stop short.

"Ugh, yes. I'm on my way now. Stupid responsibility shit." We giggle together like we did when summers were full of pool days and boys. "What are you up to?" she asks.

"I'm enjoying a gorgeous morning on the porch swing."

"That's going to be hard to say goodbye to." Leah's tone is somber, reflecting the depth of losing Nana all over again. So much of my history belongs to this house, this porch, this yard.

"It is."

"I didn't call you to bum you out. In fact, I called to fix things."

"Fix things?" I parrot.

"Yes. You need a do-over."

I blink. "I don't."

"You do!" I set my things on the railing and begin pacing. Leah's car door slams in the background. "Your night out fell flat. You didn't even get to ride his bike!"

I breathe a laugh. "I know you were hoping to distract me from everything going on and it worked for a bit. I'm not upset about what happened. Some experiences are just not as good. I envy your ability to embrace your sexuality that way. It just won't be how I embrace mine."

There's a long pause. "I just feel bad. I've had some really satisfying experiences." Her grin colors her words.

"And I'm glad. But don't feel bad. I don't. I'm not upset."

"Ok. Well, if you change your mind, I'm down for a redo. I still think we need to go again. Maybe we need to head into town."

"San Antonio has a bigger selection, but burying myself in drinks and dancing won't solve my problems."

"Ok, but someone buried inside—"

"Get to work. I'll consider it." I interrupt her train of thought as her keys clatter. She's unlocking the storefront in the nick of time, because I have no desire to continue this conversation.

Fully caffeinated, I run laundry and clean up the house. It's practical, but I'm only delaying the inevitable. Set to return for brunch this weekend, I need to get home to send proof packages out from the Halloween mini-sessions.

My two-hour drive is over in a blink, lost in thoughts of the funeral, Nana's house, and all that remains to settle the estate. My bags hardly make it through the door before I drop them to the floor and toss my purse on the bistro table. The one-bedroom apartment feels especially tiny after spending several days in Nana's house. Less cozy and more cramped.

With more aggression than necessary, I open the curtains. Natural light usually helps brighten the space, but today it does nothing for my mood.

An unfamiliar noise from the front door draws my attention.

Orange paper peeks between the door and weather stripping. I pull the paper out for inspection. A reminder of my lease renewal in December. It goes on the bistro table with the other things to handle this week.

After unpacking, I sprawl on the living room floor, using the coffee table as a desk to edit the last of the Halloween mini-session photos. I could invest in a proper desk, but it doesn't feel like a priority.

I'm not sure how long I've been working when my phone rings. Untangling myself from files, I dart for the dining table to retrieve it from my purse. Izzy's name flashes on the screen.

"Hey!" My grin is huge. It's been like I'm missing a limb with Izzy in Hawaii the last week. Not so much because I see my friends regularly—because it's an area we need to improve—but because we are often the three amigos, instead of only Leah and me. "Are you calling me from Hawaii?"

"Hey, babe." Izzy's voice immediately relaxes me. "Yes, I'm having a slow morning in the condo and I wanted to check on you."

"Okay, but first I need to hear about your trip."

Reluctantly, Izzy fills me in on everything from the elegant condo her family is staying in, to local cuisine and gorgeous beaches, to details I don't need like her brother hooking up with townies. But having the focus off me is appreciated. I'm so proud when she tells me all about learning to surf.

"You're a total badass." I easily picture her atop wild waves on a steady board, her ice-blond hair and pearly whites gleaming in the sun.

The fact my connection with Izzy and Leah survived the trials of high school, adding in long-distance friendships, is a miracle not lost on me. While Leah is a free spirit, willing to try anything, Izzy is everything grounded and thoughtful. Each of us compliments a part of the others.

"It's easier than I thought it would be. I wish you guys could have come, but it's been a trip to remember for sure." She never lets compliments go to her head.

"I'm so glad you're having fun."

Her voice turns somber. "I'm sorry I couldn't be there for the funeral."

"I told you not to worry about it. I know you would have been here to support me if you could, but there's nothing you could have done to change what happened."

She's quiet for a few moments. I exit my sliding glass door to the laundry room on my patio. "Are you back at your apartment?"

I begin moving clothes into the dryer. "Yeah, but it's weird."

"Oh?" Her voice lacks surprise. Izzy's ability to tune in to me is uncanny. It's how I imagine twins to be. Maybe sisters, but I never had one to know the difference.

"I think my emotions are just all over with everything going on. It feels like I should be at Nana's."

"Is anything going on today?"

"No. I'm supposed to meet Randi and Liv again this weekend."

"I'm sure once it's all settled you'll feel better." She pauses for a second before adding, "Unless you keep it."

I accidentally drop a pair of jeans onto the ground and whisper a curse.

"No?" She hears it for what it is. A distraction from the topic. In true Izzy fashion, she doesn't relent.

"No." She waits a few beats for me to continue. I slam the dryer door shut instead and start the cycle.

She tries again. "So you don't want to keep the house?"

"It's not up to me."

"It's not." It's not a question, but the skepticism is clear. Even from two thousand miles away, I can feel her pointed look. The way her deep blue eyes always stare until you spill truths you didn't know you were withholding.

"You're right. It's probably because everything is looming."

She ignores the last comment. "Nana's house was a second home to you."

I sweep the empty concrete porch. "That's true. I just don't know what it will feel like to not have it as a haven anymore."

"What's happening to it?"

The sliding door eases open silently as I continue. "I don't know exactly. Nana stipulated in the will that it goes to Randi one hundred percent, while Stephanie is married to Alan."

There's a deep intake of breath from Izzy.

"The focus is on clearing it out, so I doubt Randi will keep it. And I can't imagine Stephanie will leave Alan."

Izzy lets my comment hang. Sometimes I think she should've been a therapist instead of a dental hygienist, the way she helps people get to the answers they seek on their own. "All of that aside, would you want it?"

How could I not want to keep the place that always felt the most like home? Where so many of my best memories hailed from? But I have a business and a life in Austin. Things I've worked very hard for. I've managed to nearly extricate Stephanie and Alan from that life, a goal I plan to fulfill once all is said and done.

"I don't need to hold on to a house that's just going to sit."

"You'll figure it out," she says lovingly. There's more she's not saying. "I'm headed out to the beach for another lesson. I can't believe I only have three days left."

"Have fun! Before long you'll be elbow-deep in dirty mouths again," I say, referencing her career as a dental hygienist. My laugh stops abruptly, when I remember Hank. "Oh my god! Speaking of mouths—"

"Oh, this should be good," Izzy teases.

I grin but continue. "The lawyer handling the probate has the most gorgeous smile. And eyes. But you'd definitely love his smile."

"I do love a nice smile," she agrees. "Alright, gotta run. Love you."

"Love you, too. Don't forget brunch on Sunday!"

Aside from our usual texts throughout the week, I hear once more from my best friends when Leah calls me on Wednesday to discuss an encore visit to The Spur.

"I told you, I don't need a do-over." I'm preparing for two family sessions this afternoon. It feels good to be using my camera again. In some ways it's an extension of me.

"I know, I know." Leah seems ready to argue all day about this. "We won't be on the prowl! Just two besties dancing."

My fingers tap against the camera case I'm readying. I do like dancing.

"Come on. You know you want to. When was the last time you went dancing?"

I roll my eyes. "You're a terrible influence, you know that?"

Something akin to a slap comes through the line. "So...yes?"

"Yes," I grumble.

She squeals. "Yes! We're going to have *so* much fun."

I hum a response. "Don't forget we have brunch Sunday. I'll come in Saturday and we can get together, but you don't get to bail on brunch."

"Scout's honor." She's entirely too chipper.

"You weren't a scout." Our laughter mingles through the phone. "Ok, I have to leave soon so I can actually make some money. Text you later."

"Ok. Love you."

"You, too."

CHAPTER 14

SUTTON

F all calves start to arrive over the next week. Of the pregnant cows, fifteen are heifers who haven't delivered before and the other thirty-five are from experienced cows. About a third of the herd isn't expecting. Heifers sometimes have a harder time, due to size among other things, so we monitor closely for any signs of an issue.

My parents head to Dallas on Tuesday to spend a few days with Sammi and her family. I don't know if my dad has shared our discussion regarding the ranch with Mama. If it hasn't come up yet, the drive to and from Dallas will give them the perfect time to talk uninterrupted.

The rest of the crew and I are busy enough that I push everything out of my mind until my parents return. Terrence agreed to set up a time for Dad and me to tour the property as soon as we're ready.

When I head into The Big House at the end of the day on Friday, my mom is talking on the phone with someone. The creak of the oven door opening greets me as I close the front door before something heavy hits the counter.

"Thank you for calling to let me know...Ok, dear. Have a good night." The oven door slams. "Michael?"

"It's me, Mama." I round the corner.

"Oh, Sutton." Her eyes crinkle in the corners as her expression lifts. I kiss the top of her head before heading to the sink to wash up. "How was your week?"

"The usual."

She smirks as she pulls plates down and begins serving food. The front door closes again as I fill three glasses with water.

When my dad enters the kitchen, he presses a kiss to Mom's temple. "Smells good."

Her soft smile and pink cheeks shouldn't be the norm after all of their years together. Or should they?

"Everything okay?" I eye the phone to clarify my question.

She waves me off. "Oh, yes. It was the photographer for the Fall Festival. She's a sweet girl, but something came up so she can't attend." Mama's inability to sit still led to her heading the committee for the Fall Festival. It's not the biggest event in town, but it comes close.

We seat ourselves in the adjacent dining room. The leaves aren't inserted in the round maple table currently, but come Thanksgiving when Mom prepares her grandest meal of the year, they will be. My grandfather built the ten-person table, among several other pieces of furniture throughout the house. Growing up, he taught me the art of woodworking and I've continued building pieces when I have the time. A small shop near the back of the house is the perfect place to escape to.

Mama gives me every detail of their trip. What my dad and I lack in words, my mom and sister make up for ten-fold. She whips out photos of the trio on her phone to accentuate the stories.

"Look at her sweet little face!" I'm not sure if it's really as much to show me or as an excuse for her to admire them again herself. She hardly turns the phone my way and tears line her eyes. "Hasn't she grown so much?" She's still not looked up.

It's true, Viviane has grown since I saw them all last. But I can't help studying the beating heart of our family. I never realized how much she inspired Sammi's passion for life and family. That drive to be the best for her loved ones is likely what fueled the determination Sammi needed to live through her and Viviane's traumatic birth experience.

"She's a cutie." I grin over my niece when my mom looks up at me. "She looks like Justin."

My dad eats in comfortable silence until she's gone through all hundred photos on her phone. Finally, she sets it down and starts eating. Her food must be cold by now.

"Your mom and I discussed your plans for the ranch." I look between them. My mom nods through a bite.

"It sounds like you worked really hard on everything," she says. Her proud smile has returned and she sets her fork down. "I have faith that you will be successful with whatever you set out to achieve here."

Even though I want to tell her things aren't that simple, I know she knows. Before I started helping my dad as a teenager, my mom took on plenty of responsibility over the physical and mental burden of the ranch. "Thanks, Mama."

"Like I told Daddy, you two do whatever you think is right."

"You may end up with a kitchen maid soon," I tell her with a wink.

She giggles. "I don't need a kitchen maid."

"Not yet," Dad adds.

Mama moves food around on her plate. Her fork clinks against the ceramic.

"Your breakfast crew is small compared to what it could be." I give her a pointed look. "If we maintain the same ratio of employees, you'll need another table."

She assesses the room with a smile.

Dad and I stand, our chairs scooting loudly over the floor. "What do you have going on this week?" I hold my hand out for her plate.

A sheepish grin crosses her face and she holds the plate up for me to take. My dad rounds the table, giving her a kiss and thanking her for dinner before he disappears down the hallway. She follows me into the kitchen and starts rinsing dishes.

"I'm going to be working on prep for the Fall Festival. That means you and Daddy need to stay out of my way." If only I could take her stern voice seriously. I can almost smell the jams cooking and breads baking.

"Let me know if you need anything." I kiss her on the head.

"Sutton." She grabs a towel from the counter to dry her hands and bumps the dishwasher closed with her hip. "Don't work your life away."

My brows furrow as I halt in the doorway. "I'm going out tonight."

She snaps lids onto the leftover containers spread on the counter and opens the refrigerator, placing them neatly on the shelves. "That's not what I mean."

Shuffling condiment bottles fill a few moments while neither of us speak. We both know the condiment bottles haven't moved recently. "Come to the Fall Festival. Maybe you'll meet someone." The last part is said quietly.

"Mama—"

Knowing I'm going to protest, she stands suddenly and gives me a look I know better than to argue with. "How are you supposed to fall in love if you spend all of your time with cows?"

My eyes bug and I release a full belly laugh.

"Just think about it."

"Yes, ma'am." Thirty or not, I know when not to sass Mama.

She flips the light off on her way out of the kitchen and I swear she mumbles something about *pretty babies* as she heads down the darkened hallway to my parents' bedroom.

Cool night air greets me when I head out to my truck later. I roll the window down and embrace the reprieve from the grueling sun. After a busy week, a few beers with Nick is just what I need. Never mind that Saturdays are my least favorite time to visit The Spur. Second least. Fridays are the worst.

Available parking in the first row is a surprise since everybody in town seems to be here tonight. I am not looking forward to fights and bullshit, so I plan to have a few beers and get the hell out of Dodge.

A cold rain begins to trickle down. As I reach the door, it becomes a steady shower and squeals burst out behind me. Knowing someone is about to be drenched, I pull the door open wide and press my foot against the bottom of the door, stepping aside. Two women are hightailing it across the parking lot with their heads ducked, squeezing between my truck and a long set of motorcycles. An abrupt gust of wind whips through the parking lot, splattering all three of us with ice-cold raindrops as it blows. One of the women shrieks.

"Thanks!" she yells over her shoulder as she barrels past. I wonder if she's rethinking her dark denim shorts.

Her friend is moving a tad slower. She pushes her windblown hair out of her face as she passes. Her laugh and bright smile greet me over her shoulder when she turns to say something.

Maci.

She stares back at me, her face nearly glowing, and whispers a thank you.

My heart stutters awkwardly. I lick my lips and give her a stupid nod because she's the last person I expected to see tonight. And also because while I assumed Happy Maci would be beautiful, she's intoxicating.

A light wash denim jacket covers a white dress with flowers on it, cinched around the middle with a brown belt. She reminds me of a 90s country chick-flick my sister watched when we were kids.

I can't pull my eyes from her bottom lip as she bites it. It's doing things to me it shouldn't.

"Sutton." She sounds as surprised as me.

I clear my throat. "Hey. How are you?"

Her eyes flick to the pavement then back to me. "Better. Thank you." She sounds genuine.

"Good." I look behind her into the dark bar for a moment. "Can I—"

"Come on!" Her friend returns to the door, yanking her through. "We're going to miss it!"

"Ok!" A playful laugh escapes her and she waves at me as she's pulled inside. For a few seconds, I'm rooted to the doorway with the wind throwing icy water at me, watching her disappear into the dark.

Shaking my head like an idiot, I step inside, allowing the door to close. A mammoth of a bouncer sits on a tiny stool not far from the entrance. He eyes me like he's seen the entire exchange and thinks I'm in way over my head. He's right.

"Heyyyy. Suttonnnn!" Nick calls from a table not far off.

Copperhead Road fills my ears as I approach. "Hey." Without trying, I'm distracted, scanning the crowd.

"You good?" Nick asks from my peripheral, looking around the bar to find what I'm searching for. Drinking or not, Nick is always someone you want on your side. And not just because he's a Texas Game Warden. He's a solid guy with a good moral compass and has an uncanny ability to talk people down.

Movement on the dance floor catches my attention. Maci and her friend dance wildly on the far side of the room, without a care in the world. Her dress almost glows blue underneath the neon lights.

Of course. Her friend thought they were going to miss the popular line dance.

I grin. "Yeah." Turning, I clap Nick on the shoulder. "I'm good."

Nick looks at me briefly, his brows pulling together, then follows my line of sight to the two dancers. "Oh, damn." He laughs and returns the brotherly gesture.

Maci turns to her friend and laughs heartily. Her face is lit up like the Fourth of July, happiness emanating from her.

I shake my head and laugh. I already know I'm not getting out of a mini-interrogation.

"How you been?" I give him my full attention.

He takes a swig of his beer. "Good, man. The usual. Coming up to the end of archery season."

"I haven't made it out yet."

"You don't have long left. Oh man, yesterday I was out checking licenses and came across this group out past Henry Bridge." Nick carries on with his story and I divide my attention between him and Maci. The song ends and the two women make their way off the dance floor, arms linked. They're both all smiles as they order.

In no time, a biker in a black vest approaches. He has a Prospect patch on the back. Neither seem to see him as they chat before Maci's friend heads off through the crowd. I lose sight of her, keeping my eyes trained on Maci.

The guy slips into the space previously occupied by the brunette, hovering over Maci in a way that has my jaw clenching. She stiffens and stands taller. One hand reaches out for her drink on the bar top and her eyes flit around the room. She sips her drink.

"Sutton?"

"Yeah." I don't take my eyes off Maci as I respond to Nick. The biker leans comfortably against the bar top. My frustration builds over her tense body and uncomfortable stance. On their next sweep, her eyes land on me.

The man seems to call her attention back, but I'm over this bullshit. Something is going on and I'm going to find out what it is. Fights at this bar are a dime a dozen and somehow I've stayed out of most. But if he so much as blinks at her wrong, I'll lay his ass out.

"I'll be right back, looks like I've got some catching up to do." I gesture to the dark bottle he holds and grin as I head to the bar. "Watch my six."

"Always." Nick salutes with his beer.

CHAPTER 15

MACI

I can't contain my laughter. Dancing is so freeing and the atmosphere is pulsing in here tonight. The look I got from Sutton may be adding to my high.

When Leah's number one pick of the night ends, we make our way to the bar for drinks. She shouts our order over the music and I take in the place. I may or may not be looking for a particular cowboy.

"God, I've missed you!" Leah squeezes me tightly. Her head shifts to one side of me and her eyes focus past me. "Hey, are you good if I go say hi to Pete?"

"Of course!" I wave her away as our drinks appear on the bar. She grabs hers and heads through the crowd.

Out of nowhere, Colt slides into the space before me. "Colt." Surprise colors my voice. I hadn't thought of him since our trainwreck of a one-night-stand.

The corner of his mouth tips in a smug way. "Hey. You came back."

I take a sip of my drink, checking out the rest of the bar and I hum a non-committal response.

"Couldn't stay away?" He leans against the bar.

My reaction to his smirk isn't like it was last time I saw him. "I'm here with friends."

107

"I'm glad you are." His voice is lower. I'm surprised I can hear it over the music. It doesn't have the desired effect.

The feeling of being watched washes over me and I avert my eyes again. "Look—" My eyes find Sutton's. He's standing at a cocktail table near the entrance. "I'm not really looking for anything serious."

The cowboy's eyes blaze into mine, but he doesn't look happy. In fact, he looks the least happy I've ever seen him, and that's saying something, because his expressions are mostly indifferent.

Except for when he held the door open tonight.

Colt shifts closer. "Neither am I. Doesn't mean we can't have some fun. Let me take you out while you're still here." He reaches out with his empty hand and trails his fingers down my hip.

"No, thanks." I jerk back.

He ignores my vicious tone, chuckling at me. "You didn't have fun?"

"I said no." I knock his hand away, since he isn't getting the hint.

He swallows deeply, setting his jaw tightly. His eyes don't waver as he stares into mine before he looks into the crowd casually. The move isn't casual, though. It's deliberate. An effort to keep something locked away.

For a moment, he rubs at his temple in frustration. Maybe trying to stave off a headache?

He empties what remains of his beer and slams the bottle forcefully onto the bar, saying nothing more before walking away. He may as well have had smoke pouring out his ears. It reminds me of Alan in the kitchen last week.

A heavy breath forces itself from my lungs and I lean heavily into the bar. The drink goes down in one gulp after I yank the tiny straw from it. Tawny passes and I gesture to her with the empty glass.

"You good?" A deep voice nearby startles me.

Sutton's steely eyes are trained on me. His body mimics mine, facing the bar top itself. "Yeah, thanks."

Tawny sets my drink down and I throw it back like a shot.

Sutton moves closer, orders a few beers from Tawny, and gestures to my glass. Then he turns to me. "Where'd your friend go?"

My eyebrows jump. Does he mean Colt or Leah? He tilts his head toward the front door in a silent answer, pressing his lips together like he's hiding a smirk.

I purse my lips. "She's with another friend."

Things are already more complicated than is necessary. I throw a look over my shoulder to see if Colt is with Leah and the rest of the MC. They occupy the space around the pool tables in the main room. Leah is racking the balls. As if feeling my eyes, she looks my way.

She gives me a questioning thumbs up to check on me, but doesn't see my responding thumbs up because her eyes shift to Sutton standing next to me. Her eyebrows raise followed by a mischievous wink. I don't see Colt among the group.

Sutton and I reach for our drinks at the same time, our hands grazing. He's like a human heat rock. My eyes shoot up to his face.

"You're hot."

His eyebrows jump before he smirks. My cheeks flame, but I don't bother trying to correct the mishap.

Pressing the bottle to his lips, he takes a long drink and I'm curious what they feel like. I watch his Adam's Apple bob as he drinks.

Holy shit, I think my panties just spontaneously combusted.

Well, that was unexpected.

He studies his hand. Maybe it was my hand that was cold and not the other way around? Without warning, he stands fully and offers an upturned palm to me. "Dance with me."

It's not a question but he waits for my agreement.

I stand and take his hand. His grip is firm, but not unpleasant. My eyes fall to our fresh drinks.

"They have more," he says into my ear, pressing his front to my back. With our hands clasped in front of me, he leads by following. Something I've never experienced before.

I've barely stepped over the threshold when he tugs gently at my hand, pulling me against him and wrapping his other arm around my waist. My free hand grabs the back of his arm instinctively. Our height difference becomes a little clearer knowing my hand usually rests on a shoulder.

Over the years, I've danced with my fair share of men. Sutton is the first to immediately manipulate my body and I'm unsure yet if that is in my favor or not.

My eyes slide up his chest as he swiftly guides us around the dance floor. His touch is gentle, secure, and comfortable. I admire his scruffy facial hair and strong jaw.

"Why are you looking at me like that?" There's a sparkle in his eyes. His voice stays low, unbothered.

"I—" A memory floods me. My eyes linger on the bar tables, but I can almost feel the warm breeze as Nana and I swing on the front porch. She told me about dancing with my grandfather when they first started dating. She always talked about how much fun they had together.

My mouth pulls into a smile at the idea of a sort of shared experience with her.

When I draw my eyes back up, Sutton is still studying my face. "I was remembering something my grandmother told me."

As we move through a corner, he releases his grip on my waist, gliding his hand along my arm as he pushes me out for a spin. My body moves willingly, expecting him to pull me directly back in after an easy double spin. Instead, he leads me across his body as he turns in a circle. My hand slips from his and slides along his lower back as we move around each other.

For a split second, I think of the rotating Earth and the moon orbiting it. Facing me again, he secures my hand and pulls me firmly back into him.

"Are you trying to impress me?" I attempt to hit with more sarcasm and less awe. This isn't my first rodeo, but I'm wondering if I'm in over my head.

"You haven't had a proper dance?" He grins down at me. Before I can respond, he's tossing me out for another fancy spin series.

Laughter bubbles out of me. It's like being on a roller coaster. I have no choice but to give in to the glee tunneling through my body. When he pulls me back in, I let the laughter flow from me. "I've had plenty of dances before. Nothing like this," I finally admit.

"I think it's going to take a lot more than this to impress you." His smile is playful and his eyes never leave me. He tips his head down. "You were lit up like a sparkler out here earlier. I was hoping to see that fire again if I brought you."

The heat in my cheeks isn't the only heat I feel now. As if knowing, he tightens his grip on my waist.

I've experienced butterflies before. But the sensation his rugged looks and sure hold ignite is less chaotic, more delicate, and highly flammable. My body warms from the core outward.

How did I miss this last week? Everything seemed so off-kilter. It's as if I'm looking at the world with fresh eyes.

"Should I be keeping an eye out for an angry biker at my back?"

My eyebrows shoot up, but I recover and shake my head as we make another circle. "No. I think he left." I sweep the area where Leah is once more.

"Boyfriend?" His eyes flash.

I shake my head again. "Just a guy who doesn't like hearing no, apparently."

His jaw tenses even though his eyes stay soft on me as he continues to effortlessly move us around the floor. It's packed tonight. His eyes never leave me and yet I'm not concerned we'll crash into anyone.

"One more question." Sutton waits for a response. I cock my head to one side and stare up at him. "Do you trust me?"

"I trust you enough to dance with you."

"That's all?" He teases as we move into another corner. I purse my lips playfully, not giving the reason for his question much thought.

The last bars of the song play. Sutton's eyes stay laser-focused on me. He sends me out for a final double spin, eliciting a smile. Both of my hands come back to his and he pulls me directly to him pinning my hands behind my back with his.

My breath catches. Neither of us moves as people exit around us. It's only a second before a new song will play and I know we need to move, but I can't bring myself to break our contact. His eyes drop to my mouth. Just as quickly, they move back up and he slowly releases my hands, sliding his own forward on my hips and then releasing me.

I immediately miss the warmth of his body and his hands on me. When he extends his hand, I grasp it without hesitation.

I'm so screwed.

"Your friend okay?"

We wait for a new round at the bar. Leah is still playing pool with Pete and Colt is nowhere in sight, both of which I verified as soon as we came off the dance floor. "Yeah. She's playing pool." I gesture in the direction of the two pool tables.

Sutton gives a cursory glance. "You want to join them?"

He's being subtle, but I don't know why. He doesn't strike me as the type to beat around the bush. "If you have somewhere to be, don't worry about me."

He straightens and closes the small gap between us, looking down at me with those intense eyes again. "Worry isn't the word I would use." His voice skates over my skin, low and enticing.

"Oh?" I snatch my glass off the bar and take a sip in an attempt to hide my surprise.

"No." Leaning his weight back on his heels he adds, "But if you want to play pool or hang out with your friends, then I won't stop you."

I steal another glance. Leah is in her element, pushing Pete's shoulder with exaggerated flirtation and likely winning the round. "Leah's my friend. But the others aren't really."

There's a question in his eyes. I don't offer and whatever it is doesn't get asked. After a beat, he says, "Well, you're welcome to come with me, then. I'll introduce you."

With my free hand, I motion for him to lead the way. His palm warms my lower back as he guides me toward the table where I first saw him.

A broad, blonde man stands with his back to us. He's wearing jeans, a navy tee, and dirty ball cap, mingling with a few people.

Past them, on the front wall is an arcade game that measures the force behind a punch. Someone swings at it and I stop in my tracks. Sutton turns sharply, looking me over. Finding nothing amiss he takes a step toward me, cocking his head to one side in question.

"You're not going to hit that, are you?" My eyes dart past him, to the game, before returning to his. I'm forced to look directly up at him when he closes the remaining distance between us.

The corner of his mouth kicks up. "Do you have something against that machine?"

"It's a tool machine." My drink nearly sloshes out of my glass when I abruptly cross my arms in an effort to appear sassy. The last thing I plan to do is spend time with guys who think they're tough because of a high score on a simulated punching bag.

His returning grin is everything. "Do I look like a tool to you? Be careful how you answer."

I laugh. "No. But I've been fooled before."

"I don't seek validation from inanimate objects."

"Who do you seek validation from?" This time I take a small step forward. It's not a challenge. I'm just trying to cover up my own surprise at asking a very pointed question.

Sutton gives me a sexy half-smirk. "Not many."

His hand falls against my back again and we continue walking. The blonde turns and catches sight of us. A flash of surprise crosses his features before his face splits into a boyish grin.

"Hey, man, I thought I lost you." His smile never falters.

"Maci, this is my best friend Nick. Nick, this is Maci."

Nick reaches across the table and gives a smooth, confident shake. "Ma'am."

"Oh no, don't do that." I laugh awkwardly.

"No?" His face remains pleasantly curious.

"No, please. I'm way too young to be a ma'am." Nick opens his mouth to protest, but I put a hand up to stop him. "I know, I know. Southern habits die hard. I do it, too. But please—just Maci."

Nick nods with a thin-lipped smile and eyes Sutton who hasn't taken his eyes off me. "Ok, Just Maci."

I grin. "One more thing, Nick. And this one is really important, so be careful how you answer." Sutton's eyes spark when I use his words. "Are you going to hit that machine?" I hike an eyebrow to indicate the space behind him.

He immediately laughs. "No ma-No. No, I'm not. Do you want to hit it?" He gives me a boyish grin and laughs at my returned expression.

All I can think is how different tonight is from the last time I was here. The company, the atmosphere. I catalog Leah's whereabouts again.

The next few hours fly by. I take turns with Sutton and Leah on the dance floor. There are constantly new people coming up to Sutton and Nick. Sutton introduces me to a few who seem like more than acquaintances, but overall the conversations are short and surface level. It's how I would assume it would feel to hang out with celebrities.

Around one, Pete and Leah make their way over to us. Pete is supporting Leah who is more than a little inebriated. My jaw clenches and I set my current glass on the table. Nick and Sutton also zero in on the movement.

"I offered to take her home, but she wouldn't let me." Pete's muttering an explanation to me and I'm curious if he thinks Sutton and Nick might kick his ass. Leah is too drunk to be safe. Guilt washes over me. We've never split up before. I should have kept a better eye on her.

"She's really drunk." My voice doesn't carry much weight. I cup Leah's face in a hand. "Do you want to stay with me tonight?"

"No, I'm ffffine." She sways on her feet as Pete removes her arm from around his shoulders. She pats Pete's cut, just above his Member patch. He presses his lips together in defeat and turns to make his way back to what's left of the MC at this hour.

I slide my arm around Leah's waist and turn to Sutton. "We need to go."

"Agreed." His jaw is tight and his serious gaze flits between Leah and me.

"We'll help." Nick scoops Leah up with one arm under her legs and one behind her back.

"Wha—" I'm equal parts stunned and grateful. It's not like I could've gotten her easily out to my Jeep. Her protest is mumbled at best and her eyes fight a losing battle to stay open.

Outside, I take in a huge breath. The air inside had become thick and stifling, and I relish the cool wind filling my lungs. A crisp chill has replaced the rain.

"That's my Jeep." I point to the second row and use the key fob to unlock it.

Nick expertly navigates the thinning cars. Somehow, he manages to open the back door, without dropping Leah, before setting her gingerly in the backseat. His wide frame disappears inside as Sutton and I approach, and I hear the distinct click of the buckle before the door shuts solidly.

"Thank you." Once again, I'm met with the inadequacies of my words.

Nick gives me a two-finger salute. "Hope we get to see more of you two." His voice is genuine and he touches me on the shoulder as he walks back to the bar.

Over his shoulder, Sutton says, "I'll meet you back inside," as I lean in to start the car.

"Thanks," I say, standing again.

"No thanks needed." He steps forward, closing the gap between us. "When do I get to see you again?"

Knowing he's interested in seeing me again boosts my confidence. The practical side speaks first. "You know I'm not sticking around. I'm only here now because Leah begged me to go out with her this weekend. And we have brunch tomorrow."

"So you'll be here tomorrow." He smirks.

"I'm getting the impression you have selective hearing." I wet my lips and his eyes narrow on my mouth.

An all-consuming tension builds as he drags his eyes back up to mine. "Not at all. I prefer to have a solution-based mindset."

"Mm-hm. And what seems to be the problem?" The door is cold against my back as I lean into it, crossing my arms over my chest. Both actions are an attempt to ease the magnetic pull between us.

He ignores my question. "Do you want to see me before you leave?" He's giving me an out, while simultaneously backing me into a corner. I can't play coy if I admit a desire to spend more time with him. I don't know what the point would be anyway.

I uncross one arm and turn my hand over, channeling my inner Leah. "Phone." I bend my fingers up and down a couple times indicating for him to hand it over.

In the shadow of his hat brim, his eyes soften as he looks between my upturned palm and my face. He obliges, unlocking his phone and offering it to me. A stunning sunrise fills the home screen. My eyes flick up to him. He watches me with dark eyes.

I quickly program my number in and hand it back.

Without checking, he pockets the phone, holding me in his magnetic gaze. "One more question."

I squint at him.

"Do you trust me?"

A breathy laugh pushes out of me. How could I not after both he and his friend made sure Leah and I were safe tonight? I don't know what's so important that he's asking for a second time.

I bite my lip, determined to keep the upper hand somehow. "Mostly."

"Good." Sutton slides a hand onto my hip and leans down to kiss me. It's warm, and tender, and brief. I think he's going to leave it at that until he comes back in for a second kiss, and this one is everything.

His other hand presses against my neck, fingers tangling in my hair like an anchor. I grab the front of his shirt with both hands, pulling myself closer to him and his intoxicating warmth. Too soon, he pulls back.

"In case you change your mind about seeing me again," he says.

I'm certain I can't after that.

CHAPTER 16

SUTTON

"Who was that?" Guaranteed, Nick has been dying to interrogate me about Maci since I introduced her. I barely make it back to the table before he asks.

"Maci. I introduced you." I down the rest of my beer.

"That's not what I asked and you know it." He crosses his beefy arms. Even though we played baseball together, somehow he turned out looking more like a cage fighter.

"Don't try to intimidate me. We both know you're more golden retriever than bull." I side-eye him. "My mom knew her grandmother who passed recently."

His expectant face doesn't change. When I offer nothing else, he prods me further. "Uh huh. And?"

"And I went over there to take my mom when she dropped food off. Tonight I happened to see some asshole making Maci uncomfortable and offered to dance with her."

Nick's eyes narrow. "You're not telling me everything. But fine."

Shrugging, I toss the bottles from the table into a trash can not far away. "I'm closing out my tab."

"Alright, I'm headed out. Call me this week." A teasing grin spreads across Nick's face. "Unless you're busy."

"Yeah, I'm expecting several calves this week."

His face falls when I don't take the bait. "Fine. Keep it locked up. I know you'll tell me when you're ready."

I only wave him off as I head to the bar.

When Sammi and I were teenagers, Mama would wait up for us, often sitting in her recliner with the reading lamp on, crocheting something. She always needed something to do with her hands. She'd kiss me on the cheek and head straight to bed, dropping whatever she was doing unless I had something to tell her.

Tonight, the glow of the reading lamp shines down the hallway from her chair and out the front window like a lighthouse beacon. It's what draws me in before heading to my entrance.

"Mama? You good?" The front door closes with a snick and I make a point to soften my steps.

Her legs are curled up beneath her. "Of course, honey." She gifts me a loving smile. "Did you have a nice time?"

I lean down and kiss the top of her head. She pats my arm.

"I did…" It's an effort to keep the suspicion from my tone. Her question is subtle, but she's eager to get some details. Her slippers tap softly as she follows me into the kitchen.

She leans her head against the doorframe. "Mmhmm."

The night didn't go as anticipated. What should've been a few drinks with my best friend turned into something far more significant. I down a glass of water and stare into the dark dining room. Visions of Maci wrapped in my arms fill my mind.

"Nick's good?"

I blink. "Yeah." *She knows.*

My eyes slide to her. She presses her lips together. Her expression is otherwise blank. Ironically, that's what gives her away.

A silent shift is happening. Without question, my mom has always been *the most* important woman to me. The most beautiful, inside and out. I've always envied the steadfast love she and my dad share.

A nervous sensation springs up inside. My mom has never judged me for my mistakes in life. So why is there a tiny piece of me worried she may deem me crazy when the words in my head tumble out?

A sparkle lights her eyes, despite the low light. It hints at a held secret. Unconditional love radiates from her.

"I saw Maci tonight."

A tiny flicker of surprise crosses her face, but it's replaced quickly with a happy smile. "Oh? How is she?" She moves into the kitchen, leaning against the counter across from me.

"I'm gonna marry her."

She nods knowingly and presents me with a proud smile.

My mom didn't offer any other conversation to me. She gave my arm a gentle squeeze on her way out of the kitchen and left the reading lamp on as she headed down the hallway to bed. After a minute of quiet contemplation, I downed another glass of water and then locked the front door behind me, making my way around to my entrance.

Already, I want to talk to Maci again. I find her name in my contacts, easily. She's listed as 'Maci' as if she wanted me to find her. Before texting, I rename the listing.

Me:

I assume you made it home safely.

Less than a minute passes before three bubbles appear.

Firecracker:

Who's asking?

Me:

Your trusty dance partner.

Firecracker:

Oh, yeah. There was some random guy I danced with tonight.

I did. I'm tucked safely in bed.

Me:

Good.

Sweet dreams, Firecracker.

Firecracker:

Good night, Cowboy. >TNT emoji<

CHAPTER 17

MACI

I'm blinded awake by the sun squeezing between the closed wooden blinds. The Grandmother clock opposite the foot of the bed indicates an hour before brunch. Which I'm hosting.

After a quick shower, I tie my hair up in my favorite style of braid and head into the kitchen to start cooking. Songs from dancing last night replay in my head and I hum them while I work.

The first time we met, Sutton seemed stoic. Last night, though, I'd felt like the only person in the world, important, as we danced.

Leah and Izzy arrive as I'm setting the French toast onto a tray in the oven to keep warm.

They hardly wait for me to yell, "Come in!" after knocking before I hear the door open, the handle smacking the wall.

"Good morning!" comes Izzy's cheerful greeting, with Leah on her tail grumbling and less than sparkly. That explains the aggressive door opening.

I dropped her off at her house, leaving water and Tylenol by the bed. It was the best I could do since she strongly opposed staying with me.

Izzy sets what she's carrying on the packed island and wraps me in an all-consuming hug. Leah grimaces behind her dark sunglasses.

"I see you're feeling the effects of last night." Izzy and I exchange knowing grins.

Leah grumbles, "Do you two have to be so damn loud all the time?"

Izzy gives a loving roll of her eyes. "Dining room?" She lifts up the insulated bags she brought in.

"Yep." I plate the bacon. Leah plunks orange juice and champagne on the dining table, as Izzy pulls bowls of various berries and a tray of breakfast sausages from the carriers. My eyes catch briefly on the drinks.

"I've missed this." Izzy's voice is soft. I turn to see her folding up the insulated bags before coming back over and pulling serving trays from the cabinet naturally.

"Me too." I lay my head on her shoulder.

"Remember when Nana taught us how to make chicken noodle soup?" Izzy's head presses onto mine.

"Yes! We felt like real women." We fall quiet, both remembering the summer we turned sixteen.

"I'm starving." The champagne glasses clink against the counter as Leah pulls four down from a cabinet behind us.

Izzy and I look over our shoulders. "I'm surprised you can even think about food."

Leah doesn't respond, just grumbles her way back to the dining table where she plops down and fills her glass.

"Liv's still coming?" Izzy's voice is hopeful. She's taken over placing the French toast on a platter, and without discussing it, we both start moving food to the table.

"Yep. Should be here any minute."

"Fabulous," Leah grumbles, "more noise." Izzy rolls her eyes again. "Keep rolling your eyes like that and they'll get stuck."

We snicker at each other. I set a platter heavily onto the table. "I don't know how you can see past those glasses."

A soft tapping on the screen door precedes footsteps approaching the kitchen. Liv rounds the corner. "Sorry I'm late."

She holds up a container carrying a veggie tray in offering, which Izzy swipes before hugging her gingerly.

"Not at all!" My hug is tighter. "I'm glad you could come." Our similar age didn't equate to the same friends growing up, even though my best friends lived in the same town with my cousin. Liv was more reserved and stayed busy with math teams and other academic enhancements. Most of my friends at school were surface-level at best, but my time with Izzy and Leah was always unparalleled.

The four of us settle around the table, catching up on life as we eat. It's incredibly comforting after the last ten days. And it's what the house needs to feel like a home again. I recall Izzy asking me about letting this go, before pushing it from my mind.

"Liv, how's school going?" Izzy sips her mimosa.

"Oh, boy." Liv inhales deeply. "It's been a year. This class is giving me a run for my money."

Izzy smiles. "I'm sure it's because you make them feel comfortable."

Liv blushes and changes the subject. "Well, Leah, you look like you're feeling better. Rough night?" It always surprises me when Liv teases people, but it's even more adorable coming from her.

"She *sure did* tie one on." I can't help but laugh at Leah's expense.

"Oh you're one to talk, Twinkle Toes." She raises her mimosa in challenge, her grin matching mine.

Liv's head whips between us, realizing she's missed something. "You both went?"

"Leah strong-armed me."

Izzy chews quietly, watching the exchange. We've had our fair share of ladies' nights over the years, but always with a solid plan. No doubt Izzy has questions about what went down last night. The worry written on her face is similar to the frustration I felt last night having Leah mostly slung over someone's shoulder as she was deposited to me. Never mind having to be fully carried outside. I don't even know what she remembers.

"I didn't see you complaining when that stud of a cowboy swept you onto the dance floor." Leah pointedly moves the heat to me. She takes a long gulp of her mimosa in quiet celebration and raises her eyebrows as if to say *so, there*.

"Stud?" Izzy parrots. She shoves my chair with her shoulder. Her blue eyes sparkle at me.

"His name is Sutton, and he's a rancher."

Izzy's mouth falls open.

Liv cuts in. "As in Sutton Strickland?" Her eyes are huge.

My brows pull together. "Yes? Why are you saying his name like that? He was just here last week."

"Not as a date." Liv grins.

"It wasn't a date."

"He can *dance*." Leah can't help but stir the pot.

"Yes he can." My eyes rest on the uneaten food centered on the round table. "It wasn't what I was expecting for the night, that's for sure."

Leah refills her plate while Izzy and Liv continue to stare at me. Neither of them dares to ask anything.

"I met Sutton after Nana passed. He came with his mom when she brought over some food. She's very sweet." My mouth tips at her warm nature. Everyone should be so lucky to have a mom like her. "He happened to be at the bar last night."

"Well he scared Colt off, anyway." Leah speaks through her French toast.

"Colt?" Izzy is looking between us again. She and Liv shrug at each other.

"The biker?" I offer this information as if it will give them an inkling as to who he is. "Oh, really? Everyone knows Sutton, but no one knows Colt?"

The town is small, but I can't assume that between the four of us we'll know everyone. Although it's starting to feel that way with each person I meet. *Stupid small town.*

I take a bite of the crispy bacon on my plate. "What about Pete?"

A thud echoes under the table and I snicker at Leah trying to kick me.

Liv grins widely as Leah and I stare each other down playfully.

No one bites on the Pete comment, so I give in and keep going. "It's moot anyway. Sutton didn't talk to him. Colt was angry with me."

"You pissed off a biker?" Izzy's mouth tightens.

"It's not like that..." *Maybe it is like that.* "Whatever. He can fuck right off."

Liv's eyebrows raise and she suppresses a laugh. My eyes fly to her. "I love when you're yourself," she promises and pats my hand on the table. She spears a strawberry half with her fork and pops it in her mouth. "Are you going to see him again? Sutton?"

Leah's sunglasses sit loosely atop her head, day old makeup visible around her eyes. "That man was watching Ms. Maci like she was the only woman in the world."

We can always count on Leah for the drama. I roll my eyes. "He was a little intense, but I wouldn't go that far." I can't hide my smile. "I gave him my number."

Liv grins excitedly.

"Intense?" Izzy's questioning this time is playful.

127

"He—" I halt, rolling my lips in and trying to determine how best to explain Sutton's interactions.

Leah snorts at the same time. "It was some love at first sight shit."

"Oh God, Leah, that's a bit dramatic." Laughter spills out of me.

Leah shrugs. "I just call 'em like I see 'em."

"I don't know how you saw anything, quite frankly. Between pool, flirting with your own *biker,* and drinking."

"And there it is," Izzy says with a shake of her head. "You two can't be trusted anywhere."

Full to the brim, sore from laughing, and a little tear-streaked from stories about Nana, brunch finally comes to an end. Izzy and Leah head out together. Liv fakes looking busy until we're alone. We cleaned up before the others left, so there's nothing for her to do.

"What are you going to do about this place?" Liv's eyes trail around the kitchen.

I look around the space until I realize what she means. I'm surprised this is coming from her, too.

"It's not up to me." My shrug is a little more defeated and a little less careless. I try to turn her question around. "What is your mom going to do with this place?"

Liv pins me with a look.

"You look just like Nana right now." My smile stretches so wide it hurts, and my eyes blur.

She hugs me tightly. "You know that's not what I mean."

Tears flow down my cheeks and I squeeze her tighter instead of responding.

She talks softly into my ear. "Your heart is in this house. More than any of the rest of us. And that's okay. Yes, our moms grew up here, but it's been years since they spent any solid time here. They built their own lives. Just like we are."

She pulls back, but doesn't give me long to digest before continuing. "For what it's worth, I loved Nana and she will *always* be special to me. But she was your grandmother. You know?"

"She was your grandmother, too," I argue quickly, looking into her hazel eyes.

"I know. I mean that your bond with her was different. I know Nana loved me, too. That's never been a question. I'm not worried about favorites. Y'all's relationship was different."

"Yeah." I don't need to add how desperately I wish to talk to her or hug her one more time, or how deeply the loss has impacted me. Maybe this is what most people feel like losing a mother they're close to. My reaction to losing Stephanie will never compare to this and I can't bring myself to feel guilty about that. "What does all of that mean?"

"It means, I think you should consider if you want to keep the house." Liv shrugs like the answer is plain as day. She pulls away softly and turns to close up the dishwasher.

My eyes widen at her back. "What would I do with it? My business is established. I have my own place." An apartment with a lease I need to renew. I never signed the form this week.

"Don't be silly, Maci." She takes too long to dry her hands on a hand towel. "You can move your business."

Her hand comes up to stop my anticipated protest. "Yes, you would need to transition. Maybe you could travel between here and Austin until you've built a large base. You don't work a nine to five." Her eyes are piercing again in that honest way Nana used to do. "And an apartment hardly ties you to any one place for the rest of your life." She leans against the counter and crosses her arms.

"Ok, you're right about that." My eyes drift and I trace the grain of the butcher block counter with my fingers. "I'll think about it."

Liv gives a sharp nod of approval. "Good. Now take the trash out." We laugh, but I wrap her in another tight hug before following orders.

"I love you."

"I love *you.*"

CHAPTER 18

MACI

Crickets chirp outside the living room window as I sprawl on the couch, reading one of Nana's books. When my phone vibrates from a text, I jump. It's on the tray table where Nana used to keep hers. I reach for it, expecting to see something from Izzy or Leah, even though we saw each other today.

Cowboy:

How was your day?

Sutton.

Like a giddy teenager, my heart rate kicks up and I bite my lip. I thought about texting earlier, but I didn't want to bother him if things were busy at the ranch. I have no idea what those things would be, because I'm not even sure what kind of ranch his family has or what his role is, but it seemed safer to wait him out.

Me:

Good. Hosted brunch. You?

Cowboy:

Sounds like a party. Just got done with family dinner.

That sounds nice.

I feel a pang of envy. What must it be like to enjoy your family? To have loving meals together and feel comfort in their presence? Belatedly, I realize I have nothing to feel envious of. I have my family, even if they aren't all blood-related, and I do get to enjoy beautiful meals with them. Today was proof of that.

My phone ringing in my hand startles me and my heart does a little jump at *Cowboy* on the screen. I accept the call and put the phone up to my ear, willing my breathing to even out. "Hi."

"Hi, yourself." Flutters. I'd almost forgotten how his deep voice is, both gruff and soothing at the same time. He doesn't give me a chance to say anything else. "What are you doing right now?"

A grin fills my face. "Talking to you."

"Did you eat?" I get the impression this isn't the information he's really seeking.

"Yes."

The ensuing pause seems calculated. "What's your favorite food?"

"Hmm." Jumping off the couch, I head into the laundry room to switch the linens while we talk. "Probably Indian cuisine."

He chuckles. "I wasn't expecting that."

"I hope you weren't expecting salad."

"No. Maybe steak or carbs."

"I'll never turn down either. Especially sweets." A door closes on his end of the line, followed by crunching. "Am I keeping you from something?"

"Not at all." There's a dinging from his end and when he speaks again, his voice echoes a bit. I suspect he's transferred the call to the speakerphone in his truck. "I want to see you."

"Ok. You said as much at The Spur."

"Now."

Settling back on the couch, my heart rate picks up again. My eyes trail over my gray ribbed loungewear. It's not unpresentable, though it seems out of order to show him this prior to a first date. Then again, I've told him I'm leaving. My stay here has an end. Why present him with a polished version, something he can't have, anyway? And is it even fair to give in to these whims, when it will ultimately lead to nothing?

He's a grown man, though, who can make his own choices. I've been honest, so a little fun won't hurt anyone, right?

"Ok."

"Yes?" He seems a little surprised.

"I'm not really dressed." He doesn't respond right away so I add in a hurry, "I mean, I have clothes on," A nervous laugh escapes me. "I'm just not *dressed*. I wasn't really planning on company."

"I'm not interested in your clothes. I'll be there in twenty minutes."

Twenty-five minutes later, a large pair of headlights crests the hill onto the driveway and Sutton parks his dark truck next to my Jeep. I may not have changed clothes while he drove over, but I did fluff pillows, light a candle, and turn on a TV show for some background noise. I have no idea what his plans are, but I couldn't sit still while I waited.

It feels silly to wait for him to knock when I can clearly see him—something he knows given the open living room blinds. So I open the front door, but leave the storm door closed until he reaches the porch before pushing it open wide. "You're late."

He stops in front of me, his gaze taking in my face. I suspect he has on a fresh shirt, but his jeans and boots are dusty, hinting at a busy day. I wonder if someone else would be put off by him not changing completely. I find his realness appealing.

His signature hat rests atop his head, somewhat shielding his eyes in shadow. Warmth pours through my body.

"Then let this be my first apology offering." From his side, he produces a square, plastic container I hadn't realized he was carrying before. I blame it on the dark and not the sheer effort of taking my eyes off his own.

"What's that?"

He holds it out without responding. A single piece of New York Style cheesecake sits perfectly in the container. My eyes fly up to his. "Cheesecake?"

"I assumed traditional was the way to go on flavor. Unless it's too soon."

Words leave me. I shake my head and step back, silently inviting him inside as. Did he really hold onto that tiny piece of information? Something I shared in an emotional fit?

He eyes the foyer, seemingly searching for something, then glances toward the porch swing. His skin is warm as he takes one of my hands and gives me a gentle tug. It's reminiscent of how he led me at the bar and I'm grateful there's no awkwardness.

The storm door rattles its close as I follow him toward the swing, where he eyes me and jerks his chin for me to sit.

There's an ease to our interactions, his directions. They're sure, but never pressured.

"I need to grab a fork. Unless that's for later." I grin at him.

His eyes dart to my mouth then return to mine. "Sit." There's a hint of a smile on his lips.

Curling my legs in front of me and leaning my back against the arm of the swing, I face the space I've left open for him.

With his now free hand, he pulls a black, plastic fork from his back pocket. I gape before slamming my mouth shut. He sits casually, spreading his feet wide, before opening the lid of the container, stabbing the fork into the center of the slice, and passing the tray to me. Draping his left arm along the back of the swing, he gently rocks us as he takes me in.

"Are we sharing?"

He smirks. "Nope. That's all for you, Firecracker."

I raise an eyebrow in question at the nickname, but then deliver the first bite of cheesecake to my mouth and my curiosity is forgotten. It's been too long since I've had this simple pleasure and a tiny moan slips free. His eyes narrow. I pretend not to notice and go in for another bite.

I couldn't bring myself to gorge myself on the whole cheesecake Nana made. I donated it, along with some of the other untouched food, and the stupid flowers I was happy to orphan, to an assisted living home on my way out of town Monday.

His eyes bore into mine, stoking the fire inside. My nipples peak and I'm reminded I'm not wearing a bra. If he notices, he doesn't show it. I can't imagine he doesn't. The girls are good-sized and the shirt of my matching loungewear set is snug.

A couple of his fingers begin to brush swirling patterns on my shoulder. The sensation is both soothing and enticing, and my eyes flutter before I compose myself.

"How long are you in town this time?" His voice is softer, though I'm learning he doesn't ask me what he wants to know. Again, I feel this is outside of his personality which I assume to be direct.

"Tomorrow afternoon. I'll be back this weekend."

"That doesn't work for me." There it is.

A startled laugh breaks free of my throat. "Oh, it doesn't?" One side of his mouth kicks up. "What are we going to do about that?" I pop another piece of cheesecake in my mouth.

He zeroes in on my mouth and heat shoots to my core. "Stay until Tuesday."

"Why?" Who am I kidding? I'm not going to tell him no.

"So I can see you tomorrow."

I raise an eyebrow at him. "I dare say you're developing an addiction, Cowboy. It's wholly unhealthy."

He grins. "One more hit."

"Fine." I really should learn to fight him harder. "What do you have in mind?"

"You'll see," he says.

I hate surprises. "What should I wear?"

"Whatever you want."

"Not helpful." Approximately two bites worth of cheesecake stare up at me from the single-serve container. Briefly, I look between the cheesecake and Sutton. His brows furrow. I fork half of the remainder into my mouth, savoring the taste on my tongue with closed eyes. When I open them, Sutton's steel blues blaze as he watches me.

With the last piece of cheesecake speared onto the fork, I lean forward. Sutton's eyes flick between the fork and my face. "Open up, Cowboy." Like magnets, our eyes stay locked as he opens his mouth. I slip the cheesecake onto his tongue, and he closes his mouth slowly, as I willfully refrain from telling him he's a *good boy*. But I can't hold back from staring as he chews slowly, swallows deeply, and licks his lips.

There's no denying the wetness gathering between my legs.

"Mm, my favorite." His voice is husky and my eyes widen.

"Is it really?" He drops his chin as his eyes roam over my face. "Then why didn't you get a slice? Or tell me and I'd share?" A small part of me feels insecure that I should've offered a second time.

The hand on my shoulder wraps a few pieces of my loose hair around it, sending tingles down my spine. "Watching you enjoy it was treat enough."

I clear my throat and lick my lips, averting my eyes to soften the intensity of the moment. He claims a growing addiction, but I'm a moth to a flame.

"Tell me about your family." His voice is clearer and his fingers rest on the back of the swing, releasing me minutely from his captivating hold.

My chin falls to the side, a deep breath filling my lungs. The fork fits perfectly into the plastic container and I seal each of the four corners before I speak.

"Nana was my mother's mom. You may know, Randi, my aunt." Randi has worked at the high school since we were children. He gives a small dip of his chin. "They grew up here."

I eye the window into the living room like it tells a story. In some ways, it does. But I don't know what he wants to know and my words cease.

"What about your dad?"

I wouldn't know him if I saw him. I hardly know if he's even alive. "My parents weren't together long. I don't remember much about him."

Stephanie's words fill my head. "My mother said he turned out to be a criminal. I was really little. I remember that he was big—not fat, just...imposing. I think I used to play with his beard." Longing washes through me and my eyes trail over every inch of the porch, while instead seeing the hazy memories my young mind retained. "He would tickle me with it." I touch my neck marking the spot. "I don't remember him ever being harsh or anything other than loving."

An image I've not thought of for a while fills my vision and my eyes feel full. I blink away any tears trying to force their way forward. "I think he really loved my mom. I vaguely remember him whispering in her ear once when he came home and her laughing." The sound would seem foreign if I heard it now.

"Have you tried to reach out to him?" Sutton's voice brings my eyes back to him.

I shake my head. "No. I guess I assumed if he wanted to reach me, he would."

Sutton gives that a little thought. "And your step-dad—you don't like him."

Anger rockets through me and I jump up to start pacing. Sutton's hand tangles with my own. I trail my eyes from our connected hands, up his chest, to his face.

"Come here." His voice is low and soothing. This time when I sit and start to pull my legs up, he eases them over his lap, where he rests both hands atop my knees. "I didn't mean to upset you."

"You didn't," I promise. "He's a sore subject."

"Because he's a prick." He raises an eyebrow at me, shadowed under the rim of his hat.

"Yes," I agree with a smile.

"I caught as much when everyone was here after the service. How long has he been around?"

I inhale deeply, squashing the rising frustration. "Since I was a teenager. Late middle school."

"You have siblings?" His left arm comes to rest on the back of the swing again, while the other stays firmly in place on my legs.

Absently, I trail my fingers over his arm this time. "A step-brother, but I've never met him."

"How does that work?"

"Stephanie and Alan weren't married long before we moved and his mom wouldn't let him visit. I guess the issue never got pushed." I think back to the new revelations my mother shared with me. I missed so much right in front of my face.

In some ways, it felt like sharing the reason for our move had been an attempt at an apology. Yet, Stephanie never actually said that. Instead, she continued to stand firm in saying she had done what was necessary, what she thought was right.

Nana would never have thought those decisions, or the treatment of me that followed, was the right choice. In fact, she didn't. I finally understand Nana's hatred of Alan aside from my own. Did that play into her decision about the house? Keeping his hands off it was the obvious goal.

"When I was younger, it was a little odd that even as an adult, my step-brother never came around. But I try to avoid Alan like the plague, so maybe he hates his dad, too."

Sutton sits quietly without pushing further. A minute of comfortable silence passes.

Our conversation picks up and he shares a little about his sister. I tell him about Izzy and Leah. I do the majority of the talking, coaxed by his interested questions.

Eventually, he gives my knee a gentle squeeze. "I need to get back to the ranch."

I lower my legs and walk to the top of the stairs. He follows, using the opportunity to back me against a porch post, leaving an indistinguishable gap between us.

The air between us is charged, my heart beating in anticipation.

He slides a warm hand into the hair at the base of my neck, lighting my entire body on fire, and leans his head down to press his lips to mine. My fingers grip his biceps, grounding me, as his grip tightens in my hair and his free hand finds my hip.

When his tongue slides along the seam of my lips, I open for him. A hint of cheesecake infuses with the hungry clashing of our tongues as they roll and dance together.

When he finally releases me, planting a small, soft kiss on my lips, I'm breathless.

Sutton slides his hand down my neck before running his thumb along my bottom lip. "I need to tell you something." He drops his hand slowly.

A tiny part of my brain is yelling that this is the part where he comes clean about why I shouldn't trust him. I tell it to sit down and shut up.

Once again, his eyes bore into mine, set ablaze. "I didn't graduate Kindergarten." His tone holds a hint of teasing.

My brows scrunch. "Am I supposed to know what that means?"

The corner of his mouth tips up. "I don't share."

My face must be astonished because his smile grows. I can't help but laugh, asking playfully, "Are you staking a claim now?"

"I am." All teasing leaves his tone. His eyes are eager for the perfect response. Once again, I feel the need to dampen the intensity of the mood.

"I'm not a toy." My voice is no more than a whisper and part of me wonders how he hears over the crickets.

Sutton leans in, placing his mouth right next to my ear. "I have no intention of treating you like one." He pulls back slowly, keeping his eyes on me. "I'll see you tomorrow."

"Ok," I manage. He gives me one last feather-light kiss before tipping his chin and walking off the porch.

CHAPTER 19

MACI

R andi and Liv arrive at Nana's around nine the next morning. I can't decide if the breakfast tacos they bring from my favorite restaurant or the 'Good morning, Firecracker. I hope you have a great day.' text from Sutton has me in a better mood.

The morning is fairly warm, especially after the cooler weekend, and the three of us decide to eat on the back porch, sitting side-by-side on the wooden swing with Liv in the middle.

"I always loved this yard." Randi crumples the foil from her last taco in her lap. "Believe it or not, Stephanie and I used to play down there. There's a creek further back and we used to run barefoot all the way from the house. Those sticker burrs hurt!" She laughs at her historical pain.

The thought of Stephanie and Randi playing as children brings a smile to my face. Stephanie was never one to play with me, except for maybe a tea party, which is fitting considering her affinity for decorum. Imagining her carefree in the brush is difficult.

"How did I never know that?" Liv asks, staring into the tree line as if she can see through the thick of it to the place her mom speaks of.

Randi shrugs then bounces her eyebrows at us. "Aunt Stephanie and I got into enough trouble as kids, I think Nana made a point to keep you two busy up here when you were around."

Liv turns sharply to me. "Speaking of, what happened to the tire swing?"

I shake my head. "I don't know. I noticed it was missing last week." I continue to chew my lip, thinking of who Stephanie was as a child or young adult. Randi must have known a much different version than I have.

"She wasn't always the way she is." Randi seems to read my thoughts. I look past Liv to my aunt. Her eyes meet mine. "Stephanie was care-free. I was the practical one and she was the free spirit."

My eyebrows jump.

"After she separated from your father, I think she made it her mission to never make a mistake again. And Mom was always on her about going back to him."

"Nana liked him?"

Randi nods with a shrug and turns back to the tree line. "Yeah. He was handsome and smitten with Stephanie. And he was a good dad. He doted on you. He was polite to Mom." She's quiet for a moment, letting her words soak in. "Maybe they didn't do things the way others in town would, but they loved each other. I never understood what could've changed Stephanie's mind so fast, and neither did Mom. Our confusion didn't help her, but she wouldn't open up to us. It was a loss all the way around."

I allow my thoughts to wander. Stephanie has always been secretive about my father and I muse at how much of a role he played in her becoming who she is today.

Liv stands and gathers our trash. I follow, stretching my arms over my head.

We file inside through the screen door of the laundry room and head into the kitchen. "I've done the laundry besides Nana's room and tried to get everything in its place, so to speak, so it's easier to go through."

Randi hugs me around the shoulders. "Where do you want to start? Upstairs?"

Liv tangles her fingers with mine. "That's a great place to start."

We follow Randi up the stairs into the loft. She smiles, looking around the space, lit by a picture window on the back wall. The sun rises on the front of the house, so the natural light is muted currently. In one corner sits a desk with an older-style laptop on it. Books rest on the reading chair, frequently lit by the lamp on a telephone table beside it.

"Mom always loved this space." She doesn't add any detail as her eyes gloss over each piece of the room.

Liv steps to the desk. "Was Nana working on anything?" She slides her fingers along the open keyboard.

"I don't think so," I say, knowing the question is directed at me since Nana and I used to frequently chat about work. She would tell me about any editing she was working on and I would tell her all about my photo shoots. "She didn't mention anything recent the last time we spoke. And no one brought it up at the service. I guess it's possible."

"I always wanted to hang out with Nana in here while she was proofreading, or just reading." Liv plops down and kicks her feet up on the ottoman. "Oof. This could use recovering." Randi joins in our laughter.

"Wouldn't this space be perfect with a few low couches and a coffee table between? Maybe a bookcase along the window?" I gesture to the back wall.

One of Liv's eyebrows quirks and she purses her lips. Randi watches our interaction silently. She wanders over to the window and peers into the backyard. "Yes, I think you're right. It has great natural lighting and it's open to the downstairs. Separate but not."

"Yep," Liv says, pushing out of the chair.

I take in my aunt. "Are you going to sell the house?"

Unbothered, she smiles softly. "I have a ton of wonderful memories here. But I love my house. I have no need for this place. And it wouldn't feel right to be here. Not permanently. Although, it will definitely feel weird not to have holidays here anymore. Or random dinners with Mom."

Liv and I exchange a wide-eyed look. She voices our combined question. "Who's going to host holidays now?"

Holidays have been a sore spot for as long as I can remember. I spend the days trying to hide away with my relatives, ignoring Stephanie and Alan. Sometimes Alan would have to work and Stephanie would be even more put out. Would they even bother coming without Nana as a buffer? Would I?

A piece of me hopes my aunt won't offer, because I can't imagine Stephanie will.

No one speaks for a minute. "Mom?" Liv prompts.

"I'm happy to host. I don't know how special that would feel in my little place, but it wouldn't bother me." She chews her lip for a minute. "I guess holidays are going to take some adjusting, aren't they?" Her glassy eyes bounce between Liv and me.

After a moment, she keeps going. "I'm not in a hurry to sell. We have months before it's even an option, but it doesn't make sense to let it fall into disrepair when it still has so much left to give."

"I guess we need to make a list," Liv says, breaking the silence after a moment. "This furniture can go. Right?"

Randi and I nod.

"I don't know how Nana sat there for very long. That is one uncomfortable chair." She stretches deeply then joins Randi at the window.

"Mom always wanted to add a fire pit out there."

"I think it's a great idea." I indicate a large oak tree on the left of the yard. "That tree would be great with a bench seat around the base, right? It's such a great space for entertaining."

Randi and Liv exchange a look. "Yes. It is."

Part of me doesn't want to encourage them, but the question tumbles out anyway. "What?"

"Oh nothing," Randi says, grinning as she turns away from the window and heads for the bathroom.

"Not you, too," I call, following as Liv snickers behind me.

Not long after Randi and Liv leave, Izzy calls.

"Hey," I answer happily.

"Hey. You busy?" Izzy's serious tone has me curious what could be wrong.

"No. Randi and Liv just left. What's going on?" I make my way to the front porch swing. With force, I push the swing backward, but as it sways and picks up momentum, I use my feet to keep us from slamming into the front wall.

"I wanted to talk to you about Leah."

"Leah?"

"Yeah. We couldn't talk yesterday, but I think we need to sit down and have a heart to heart with her. I'm worried about her drinking."

My mind flies through my interactions with Leah over the last week and a half. The multiple visits to bars, the drinking at brunch. Separately, these things aren't cause for concern, but mimosas with brunch aren't the norm for us. The last time we spent so many nights in a short period of time at bars was when we were all turning twenty-one. With a few years of drinking under our belts, it's not typically at the forefront of our interactions. And she's never gotten dangerously drunk like she did recently. I blamed it partially on my inattentiveness, but when I look at the whole picture, Izzy may be onto something.

"I think something's going on."

The swinging isn't going to cut it. I stand and begin pacing the length of the porch. "I hadn't given it much thought until now, but you're right."

Leah's family has its share of drama. Far different from mine. Her mother, single and raising two daughters, has struggled with substance abuse for as long as I've known Leah. Her sister, only a couple years older than the three of us, has several children with different fathers. Both women seem happy to take whatever the men in their lives are willing to provide for the time being, while Leah has always distanced herself from their choices. Unfortunately, she's not always above self-medicating and I feel guilty for not checking in with her in recent weeks. Not the way she needed.

"Has she said anything about her mom or sister?" My voice is quiet and guilt-ridden.

In pure Izzy fashion, she calls me out before I can spiral too far. "Don't beat yourself up. You've had plenty going on and I've been out of town. And you know Leah doesn't ask for help. But I do think we should find a time to talk to her together."

CHAPTER 20

MACI

Me:

You showing those cattle who's boss?

Cowboy:

Depends. Who's asking?

Me:

>crying laughing emoji<

Cowboy:

Don't worry, they won't hurt me too badly before tonight.

Be ready at 7.

Me:

Yes, sir.

Care to tell me where we're going now?

Cowboy:

>zipped lips emoji<

Standing in my bedroom with the closet doors flung open, I curse Sutton for keeping me in the dark. How is anyone supposed to dress appropriately if they don't know where they're going?

I wonder if I've given him the impression of needing to be wooed or impressed, or if this is just his nature.

The temperature has dropped again, so after entirely too long contemplating, I pull on some jeans and a pumpkin-colored, cashmere sweater. I'm still determined to strong-arm Texas into playing fair with the seasons. It's not lost on me that I'll lose.

Going through the house with Randi and Liv today was refreshing. Randi shared more stories with us from her childhood as Liv and I laughed and cried appropriately throughout. A large part of me feels like we honored Nana, did the house justice, by going through and talking about all the beautiful memories. Between today and the high of seeing Sutton again, nothing can dampen my mood.

About the time I throw myself onto the couch and turn the TV on, headlights crest the top of the driveway. The blinds are closed, so it's just the shine that I notice, and this time I wait—quite impatiently—until Sutton comes to the door.

The rap of his knuckles against the wood sends electricity shooting down my spine.

It's an effort to contain my giddiness as I open the door and take him in. He's wearing a blue Henley that matches his eyes, jeans, and a light-colored felt hat. Authentically him, but all cleaned up. My mouth waters.

"Hi," I say, pushing open the storm door.

"Hi, yourself," he says, a hint of a smile playing at his lips. Once again, he pulls out an offering.

"Oh you brought me—" The words begin to tumble from my lips, expecting typical flowers, until my brain catches up to my eyes. I lean forward in the doorway examining what he holds more closely as my face scrunches in confusion. "Is that a cactus?"

My eyes fly up to his and he takes a step forward, gauging my response.

Sutton holds a small painted bowl with a tiny, purple-tinted cactus, the top of which is softly shaped like a heart.

"I came across it at the ranch." He extends the bowl to me. "It's a prickly pear."

"It's beautiful." My weight shifts as I study the contents of the bowl in my hands, and like a magnet, Sutton shifts forward, stepping over the threshold. His eyes heat my skin.

"I know your stance on flowers."

My mouth falls open and I catch a breath, my eyes shooting back to his. The corner of his mouth tips up and he presses his lips together, trying to hide a smirk.

My cheeks heat. He heard me. And he remembered.

Nana loved plants. She would talk about propagating cacti, among other things, and how to properly transfer them. This is no last-minute flower stop. My throat thickens. "Thank you."

"Mhm." He ducks his head to kiss me on the apple of my cheek. "You ready?"

"Yeah." I'm already on fire. "Let me put this inside." Thankfully, Sutton moves back so I can think straight. I take the cactus to my room, placing it on the bedside table.

I grab my cross-body bag from the foyer table and lock the door as we step onto the porch. He offers me a warm hand and leads me out to the truck, where he opens the door and waits for me to climb in so he can close it.

His truck smells divine. I know it must be a particular woman who enjoys the smell of hay, livestock, and leather, mixed with his cologne, but I inhale deeply. In high school, Izzy showed pigs, something no one would believe by looking at her. The scent of the Ag barn, livestock shows, and rodeo are seared into my brain. It's a welcomed scent that feels like coming home.

My eyes appreciate his body as he rounds the front of the truck and climbs in.

When the truck comes to life, I'm not even a little surprised when Alan Jackson is playing quietly on the radio. Sutton shoots me a grin and I bite my lip to keep from smiling too wide.

He throws the truck into reverse and puts his right hand on the back of my seat. His smile widens when he sees me eyeing him.

In a single, swift motion, he backs up the winding gravel drive to the street. These panties are ruined. Why is that so sexy?

"Why are you looking at me like that?" He pauses momentarily before putting the truck in drive, expecting me to answer.

"Like what?" I fib, turning my eyes to the street.

He breathes a laugh and interlaces our fingers on the console. I refuse to ask where we're going. At this point, I'm just along for the ride.

His voice is quiet and deep. "You like barbecue?"

I glance sidelong at him.

He grins. "Alright, then." After he takes two lefts leaving Nana's, I have an inkling where we're headed. Granger's BBQ is the best in town and I'm pleased when he pulls in and parks alongside countless other trucks. I move to get out with him, but he squeezes harder on my hand, holding me in place. I nearly get whiplash when I turn back to look at him. What the fuck?

His eyes are deadly serious, his chin lowered like a puma preparing to strike. "Don't touch that door."

Pulling my head back, I blink. "I thought—"

Releasing my hand, he holds my gaze. His voice is lethal, but a different tension builds in me as he enunciates each syllable. "Do not touch that door." Then he gets out of the truck.

He extends a hand to me after opening my door.

"All you had to do was say you wanted to open the door," I grumble, taking it.

The truck door slams closed behind me, not as hard as I interpret, and Sutton leans into me with his lips by my ear. "I wanted to open the door."

A mischievous gleam fills his eyes when he puts space between us.

One side of my mouth tips up. "Yes, sir."

Something flashes in his eyes. His hand is warm on the small of my back as he guides me toward the door. I don't need a chaperone or a guide. I haven't needed anyone for a long time. But I don't move away from his touch, frankly, because it's driving me a little bit wild and my core is throbbing already. Fiercely independent or not, Sutton is charming, especially given that nothing feels forced. His actions seem as natural as breathing for him.

The warmth disappears as he opens the restaurant door, allowing me to pass through.

During the two-minute wait to order at the counter, a couple of middle-aged men at a corner table wave politely. Sutton gives them a returning two-finger wave. Habitually, I scan the seating area, but the place is broken into smaller rooms and I can't see much. Something is setting me on edge.

At the counter, Sutton gestures for me to order first. I opt for a sausage wrap. He glances at me briefly as I order from the clerk and follows up with his own request, which includes over a pound each of brisket, sausage, and sides. I can't imagine he's going to put away all of the food he's ordered and I purse my lips. Far be it from me to judge another person's eating preferences.

The cashier gives us a table number and Sutton leads me to the only available table, not far from the men who greeted him earlier. We have to pass their way, so he casually stops and has a short conversation about cattle, something I know close to zilch about. I tune in as best as possible. He makes a point to introduce me, but between my lack of knowledge on the subject and the feeling of being under the microscope, I can't fully focus. Plastering what I hope is a bright, casual smile on my face, I continue to scan the room as nonchalantly as possible.

We move to the table by the window. The front door dings as someone exits and the cashier from the front counter comes around with our food. I'm even more sure now that I see what all Sutton ordered that he will not be eating all of it.

I eye the food speculatively. He sends an inviting look across the brisket at me. "If you ask nicely, I'll share." That mischievous grin has returned and fiery butterflies take flight in my chest.

I hold my sausage wrap up and show it off with a little shake. "I'm fine."

An engine revs nearby and my eyes shoot out the window. At the exit of the parking lot, Colt is on a motorcycle about to pull onto the street, but his eyes are on me and he winks. A shiver runs down my spine as I turn my gaze back to the table.

Sutton's eyes narrow. He looks out the window and back to me questioningly.

I shake my head and lean forward to take a bite of my wrap, held over the disposable tray to avoid dripping grease everywhere.

"Maci." My name on his lips does things to me it shouldn't. I meet his narrowed eyes. "What was that?" It's clear from his tone he isn't going to be brushed off again. Reading my mind, he says, "And do not tell me nothing."

I hold his gaze for a moment, deliberating.

Sutton's attractive, intuitive, and kind as far as I can tell. He grounds me in a way I haven't been in too many years. Still, I don't know what he's getting at. No one threatened me. It was just a creep on a bike.

He continues to wait. His jaw ticks and I know he wants an answer.

"Colt," I mumble, setting my wrap down with a little more force than necessary. His cheeks twitches below his left eye, though he says nothing. "The biker."

"I know who he is," he says. He releases his hold on his own food, of which he hasn't taken a single bite, and leans his back against his chair. One hand disappears below the table and his boots slide further apart. I imagine he's rubbing his leg as a calming gesture. His uninterrupted focus causes pooling between my thighs. I press my lips together.

On the surface he looks calm, no one in the restaurant would glance twice at his demeanor, and yet there's a tension in the air. He wants to understand what's going on, but also never truly makes me feel forced or uncomfortable about sharing.

"He bothered you."

I avert my eyes, deliberately turning my head to look around the room.

"Hey." This time, his tone is softer and I immediately find his eyes again. His jaw is relaxed and he leans toward the table, setting his arms atop it, like we're about to share a secret. "What happened?"

"He was just leaving."

Without missing a beat, he says, "Don't do that. Don't act like you don't know what I'm asking. Don't shut me out." His face is both serious and soft as he stares at me for a long moment. The way he reads me is too intense. I always try to keep things surface-level. Safe. But he's too good at seeing through my shields. Knowing that he *wants* to know what I keep hidden is equal parts terrifying and exhilarating.

A chosen few get through my barriers and those people have been in my life for years. So why do I want to let him in after a few nights?

I take a deep breath to steady myself. "He just winked." I shake my head, annoyed at myself *and* Colt.

"What happened at the bar?"

I lick my lips. "He asked me out. I told him no. He was angry." I study the dingy tile on the floor for a moment and then look directly into his still waiting stare. Once again, I consider the limited time I plan to spend here. I'm not going to skirt the choices I've made, to avoid discomfort with someone who isn't even going to be in my life that long. If he wants the truth, he's going to get it.

"He bought Leah and me drinks one night when we were out. That's how she met Pete. We hung out with them. I suspect a drink for her was collateral, either to get us both to come over or to distract her with Pete."

Talking about exes with people I'm dating isn't really an issue. The past is the past and if they have hang-ups about it, that's on them. Talking to a man I really like, about a really stupid decision, feels vastly different.

"We hooked up one night. It was stupid and less than satisfactory, but I was trying to get out of my head." He masks the surprise well if there is any. "I told him it was nothing. I didn't even think it was an issue. He didn't exactly strike me as the type to stick around."

"Anyway, what you saw was him trying to be charming and ask me out. He was pretty pissed I said no." The unease from the night at the bar slithers beneath my skin. "I haven't seen him or talked to him since then."

I say the last part for my benefit, not Sutton's. Convincing myself there's no reason to be concerned. Colt was just being a dick because he happened to see me again.

I stare at my wrap like it's the reason behind all of my irritation.

"Maci, look at me." His voice remains comforting and sure.

I do. So much is swirling around in his eyes.

"You're not stupid. And you don't need to justify any decisions to me. Or anyone else." His face hardens. "You deserve to be satisfied, not scared."

He rises and walks to the front counter before returning to the table with black to-go containers. He makes quick work of boxing everything up and putting it into a bag. "Come on."

I take his hand willingly when he reaches for me. It's a new normal that I gravitate to, enjoying the comfort he infuses into me with touch.

At the truck, Sutton situates the food on the back floorboard before opening my door, never letting go of my hand. He wraps his arm around my waist and pulls me close to him. Those perfect eyes twinkle mischievously as he studies my face. "Do you trust me?"

I can't help but smile and whisper, "Yes."

"Good." His other hand grips my neck and tangles in my hair as he leans in to kiss me. It's possessive, and warm, and over faster than I want. He pulls away and kicks his head toward my seat, indicating that I should get in, which I do without hesitation. Hoping to create some friction, I cross one knee over the other to ease the ache he's created.

CHAPTER 21

COLT

I'm minding my own damn business, grabbing a bite to eat after a really long fucking day, when I spot Maci come through the front door of the restaurant. I'm situated in a darker side room, able to see through the cutout window of the wall because of my height.

Her sweater hangs loose off one shoulder. My mouth waters. But then some asshole in a cowboy hat follows her through the door.

What the fuck?

When she told me she wasn't interested in going out at the bar I was pissed, because she was fresh meat around here and really fucking hot. Even if she did insist on the damn condom. But I decided to let it go because I figured she was bummed we weren't closer.

Now I see she's a lying slut. If she thinks that boring ass cow-fucker can get her wet like me, she's going to be sadly mistaken. She'll come looking for a ride by the end of the week. And I'm gonna make her beg. I bet she's sexy as fuck on her knees.

She's scanning the place like she did when we were at the bar. Probably looking for her next ride. The brisket suddenly tastes dry in my mouth and I toss the piece in my hand back into the tray.

He shows her off like she's a prized fucking cow as they head to a table. In or out of town, she's way too wild for him. She looks bored as fuck already.

I toss my trash, throw the tray on top of the shelf, and head out to my bike on the side of the building. On my way out of the parking lot, I glance back, spotting the two of them through the window seated at a table. She never smiled at me like that. She's laying that shit on thick.

I rev the bike and her eyes dart my way, so I toss her a wink as I pull onto Main. She'll be on her knees in no time.

CHAPTER 22

SUTTON

Maci is tense as hell after seeing Colt.

Dusk is being overtaken by the night as we turn by the bank onto the county road. Maci's face is almost pressed against the truck window, presumably looking up at the few stars winking into existence. I let her be, aside from holding her hand as I drive.

"Where are we going?" Her voice breaks the silence about ten minutes later as we turn onto the farm-to-market road that leads past the ranch.

"You'll see." I grin at her and her lips purse. It's a little thing she does when she's frustrated or thinking things through.

I didn't plan to bring her out to the ranch tonight, but I need to get her out of her head. Which I'm doing in a way that keeps her all to myself because I'm selfish.

I don't consider myself to have a short fuse, but if I find that asshole hanging around, I'm going to take care of that problem right quick and in a hurry.

"This is where you kill me, right?" My eyes widen momentarily before I laugh. A flash of surprise crosses her face, replaced by a void of emotion. "I knew it. Charming cowboy, good dancer, too good to be true."

Lifting our entangled hands to my mouth, I kiss the back of hers without thinking. Her eyes zero in on the action. "Believe me, if I wanted you dead, I've had plenty of opportunities before now."

"Oh my God!" Her panicked voice is tinted with amusement. "You've even thought about it!"

She's more animated than I've seen her and I'm enthralled. Even the first night we danced she was more subdued. It's like she's finally letting me see sparks from the fire hidden inside. My smile widens.

"I've thought about doing a lot of things to you," I tell her honestly, "but taking you from this world is not one of them." I rub a few circles on her hand with my thumb for good measure.

She's undressing me with her eyes. "There's that look again." Equally hard to ignore is when she calls me *sir*.

"I don't know what you're talking about." Her attitude turns petulant, and she faces back out the window. I like this playful side of her. I'm hopeful it's not shock, but that she's finally relaxing with me.

A minute later, we pull up to the ranch. The lights on the limestone pillars flanking the gate are lit up, casting a glow on the gate and cattle guard. Using my free hand, I press the button on my visor and the iron gate slowly swings open.

We aren't going anywhere near The Big House tonight. Instead, I turn left at the first branch off the main driveway and head toward the furthest pasture. The caliche kicks up behind the tires, filling the air and coating the truck with a thin layer of cream-colored dust.

"Hang tight." Throwing the truck in park, I jump out to open a gate for one of the pastures not in use.

Maci mutters, "And here's my final resting place." But when I shoot her a look, she's grinning at me. *That mouth.*

The idea of anyone else getting to experience that perfect mouth is not something I'm willing to entertain. I know she plans to leave soon. For good. That doesn't work for me.

With the gate open, I switch to low beams and pull in. My favorite country station fills the night air when I roll the windows down. I throw Maci a warning look as I park and prepare to get out. She holds her hands up in supplication.

"Good girl." Even in the darkened truck, I can see her cheeks color and her mouth fall into a small O.

Before helping Maci out of the truck, I grab a blanket from underneath the backseat and quickly lay it on the open tailgate. She takes my hand willingly and slides down. At the back, she doesn't wait for me to speak before hoisting herself easily into the truck bed and giving me a glorious view of her perfect ass in those jeans.

She turns to me, hands on her hips and her sweater falls off one shoulder. With a proud stare, she dares to say, "Do you need help getting up?"

Trying to hide my amusement, I grind my jaw back and forth. Her lip catches between her teeth to stifle her own grin. So much for sitting back here. Nothing is keeping me from getting my hands on her now.

Grabbing her around her thighs, I throw her over my shoulder like a bag of feed as she squeals my name and grips the fabric of my shirt in her hands. After one good circular spin, my hands slide up the back of her thighs to her hips and guide her down my body, which is stupid because *fuck she feels good.*

Her hands drag down my chest as she goes, eyes flashing as she goes to shove me. Instead, I grab a wrist in each hand and pull her flush against my body, her arms pinned between us.

Her breathing catches and her eyes soften.

"You have a smart mouth, you know that?"

"Oh, yeah?" She's trying to play tough, but her voice is a whisper. "What are you going to do about it?"

I slam my mouth onto hers. She returns the kiss with every ounce of pressure I'm pouring into her, clenching the front of my shirt in her ensnared hands. Releasing her wrists, my fingers trace down her forearms to her elbows, tucked against her ribs. I take in the way she arches and shivers as I skim my hands down her sides, loving how receptive she is to me.

I haven't even started.

She continues to kiss me with fervor and I move my hands over her ass, gripping her thighs and lifting. Her legs wrap around my waist eagerly. No doubt, she can feel what she's doing to me.

Our kissing deepens and my hands find their way up her back and inside her sweater. Her arms snake around my neck as I step blindly forward and set her on the tailgate. I didn't bring her out here to have my way with her. I will maintain that boundary. For now.

Something registers all of a sudden. "What is that?"

"What's what?" Her voice is breathless between kisses.

"On your lips." I press my lips against hers again, dipping my tongue into her mouth.

"You're on my lips," she manages when I release her to skate my mouth along her jaw, toward her neck.

"Not yet I'm not," I whisper into her ear.

After a catch in her breath, she lets out a low laugh and my cock jumps. "Naughty Cowboy."

I nip the skin just below her ear and she yelps then giggles. The weight of my hat leaves my head. When her hands dive into my hair, my momentary concern vanishes. I reconsider ever wearing the hat again. She can burn the fucking thing for all I care.

I savor every kiss, lick, and suck on her skin, trailing down her neck to the soft bend and over her shoulder. Her head tilts away, granting me easier access. She doesn't know it yet, but she's mine. No one is ever getting this close to her again.

From the corner of my eye, I spot my hat lying upside down on the tailgate. I'm unsure if she knew to do that or if it was accidental.

She still hasn't answered me. "Woman, you're testing me."

"Oh no," she hums.

She shivers as I remove one hand from her back. Her sweater is soft and cool under the palm I sweep up the front of her chest to her neck. Her jaw fits perfectly in the crook of my hand, causing her mouth to fall open and her eyes to blaze. Her grip on my hair tightens.

I repeat my question. "What's on your mouth, Firecracker?"

"Lip balm. Salted caramel." She stares back at me. The soft sweater doesn't hide the heavy rise and fall of her breasts.

I brush my lips along her open mouth, teasing her as I ghost them slowly back and forth. "Thank you," I whisper, before planting a last soft kiss on her mouth. "Hungry?"

She studies me silently for a moment before tucking her lip into her teeth and shaking her head. Without giving her a chance to argue, I give her hips a squeeze and set her on the ground. "Come on."

Sitting on the tailgate isn't an option if we can't keep our hands off of each other.

On the way to the front of the truck, I yank open the door and turn the radio up. She quickly catches on as I pull her body tight against me and wrap my free arm around her back.

Unlike dancing at the bar, she isn't on edge out here. Her body instantly molds to mine. She reaches up to rest her hand on my bicep as she did before, releasing a breath. "It's gorgeous out here."

"Mmhmm."

She looks up and finds my eyes, then swats my arm with a laugh. "Not me, silly."

"You can't tell me otherwise." But I look past her at the expanse of land and sky. There isn't another light or building in sight, save for the stars twinkling overhead. It's a relatively clear night, cooling quickly.

She doesn't respond. I spin her once, earning me a grin. "I bet you bring all of your dates out here to woo them with dancing beneath the stars," she mumbles close to my chest again.

It's not lost on me that she's not making eye contact. I know very well what she's doing. "Yep. Then we screw in the back of my truck."

Her eyes bug and she gapes at me.

I chuckle at her expression, but I don't need her thinking this is a schtick. "I've never brought anyone out here. Hell, I wasn't going to bring you out here tonight. You needed to release some tension. Dancing does that for you. It was improv."

She grins at me and I toss her out for another spin. On her way in, I dip her. Excitement sparkles in her eyes when she rights herself, and she leans up to kiss me. It's the first time she's initiated contact and pride swells in my chest. I have to figure out how to keep her.

CHAPTER 23

MACI

After our date, Sutton brought me back to Nana's, walked me to the door like a gentleman, and then pressed me into it hard, kissing me very much unlike a gentleman. I didn't invite him in and he didn't ask. Then he waited for me to go inside before he stepped off the porch.

I knew I was screwed before, but I'm royally fucked now. Walking away from him when everything is done here is starting to seem like it will hurt instead of just being a bummer.

That's a problem for another day.

Uncharacteristically, I lie in bed playing on my phone Tuesday morning. I should be packing up to head home today. A text notification comes in.

Leah:

Maci, what are you doing today?

Me:

Driving home.

Izzy:

You are home.

Have all the women in my life set out to conspire against me? I don't know where they get the idea that I can simply keep this house because I want to or have an emotional attachment to it.

Me:

>.<

Leah:

Ok, fine.

Let's do Taco Tues. before you go.

Izzy:

I second this motion.

I chew my bottom lip. Another day with my besties is never a bad thing, and after my conversation with Izzy yesterday, it could be the perfect time to see what's up with Leah.

Orders from the Halloween mini sessions and my two family shoots last week are trickling in. I decide to complete the orders I have today and use dinner with the girls as a reward. Plus, it will be the perfect time for Izzy and me to check in on Leah.

Me:

Taco Shack at 6?

Leah:

(three high five emojis)

Izzy:

It's a date.

Me:

Speaking of dates. I have one to tell you about.

A welcomed breeze blows through my hair as I shut the door of my Jeep. Leah and I lock eyes across the parking lot of our favorite taqueria on Main Street. She's selected a table on the patio and calls out, "Taco Tuesdayyy!" from her chair, waving her half-full margarita at me.

"Be right there!" I shout back with a grin, before hurrying through the heavy glass door at the front of the building. The scent of homemade tortillas, salsa, and fajitas washes over me as I soak in the soothing familiarity. Behind the peeling Formica countertop stands a beautiful teenage girl with jet black hair and eyes. She wears a bored expression.

I don't let her lack of enthusiasm dampen my mood. It wasn't long ago that I was sixteen and hated a job in the service industry. Instead, I smile brightly, rattling off my order.

Behind the cashier, someone presses a service bell and places a large paper bag of takeout in the window separating the kitchen area from the checkout area.

The girl swipes my card without acknowledging her co-worker or the food, then hands me a plastic number on a placard and my card wrapped in a too-long receipt. Her *thanks* is half-hearted at best.

On the patio, Leah is texting when I slide into the seat beside her. Two foil wrappers are smashed into tiny misshapen balls on the table and her margarita glass is nearing empty.

"We said six," I tell her, raising my eyebrows because it's only a couple minutes past the hour.

Leah sets her phone aside. "Yeah, I know." A gust of wind blowing through the covered patio sweeps her dark hair out behind her. The foil balls rattle in the grated table, but go no further. "I was starving!" Leah drops her chin indignantly.

I shake my head, unsurprised. "Where's Izzy?"

"I'm here, I'm here," Izzy says, pushing open the glass door. She's still in scrubs and her ice blonde hair is pulled up in a beautifully curled ponytail. One section of hair is intricately braided starting above her temple and wraps around the hair tie. "Sorry—" Her trendy bag gets tossed into the fourth chair at our table as she sits next to me. "My last cleaning was the sweetest little boy who was terrified, so I took some extra time with him."

"Well, as usual, Leah couldn't wait for us." I'm joking, but Izzy and I cross our arms in unison, pinning Leah with hard stares.

She shrugs. "If it makes you feel better, I'm happy to order another round of tacos."

"This little piggy went to market," Izzy says with a loving laugh. Leah grins back.

The cashier pushes open the patio door and sets a tray of tacos between Izzy and I.

"Thanks!" I call at her retreating backside. "How did she manage both of ours at once?"

"I pointed you out when I ordered," Izzy says matter-of-factly. Because, of course she did.

"I'm going in for another round. Need anything?" Leah stands abruptly and looks between Izzy and me. Our eyes lock.

Leah's eyes flit between us when I turn back to her. "Maybe you could wait?"

She furrows her brows. "I'm just running in real quick. You can tell us about your date when I get back."

"It's not that."

Leah's frown deepens and she eyes Izzy.

"Can we talk a sec?" Izzy gestures at the empty chair.

Leah sits without speaking. Her posture is guarded.

"Izzy and I want to check in with you. It seems like maybe you're going through something you haven't mentioned." I don't want Izzy to always have to be the one to say the hard things, so I dive in.

As expected, Leah throws herself against the metal back of the patio chair and crosses her arms. "You guys are so ridiculous sometimes. I don't need an intervention." Her tone lacks true anger.

"We aren't saying you do," Izzy argues, leaning forward. "We just want you to know we're here for you."

"I haven't been good at checking in on you." I chew my lip.

"You don't need to! You're dealing with Nana's passing." Leah's face turns red and she looks away from us.

"I think we're all dealing with that," I offer softly. "Still, if there's something else going on with you, I will always make time to listen. You know that. You guys are my best friends. My sisters."

Izzy squeezes my hand from next to me.

Quiet hangs between us all. When Leah finally speaks, her words are quiet and her eyes stay on the stained concrete floor. "Lily called and wants to move in with me. She says it's temporary, but we all know that's not true."

"What did you tell her?" Izzy's voice is also quiet.

"I told her my landlord doesn't allow people not on the lease. She thinks I'm talking to them." She sighs heavily.

I'm not surprised Leah doesn't want her sister moving in. Through the years, we've seen Lily's ability to coerce people into helping her at their expense. She has a knack for attracting drama and isn't great with general cleanliness. Not to mention the kids involved. Unfortunately, Lily also has a tendency to be persistent and I imagine Leah is under more stress than she's letting on.

"I'm sorry."

Leah forces a tight-lipped smile my way. "I'll figure it out. I just didn't want you taking on my bullshit, too."

"I will. Anytime."

"We both will." Izzy maintains her hold on my hand as she reaches over to take one of Leah's.

Leah nods at the ground. "Ok then," she says looking up at us, "I guess I'll get a soda. Damn buzzkills."

We dive into taco sorting as Leah heads inside. When she returns and plops down, Izzy and I are both chewing ridiculously large bites of our tacos.

"Spill it." She crosses one leg over the other with sass and shakes her flip-flop-clad foot at me.

I roll my eyes and open my mouth to speak, but movement behind her catches my attention. It's not so much that there *is* movement from the parking, as much as, without trying, I recognize the truck and fiery butterflies take flight in my chest again.

Leah shifts her torso to look behind her chair inquisitively. "Is that him?"

The truck settles into a spot.

Izzy sets her taco down and wipes her hands with a napkin. "Sutton?" She focuses on me while Leah stares down the truck.

My cheeks heat. The three of us watch as the driver-side door swings open in the parking space and Sutton emerges. He presses on his phone and puts it up to his ear as he makes his way toward the front door.

"Are you going to say anything?" Izzy prompts.

"He looks busy." My argument is lackluster at best. Truthfully, I know I won't be able to hide my giddy grin and blushing cheeks from my friends.

"Sounds like as good a test as any to me." Leah is facing me again, with her head cocked to one side, as she references him. I know they won't let up.

"Yeah, yeah," I mutter, standing and making my way from our table to the edge of the patio. The outdoor tables have filled up, thanks to the beautiful evening.

Sutton steps up onto the sidewalk near the patio, still talking into his phone. "Ok, Mama. We'll figure something out."

Pressing my back against the wall where the fence is attached, I lean one hip against the metal. "Hey, Cowboy."

Sutton's eyes fly to me and a wide grin takes over. His eyes light up. "Alright, Mama. I'm here picking up food. I'll be home soon." He stops in front of me, saying, "Love you, too," before pocketing his phone.

"Firecracker." Something like relief is infused in the word.

His nickname for me sliding off his tongue reminds me of last night.

"How are you?"

"Better now." He's practically touching the fence. No more than an inch separates us. "I thought you were headed back to Austin." His eyes catalog my face appreciatively. There's no way for me to stop the flush sweeping over my skin. He smirks knowingly.

I gesture over my shoulder with my chin. "Taco Tuesday."

After a beat, his gaze follows, as does mine, to Leah and Izzy who wave at him. He places a hand on his hat and tips his head forward in acknowledgment. His eyes skim the bricked patio, then slide up my body to my face.

Jesus, it's hot. Where did that breeze go?

"Everything ok with your mom?" I have to diffuse this tension before one of us jumps this flimsy ass fence.

"Yeah. She's stressed because the photographer who was going to take photos at the Fall Festival had to cancel and she hasn't been able to find a replacement."

"Oh." It occurs to me then that he doesn't know what I do. "When is it?"

"Next Saturday."

"I can help." I blurt the offer without considering. I know I don't have anything scheduled that weekend as far as photography goes, but that doesn't mean I have any idea what they need at the Fall Festival.

Sutton's eyebrows pinch briefly. "You're a photographer?"

"I am."

He licks his lips and my eyes freeze on the movement. Only the grin that follows encourages me to meet his eyes again. "Ok."

"Give your mom my number and we can work out the details."

His eyebrows jump before he clears his throat. "Yeah. Or you can use me as the middle man."

My brows dip. He doesn't want me to talk to her? "Ok. Well, I guess get me load-in info, location, and time frame. And whatever packages they marketed. I'll match them."

"Mm. I kind of like Bossy Maci." He's smothering his sexy smirk again.

"Then be a good boy and do as I say."

One eyebrow hikes. "What do I get if I'm good?" Before I can respond, he shakes his head quickly. "Never mind. Don't tell me. I'm about to have dinner with my parents."

I grin.

His eyes dart hungrily to my mouth. "I'm going to grab our food. Have fun." Before walking away, he glances once more to my friends and then back at me. "And quit eye-fucking me or you're going into the truck, too."

CHAPTER 24

SUTTON

After leaving Louisa's with our order, I head straight home. It was just as hard to leave Maci there today as it was last night on her grandmother's front porch.

Without trying, she's claimed a piece of me. No matter what happens over the next few months, I know I'll never be the same.

As I'm making my way up the steps with to-go bags, Mama pulls in the drive. She parks next to me and opens the hatch, grabbing grocery bags from the back. I shift the food to one hand and head down to help.

She smiles warmly. "Thank you, honey. Everything go okay in town?"

"Yep." I wrangle a few bags into my arms, alongside the takeout bag, and push open the front door for us, letting her pass through.

"Good." She heads into the kitchen and begins unloading.

"I'll grab the rest."

Once everything is unloaded, I wash my hands and fill a glass with tap water, setting it on the counter. I use the towel hanging from the oven door to dry my hands.

Mama snatches it quickly and snaps my leg with it. "These are decorative!" she chides playfully.

I laugh and wrap her in a bear hug, before pressing a firm, wet kiss to her soft cheek.

"Sutton!" she squeals.

"It's just decorative!" I jog from the kitchen, snatching my glass from the counter before she can whip me again with the towel. Her laugh floats after me.

My parents have always been a wonderful team, but when it comes to the kitchen, Mama is very traditional. That's her domain. Instead of getting in the way, I sit at the dining table watching her organize her haul, completely in her element.

Before long, Dad sits down at the table with me, pulling containers from the paper bag before us.

"I may have a solution for your photographer issue." My dad's eyes slide my way, but he says nothing. He pushes a Styrofoam container to me.

"Oh?" My mother's voice is muffled from her place in the pantry.

"Yeah." There isn't an easy way to do this. She's going to question me to no end either way.

After a moment, she comes into view, stopping in the cased entry between the two rooms. My father chews silently, anticipating entertainment.

"Maci." I shove an extra-large bite of food into my mouth.

Her eyes light up. "I remember now that Ruthie said she's a photographer. When did you see her?" She doesn't care that my mouth is full. She waits.

I swallow and gesture to the takeout bag. "At the restaurant. She happened to be there with some friends."

She hums a response and turns to continue with the groceries. "And you're going to be seeing more of her?"

I work to keep my face blank. We haven't spoken of my comment about finding my future wife since the night I came back from the bar. I know she's fishing.

174

"That's the plan."

My dad is studying me with an ill-hidden smirk.

"She gave me a card. You two can work out the details."

"Wonderful!" Her head pops into view again, her eyes are bright. She's definitely not referring to the Fall Festival.

Finally, she makes her way to the table to sit down. Her eyes twinkle, but she says nothing. My dad's grin is too loud next to me.

CHAPTER 25

MACI

Wednesday morning, the mailbox is full when I make it back to my apartment. There's another colored notice on my front door. I need to let them know to prepare my lease renewal.

Inside, my apartment feels vacant. Not like Nana's house when I first arrived after she'd passed. That was emotional. This is void of purpose.

Suddenly, I don't want to be here at all and I hate to admit that I'm already missing Sutton. Having extra time with my friends and family lately has also helped my heart. And probably my mental health.

Andi calls Wednesday afternoon to discuss the Fall Festival.

"Hi, Maci! How are you, honey?"

I'm thankful she can't see my blushing cheeks. Her continued kindness is so comforting, even if part of me feels like I'm keeping a secret from her.

"I'm doing well. I'm looking forward to helping next weekend. What can you tell me about the event?"

"We have a small budget for a photographer. Anyone who wants photos would show up and provide contact information. They could work out packages with you. Our previous photographer was offering three edited images for forty-five dollars."

"Don't worry about a fee for me. Packages would normally cover a session fee, but I always discount minis like this anyway."

Andi grunts a disagreement, but doesn't argue. I'm not convinced she's going to heed my request. "Will you have a backdrop? The photographer has an outside setup."

"Sure, not a problem. Anything in particular?"

"Your choice. You can load in as early as seven, but once Main Street is closed, you won't be able to get a vehicle in for load-out until four."

"Sounds perfect." I'm already dreaming up a fun backdrop. "Thank you, Andi."

"No, thank you, sweetheart. I'm so glad you ran into Sutton."

Heat rushes up my chest into my neck and face. "Me, too. I'll talk to you soon."

Over the next few days, I keep myself as busy as possible. Cleaning, laundry, and work. The latter part is easiest to do as a one-person business. I spend time preparing social media posts, responding to inquiries, scheduling sessions, and arranging printing and pickups.

Sutton and I text regularly. Easy things, like how our days are going. He always sends me a message in the morning. Otherwise, I don't usually hear from him until late in the afternoon. They're all short and sweet, which is fitting since he's most often a man of few words. It doesn't bother me. The silences with him have been comfortable without an insistent need to fill the quiet.

Saturday he sends me a sunrise picture, which is by far the most gorgeous sunrise I've ever seen and it's only a photo. Monday afternoon, I sit in the courtyard of the complex, enjoying the breezy day. One of my favorite elements of the property are the many outdoor seating areas. A noise in the distance distracts me from my book.

A sliver of the highway in the distance peeks between two of the apartment buildings. A big ass truck drives by, pulling a large cattle trailer and

I have a sudden epiphany. It's crazy and I think he's going to laugh at me, but I send Sutton a text anyway.

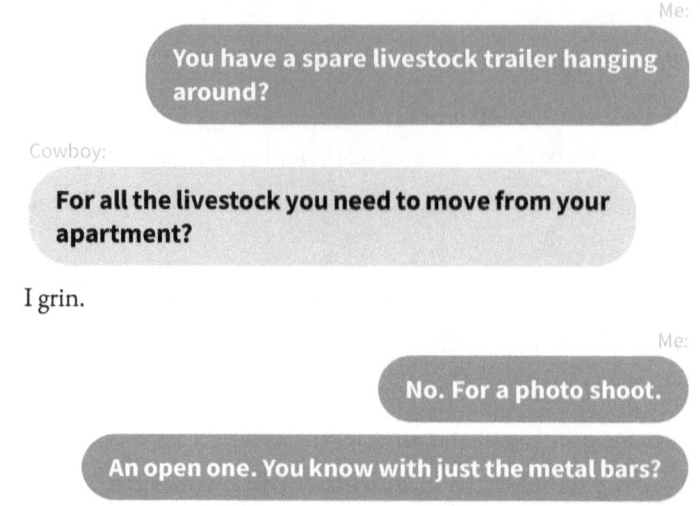

Me:

You have a spare livestock trailer hanging around?

Cowboy:

For all the livestock you need to move from your apartment?

I grin.

Me:

No. For a photo shoot.

An open one. You know with just the metal bars?

He doesn't respond right away, maybe deciding whether he wants to really indulge in this conversation or not. Or maybe he's roping some calf trying to flee the confines of a pasture. A laugh bubbles up as I picture ranch hands chasing a wild baby cow.

My phone vibrates.

Cowboy:

You want to take pictures of cows?

Me:

You're impossible.

I start to type out an explanation and decide it would be easier to call, so I do.

He picks up on the first ring. "That's a funny way of saying 'yes'."

I roll my eyes even though he can't see me. "You and I both know I'm talking about the Fall Festival this weekend. I have a plan for a setup, but I have one that seems more fitting, assuming I can get my hands on a trailer."

He doesn't respond. There's shuffling from his end and then my phone vibrates against my ear. I check the notification, assuming it's a text from Leah or Izzy, but it's from Sutton.

It's perfect.

"A simple *yes* would do," I joke. "Yes, like that."

"You realize it's had shit in it right? And real animals?"

"I do know how they're used."

"I never know with you city women."

Somehow, I know my huffed sigh elicits a grin on his end. I make an effort for a syrupy, sweet tone. "Would it be a huge inconvenience to bring it to the festival?"

"No," he says simply. Like it's already a done deal. "Do you need it both days?

"No, I'm only scheduled for Saturday."

"Ok."

Someone walking a dog passes by and the dog barks incessantly at me, bouncing at the end of its leash. I jump initially and glare in their direction.

"When are you coming in?" His tone is measured.

"I was planning on coming Friday."

"Alright, let me know when you get in. I need to get back to it. These dumb shits need every bit of hand-holding I can offer today." The last part is growled and a tingle shoots through me.

Friday morning I wake before any light creeps through my blinds, but it doesn't matter. I can't wait any longer to get back to Nana's. If I'm being honest, I want to be close to everyone again.

Pulling into Nana's drive brings a sense of peace to me. I drag my suitcase in behind me, not bothering to unload any of my equipment. In Austin, I would never leave the equipment loose in my Jeep, but out here, no one is meandering through the driveway, checking out the goods.

As soon as I step inside Nana's house, I realize that the time away has provided me with clarity. Nana's house has always been a place where I was welcomed. A second home. But ultimately, it's not. Not that the apartment is. Not long-term, anyway.

There are too many fond memories here to hand it off to someone outside of our family, and also too much love left to give for it to sit idle. For longer than I keep track of, I stand in the living room, staring up in the loft area and visualizing something different for this home.

CHAPTER 26

SUTTON

I agreed to meet Maci with the trailer on Saturday because it was a perfectly acceptable reason to see her again, and I was positive I wouldn't be able to go another day without doing so, even if that meant driving up to Austin. She's done something to me. Somehow intertwined herself into my DNA make up, leaving it nearly impossible for me to go any length of time without thinking of her. Each day she was gone I grew more and more agitated. Something everyone around me seemed to recognize as well.

Even though I explained this trailer has carried countless animals in it, and has the gashes, scuffs, and manure stains to prove it, I still try to clean up the damn thing before I haul it into town early Saturday morning.

I've backed the trailer in, according to the booth map Maci sent me, and I'm opening the back gate when she walks up. The weather is typical for October in Texas, which is to say warm for fall, but she's dressed in a red flannel shirt with a black puffy vest over jeans. She's going to be warm, but she's always in typical fall clothing no matter the weather. I'm beginning to think it's a compulsion.

Her chestnut hair is tied up in a high ponytail with the ends curled and a few loose pieces framing her face. All I can think as soon as I see her is that I want to wrap that ponytail around my fist and possess her mouth.

I compose my face and she beams, looking from the trailer to me. "Thank you. This is perfect."

A black, soft-sided wagon is parked a few feet behind her full of pumpkins and blankets. I hope she doesn't think I know what to do with all of it. She catches my look. "Don't worry. I'll handle that."

All I can do is nod and shove my hands in my pockets. The urge to touch her is almost unbearable. As she approaches, she pats my chest, her touch cool through my shirt, and electricity shoots through my body.

She sets to work placing pumpkins around the open gate and off the sides of the trailer, cocking her head side-to-side as she assesses. Then she's pulling the blankets from the wagon and interacting similarly with them.

I'm beginning to feel like an ass just standing around watching when she starts talking. "How's the ranch?" She looks up at me when I don't respond immediately.

"Busy." It's so much easier when she does the talking. "We have some big things on the horizon."

"Oh?" Her interest seems genuine, which is a little surprising because I don't get the feeling she's spent much time on a ranch, even if I do think she could hold her own under any condition. She sets a black structured backpack on a small table that the event staff must have left and begins to organize a few items there.

"Yeah. I'm hoping to finalize a purchase that will increase our land by four hundred percent."

Her eyebrows shoot up and she stops moving to look at me. "That's incredible, Sutton."

Holy hell. I have to figure out how to make her say my name again.

I swallow. "It's exciting. I have some plans to make everything run as smoothly as possible, but I feel like I'm missing something to use the properties to their full potential."

Finished with the table, she straps the backpack onto her back again, a large camera in hand. "Aside from an ass ton of cows, what goes on out there?" She smirks at me.

I shake my head at her. She may not understand everything about the ranch, but I know she's playing. Maci doesn't need to spout off facts and figures for me to know she's intelligent. "Our property is focused on cattle right now, but the property we're looking at is set up for horses. I believe they host guided hunts, too."

She tilts her head softly side-to-side, as if she's thinking on what I've said. "Are you continuing those?"

"I plan to. Cattle, hunts, sectioning areas off for leases—"

"Leases?"

"Yeah. People purchase a contract to hunt the land themselves for a season."

She considers this and moves back toward the trailer. I follow. "So what do you think you're missing?"

"I want to make sure we're using the land effectively without taxing it. Adding too many animals would give us little opportunity to cycle through the pastures. We rest several each season."

She sets her bag just inside the trailer and turns to me, stepping closer. "Are there horse trails?"

"Not especially. Maybe on the land we're adding."

"Maybe you could incorporate something like 'A Day on the Ranch' for visitors to come and see how things work. It would give you a bigger presence in the community and take advantage of tourism in the area. Plus, people would pay you to be additional manpower."

"A dude ranch." My arms cross on their own. Her lips press together in amusement like I'm being ridiculous and she places her hands on my crossed arms, the cool feeling of her palms seeping through my flannel again.

"You can do it whenever it's convenient and set the terms. Only want to deal with lay people once a month? Fine." Her emphasis on lay, as if we look down on everyone else, is obviously a joke.

"If you want to get really fancy, you could set up an area or two somewhere secluded on the property and build some smaller housing there for vacation rentals or something." Her lips purse. "I guess you'd have to consider having random people near the animals though, so maybe not. I don't know. Just a thought." Her hands fall to her sides.

Why did she immediately dismiss herself?

"I think you have great ideas. I may be able to make something like that work and I see where you're coming from. The vacation rentals do fit. To an extent." She looks up at me with soft eyes and I can't help it anymore. My hands find her hips.

"It's all about the experience. I'm sure you'll get it figured out." A fleeting smile passes her lips and her cheeks blush. I'm about to claim her right here in front of everyone.

Her eyes dart past me and she waves. "Hi!"

A woman walking up with three kids in tow waves back. That's my cue to get out of here.

"I promised my mom I'd stop by her setup." I angle my head down, catching a whiff of her shampoo. Something spicy like cinnamon greets me. "You ok if I meet back up with you later?"

"Of course!" She tips her head up to me, unintentionally teasing me with those sweet lips set in a grin. I wonder if they'll taste like caramel today. "I'll be here, snapping away all day. I really appreciate you doing this."

Does she know I'd do anything she asks? "Yep," is all I can manage. "I'll be back." I reach up and grab the end of her ponytail hanging over the front of her shoulder and give it a playful tug. Her eyes light up.

I'm so fucked.

Mama's booth is stationed in the same place it is every year. Behind her table is a collapsible shelving piece Dad built for her especially for these events. Her tiny jars of jam look so typically-country organized by color on it.

"Mama." I kiss her head as I approach from her side, wrapping an arm around her waist.

"Hi, sweetheart." She leans into me, wrapping her arms around my middle for a moment, before pulling away and hurrying around again. "I didn't expect to see you so early."

I'm not interested in having a personal conversation within earshot of everyone in town, but Mama is known to keep at something like a dog with a bone. "I took something to Maci."

I don't miss the glow that accents her face, but all she says is, "That's nice."

A woman walks up then and inquires about the flavors of jams. Mama sets to work, offering her samples and selling her heart out.

She stays busy as things pick up throughout the morning, so I wander around a bit. Nick mentioned that he'd be out here doing some community outreach-type things, and when I spot a Birds of Prey show, I decide there probably isn't a better place to find him.

Sure enough, Nick is stationed at the far end of the area sectioned off for the bird show. It seems too early for sessions and he's chatting with a family, handing out stickers and pamphlets. When they thank him and move away, I shake his hand in greeting.

"Hey, man," he says happily. "I wasn't sure if I was going to see you out here."

I nod, cross my arms over my chest, and peer out at the passersby. "Yeah. Maci needed to borrow a trailer so I dropped it off a little bit ago."

His eyebrows raise. "Nice. I like her." As if processing the latter, his brows furrow. "What'd she need a trailer for?"

I smirk. "She's using it as a prop for a photoshoot."

"She knows cows have actually shit in there, right?" He matches my stance.

"That's what I said."

"You tried to clean it up, didn't you?" It's not so much a question. His mouth quirks to one side. I don't even need to answer.

"It's a lost cause." He knows I tried anyway.

His chest shakes gently with a laugh. "You make it out to hunt, yet?"

"No. Hoping these yahoos can keep it together one day this coming week so I can get away from the ranch. Dad's checking on things today."

"You still thinking of expanding? You're gonna need to hire someone else to be you, if so. That's a lot to do."

I chew the inside of my lip. "Yeah, that's the plan. I've got some things in the works. But it's true, I'm going to need more manpower."

"Would Terrence's crew stay on?"

I shake my head. "We haven't gotten that far. I set up a meeting with him this coming week."

"Let me know if there's anything I can do to help out."

"Always." I spot a family making their way by and someone is getting set on the stage with stands for the birds, so I decide to head back to where Maci is. "We'll catch up later."

Nick throws me a two-finger wave as I walk away. "See ya."

Maci's setup has caused a backup of people watching her take photos of kids and families in the trailer. The seasonal feel she was going for is evident and pretty damn cool. No one has any idea there are stains beneath the blankets and pillows inside. The pumpkins spill out onto the ground playfully. Everything looks a little put together and a little haphazard, which makes it perfect.

I hang back, taking in the sight. The sign-in sheet on her table is almost full with a small portfolio and business cards set off to the other side. *Southern Grace Photography.*

Moving around the crowd, I situate myself beneath a tree providing some shade. It's solid beneath my weight when I lean a shoulder into it and cross one ankle over the other.

Maci is totally in her element, oblivious to everything else going on around her. She works and I watch, entranced. Before long, a prickle runs along my neck. I scan the crowd intently.

Nothing stands out, and as quickly as the sensation arose, it vanishes. Something coils itself within me. A need to protect fiercer than I've ever experienced before. Maci is mine, whether she fully understands that or not, and I will not allow anyone or anything to hurt her, come hell or high water.

Chapter 27

Colt

Why do these motherfuckers insist on ruining a perfectly good day by gallivanting through town, looking at art and buying homemade jams? Fall does not need a goddamned festival. There's zero reason to celebrate. It's just a period in time.

My frustration is beginning to boil over at the number of streets closed for this stupid ass festival. *The next pedestrian who walks out in front of me is going to experience what it's like to be run the fuck over.*

I'm about the turn, following a detour that hopefully gets me where I want to be, when I spot a familiar Jeep in the distance. I pause on the street and the vehicle behind me at the green light beeps its baby ass horn. That motherfucker gets the middle finger.

I decide to check things out. I'm already here.

The next lot is designated overflowing parking for the festival. Sure enough, it's Maci's Jeep parked in the first row. I bet she didn't see me smoking out front when she first came into The Spur with Leah. She didn't give me the time of day until I bought their round. Typical.

I wonder if she's here alone. She's probably on the prowl for her next cock.

Yet another reason I love this bike. I back it onto a grassy area under a tree on the opposite side of the lot from the Jeep.

188

The area is a madhouse. Kids with painted faces are running in every direction. Some moron in a striped outfit is selling caramel apples, and trying not to lose them all to the fucking kids constantly cutting him off. Funnel cake frying and Mexican corn mix in the air. Music plays from Town Square. I haven't figured out if it's live or not. All it does is add to all the damn noise.

I eye the booths momentarily. *Where would I be if I was a slut on the hunt for dick?* Instinct tells me to turn left. A block down I'm rewarded when the crowd seems to open up a bit. To the right is a trailer and people milling around. There's a repetitive clicking sound. I make my way closer.

There she is.

Maci is squatting at the back of the trailer where the gate is flung open. Two kids with missing teeth sit on the blankets near the edge kicking their legs. They look like trouble-makers with unruly hair and gleaming eyes. Something I relate to.

A chick I assume is their mom is off to one side. She beams with pride like they're the two cutest kids on the planet. They're not, but I don't care.

Maci moves around them for another minute, snapping photos with a large black camera. Then she stands and tells them how precious they are and how well they did. She's bullshitting, but she's decent at it. She chats with the mom for a few more minutes and motions to a table off to her left, further down the block from me. I wait for the family to walk off before I make my way over to see what's laid out.

She doesn't even notice me. Mostly because she's honed-in on the next family and getting them situated—nice little gig she's got going here—but also, because I cross behind her to her opposite side as she angles her body to where I had been.

The crowd is denser on this side and I blend in easily. As easily as a badass in all black can blend into a crowd wearing pumpkin spice banners as attire. And fucking plaid. Like there's no other color available in fall.

The table holds an open photo album and some business cards. There's nothing special about them. They're white with a name on them. But there is a QR code which could come in handy. I'm not one to share my personal business on social media, but people make it easy to find them doing that kind of shit. I smirk and pocket the card.

I'm over this nonsense and about to leave when a swift movement from my right catches my attention. That fucking cowboy is coming up. He leans casually against a shaded tree, watching her like he has something to be proud of. *Wait til she drops you like a sack of potatoes.*

My blood is beginning to boil. Seeing this bastard grates on my nerves, but there are too many people here. I'll find some other time to break this guy's jaw. Better yet, maybe I'll make him watch while I show him how wet Maci gets for me. That oughta really grind his gears.

A satisfied smile spreads across my face as anticipation dances beneath my skin. At least I have something fun to look forward to soon.

I'm heading back the way I came, further into the crowd so I don't have to deal with the cowboy prematurely, when Leah comes running up from behind me. She doesn't notice me either, which isn't surprising since the only thing I've seen her pay attention to is Pete. I don't even understand that. Dude is a wet noodle.

She yells something at Maci, and I swear it sounds like, "Maci Grace McCullough," but that can't be right. I stop in my tracks and stare.

Leah babbles on. That chick is all words and hand motions. Or hair flips. She's fucking hot, but she's also really annoying. Maci doesn't seem bothered. I guess she's used to the annoyance.

I yank the card from my pocket. *Southern Grace Photography.* No last name.

Alan only mentioned her by name once or twice. That bitch he married was a McCullough before she took his name, though. Maci Grace isn't a run-of-the-mill name, especially in this town. It has to be her. I can't believe I didn't realize sooner.

My excitement around claiming Maci in front of that cow-fucker is overshadowed by anger. If there wasn't an audience here, I'd grab her by the ponytail and drag her out with me. That slut took everything from me. She's going to pay.

I head back to my bike, bumping into anyone who crosses my path on the way. These people need to pay the fuck attention. In the parking lot, I spot her Jeep once again. The festival-goers have all vacated this area, which is good because this time I don't think. I slam my entire arm against her window, which explodes in a shower of glass, before crossing the rest of the way to my motorcycle. I have half a mind to sit and wait, so I can see the expression on her face when she sees what's happened.

CHAPTER 28

MACI

Sutton and I decide to load the Jeep and check out the festival for a bit. My photography slot was only scheduled for a portion of the day, and he won't be able to haul out the trailer for a couple more hours.

The collapsible wagon full of props rolls behind him while I carry my camera bag. Sutton refuses to let me handle it all even though I did this morning. We cut across the closed street between a coffee shop and a bank on our way to overflow parking.

The Jeep beeps as I unlock it from the key fob and step down from the sidewalk and head to the back. My feet crunch and I look down instinctively to find the cause of the unexpected noise.

"What the fuck?" Bits of glass are scattered below my door. Snapping my eyes up to the window, I find it busted in. "Holy shit!"

Sutton pops around from the other side, hands empty. "What's going—what the fuck?" His eyes scan the damage to my car and the surrounding glass.

Shaking my head incredulously, I assess the small lot. All the other vehicles seem to be intact. My eyes dart between cars as I hurry around the passenger side to put the camera bag in. I scan the interior, including the glove box and console. Nothing is missing. Not that I keep valuables in my car. I slam the door shut with more force than necessary.

"Yeah, it's the one labeled overflow parking." Sutton hasn't moved from his place near the driver-side door and is now on the phone. I mouth, *who's that?* He mouths back, *9-1-1.*

Sutton's voice is low and steady as he speaks to dispatch. I scan the exterior of my car. There's no other damage.

He comes up behind me, placing both hands on my shoulders and pulling me against his chest. "Are you okay?"

"I'm pissed," I hiss, and then take a breath, "but I'm okay." My hand presses the bulky hidden pocket on the right side of my vest. It doesn't matter. I was somewhere else entirely and what would it have done?

Sutton's hands slide around my front and I slip my fingers over his, guiding them to settle on my hips. "They're sending police this way."

I turn in his hold to face him, grabbing onto his arms. His hands haven't moved from my waist. His touch always has such a grounding effect on me.

"Thank you. I don't know how long this is going to take. You can head out if you need to."

His eyes turn furious. "Are you fucking crazy? I'm not leaving you alone. Someone bashed in your goddamned window."

He's never shown this side of himself, but then again, how well do we really know each other? I know he isn't angry at me. I press my hands on his chest. "There's nothing you can do."

"It doesn't matter. Until we figure out what happened here, you're not leaving my side." As if to punctuate his statement, his grip tightens on my hips as he pulls me closer to his body. I don't know if it's the sentiment or the touch stirring things inside me.

"I do not need a babysitter," I say carefully. "I'm wound up, too, but seriously...I'll make the report and go from there. Let's not go overboard."

"You are high as a kite if you think I'm letting you wander off alone after you've been targeted."

I push back from him. "I don't appreciate you acting like I can't take care of myself and I float aimlessly through life. And who says I was targeted?"

He takes a large step forward, pressing me into the rear fender, and angles his head down. "I don't think you're helpless, Maci. In fact, I think you're really damn strong. The fact remains that your vehicle was vandalized and I see that as an act of aggression on you. I happen to be fond of you. So you can consider me your personal ball and chain for the time being."

I stare up at him. His eyes are gleaming, and as serious as he is, I can't help but think it's the most words he's said at once. My heart does one of its stupid somersaults even though he's being ridiculous.

"Fine." My voice comes out scarcely above a whisper.

His shoulders relax minutely. "For the record, I was going to invite you over for family dinner tomorrow, but you don't have a choice now."

I can't help the corner of my mouth tipping up at him. "Little early to meet the parents, don't ya think?"

He gives me a look I can't decipher, but we're interrupted by a police cruiser pulling into the small parking lot. Sutton waves him down, giving me a pointed look. "You already know my mom."

A man with skin that looks too smooth to have ever seen facial hair steps out of the car. His brown eyes land on Sutton immediately.

"Sutton." The officer dips his chin in greeting and shakes Sutton's hand as he approaches, then places his hands on his utility belt in that way officers often do. I'm not even a little surprised that they know each other. His gaze slides to me. "I'm Officer Callahan. Casey."

"Maci McCullough."

"Nice to meet you, Maci. So what happened here?"

I show him the broken window and explain that nothing was taken. He jots down several pieces of information in a tiny notepad and shoves it into his uniform pocket when he's done. "Do you have time to give an official statement?"

"Sure," I say with a shrug.

"Okay, I'll grab a form from my cruiser. Can I get your ID to put in some preliminary information?"

"Of course." I pull my wallet from my camera bag in the trunk and hand two cards over, setting the bag near the edge of the cargo area.

When I turn back, Officer Callahan is looking at me over the cards speculatively. "Do you have a firearm on you?"

Sutton's head snaps my way. I ignore him. "Yes." Rather than reaching, I point carefully at the right side of my vest. "Do you want me to remove it?"

He looks between Sutton and me. "No, just hang tight and I'll grab the form." He starts to walk back to his car, but shoots over his shoulder, "No reaching," and grins.

Sutton's eyes haven't left me and I finally return the look, saying nothing.

"Firecracker seems so much more fitting, now." One side of his mouth tips up.

My lips press together, hopeful he doesn't question me right now. We live in Texas; it should be no surprise when someone has a gun, even if some people are surprised when that someone is a woman.

Officer Callahan returns with the form and a clipboard. Thankful for the distraction, I begin writing while he takes a few photos. "There was no other damage?"

"No, just the window."

Sutton hasn't left his post at the rear of my car, arms crossed, alternating between scanning the surrounding area and watching me. He can be a sentry if it makes him feel better. There's nothing he can do now.

When I hand over the form, Officer Callahan explains detectives will check on camera footage in the area if there is any, but I don't get the impression much is going to come of the incident for now. Much to Sutton's dismay, Casey neither confirms nor denies the idea that I've been targeted, but he advises me to be more alert for a while, just in case.

"Thanks for your help, Office Callahan," I say as we're finishing up.

"Casey," he corrects. "You're obviously a friend of Sutton's, so that makes you a friend of mine."

Sutton, watching Casey, doesn't acknowledge me as I glance his way. "Casey," I correct.

"Good to meet you, Maci. Wish it was under better circumstances."

"Me, too." He gives Sutton a nod before turning and heading back to his car as I wave.

Sutton turns to me. "You have two options." I get the distinct feeling he's about to offer me two choices he can live with. "We can do some shuffling of vehicles and I can sleep on your couch tonight, or you can stay at my place."

I open my mouth to tell him precisely how over the top he's being, but he can see it written all over my face. He stiffens and leans into me again. "Don't." His eyes bounce back and forth between mine. "Don't try to argue with me on this, Firecracker." I snap my teeth together. "Your house or mine."

This isn't the Sutton I'm used to. The quiet, part aloof, part easy going rancher. The Sutton before me is prepared for battle, determined to protect me. How foreign.

Not relenting, I whisper loud enough for him to hear, "Did you forget the part where I have a weapon?"

He shakes his head. "I don't care what you're packing. Until I see you use it and know you're not going to shoot yourself before someone else, you're not getting out of my sight."

I balk. "You are being completely ridiculous!" His signature, hidden smirk teases the corner of his mouth. My stupid body reacts with lust, which fuels my anger. I thrust my hands onto my hips. "I took a class. I had to show I could use it then. I go to the range regularly."

"I don't care what some gun-toting yahoo saw, however many years ago you got your license." His eyebrows raise in slight challenge, knowing I'll try again.

I huff and study the asphalt. I'm trying to reconcile my need for independence with someone genuinely caring so fiercely about me. It's been a long time since I could count on someone I haven't known half or all of my life. And even some of those I can't.

He bumps me playfully with a shoulder, still crowding my space and drawing my eyes back up to his. They mirror the heat building inside me and all of my resolve melts.

He smirks openly and backs up. "My place then."

Sutton gets as much of the glass out of the driver's seat as possible before tossing the blanket I used for the shoot over it. I can tell it's not his preference, but we have to get it back to Nana's and he has to move the trailer, so we make do.

Nana's drive isn't really ideal for turning around a truck and trailer, so I'm not surprised when Sutton opts to park on the street. He busies himself sealing up my window with things from the garage while I schedule mobile repair to come out.

The pumpkins find new homes on the stairs and around the front porch before I head in to pack an overnight bag.

Before long, the storm door closes quietly behind Sutton. The magnetism between us is palpable. I loved playing with magnets when I was younger. The closer they got to each other, the harder it was to keep them apart. It's the same sensation I feel when Sutton's around. It's how I know he's leaned against the wall outside my bedroom door even though his steps were silent.

"Have you ever been hunting?" His low voice floats through the doorway while he remains out of view. I suspect he's giving me privacy, just in case.

A pair of pants dangle over my open duffle as I pause to answer. "Are you asking because you're convinced someone is trying to assassinate me and therefore want to make sure I'm still alive in this room, while still providing me privacy? Or do you actually want to go hunting?"

He laughs heartily against the wall and I race to the doorway. "Do that again."

He looks so casual leaning against his shoulder and facing me with a wide grin. "Have you been hunting?"

"Yes, sir, I have." His grin disappears and his eyes turn hungry. I raise my eyebrows at him as his works jaw back and forth.

"Would you like to go again?"

I roll my eyes. "Can't you just ask what you want? Yes, Sutton, I will be happy to hunt with you." I give his free shoulder a small push before heading back into my room, feeling a playful tug at my ponytail as I do.

"I don't know if you could sit still long enough to shoot anything."

The tease brings a smile to my face.

I throw the last few items into my bag and zip it up. At my door, Sutton motions for me to pass him, snatching my bag as I do. I'm not even a little bothered. His chivalry is growing on me.

He waits at the edge of the porch while I lock up, then walks side-by-side with me out to his truck. I absolutely do not touch the door while he loads my duffle into the backseat. I'm not sure he's even noticed my restraint when he opens it for me, until I pass him to climb in and he leans in to whisper in my ear, "Good girl."

And I nearly melt.

CHAPTER 29

MACI

T he drive to the ranch is quiet. Sutton doesn't try to distract me from my thoughts, so I let them run free. My heart and brain are in a tug of war.

The sun is being chased from the sky in oranges, pinks, and purples as we pull onto the dusty driveway. Sutton lets us in the gate, closing it behind us to avoid a cow-tastrophe. When I tell him as much, he looks at me like I have three heads. "You good?"

"Yeah." I laugh half-heartedly. "Maybe a little on edge."

He reaches over the console and squeezes my thigh reassuringly.

The ride is bumpy and I watch out the window. We pass the fork we took left the first time Sutton brought me out, heading to the right instead. He continues to pass several smaller turn-offs before the road ends in a rounded area.

A beautiful, smokey blue ranch-style house greets us. With two windows on either side of the door, its symmetrical facade reminds me of houses I drew as a child. The sun setting toward the back left of the house adds to the memory. A handful of steps lead to the front door.

"Welcome to The Big House."

"Sounds like a prison."

He smirks at me. "It's the main house on the ranch. My parents' house." He barely pauses, sensing my unease. "Don't worry, I have a private entrance."

It's a feat to maintain eye contact as he studies me, while I try to school my face. We haven't exactly outlined what we're doing and though I've met his mother, being out here now seems like a bigger step.

"I will gladly take you in to say hi to my parents." My heart picks up. "But if you don't want to or you're not up for it, that's fine, too. I had already planned to invite you to dinner tomorrow and there's no reason we can't wait until then. And they didn't know about that or coming out now."

His face betrays no emotion. Does he want me to come or is he being polite because he feels some need to protect me and I'm already here? I was beginning to think I'd gotten good at seeing through his composed facade to what simmers underneath, but I can't tell what he wants.

It dawns on me. He's doing it on purpose. He's trying his hardest to let this be one hundred percent my decision.

"Family dinner." A pang of envy filled me when he mentioned it before. Now I'm filled with apprehension instead. What would it mean to join family dinner?

"Yes."

I look out my window to the front door of the house. "It won't be awkward if we don't go in until tomorrow?"

"They won't even know you're here. They don't even know *I'm* here, minus my truck."

"I think your mom will worry too much if she sees me now."

He dips his chin down in agreement. "That, or question you to death. You know her well, already. Let's get you settled then." Still, I have no idea what he's feeling. His expression softens and he squeezes my thigh again.

Sutton's portion of 'The Big House' has two rooms, a bathroom, and a small hallway. The entrance leads into a tiny foyer. I suspect at one time it was an additional closet that was opened up during the remodel. A hat rack houses hats in various colors, fabrics, and styles, not a ball cap among them.

Who needs that many hats?

I refrain from questioning the hats, and will continue to do so as long as he doesn't see fit to question me about my shoe collection.

The space has the feel of a cabin, with rich wood walls, leather and wood furniture throughout, and low lighting. Simple sconces line the hallway providing a soft amber glow.

His bed frame is made of cedar logs, sealed, and fit together with wood nails. It's captivating and I take my time looking over it. The footboard and headboard are tangled limbs, all beautifully intertwined.

"This is gorgeous." My fingers dance along the top of the footboard.

He doesn't respond from his place just inside the bedroom door. I turn to look at him and find him studying me again, my bag in his hand. I'm sure he heard me, but I want him to know I'm serious. "It's really lovely."

His face is soft and hints at wonder as he studies me. "I made it."

I gape. "You made this?" For the first time, his suntanned cheeks pinken. It's hardly noticeable, but my heart beats a little faster anyway.

He sets my bag down inside the closet, removes his hat and boots, and sets both in the hall.

"I-I don't know what to say. It's amazing."

He settles himself on the bed leaning back against the headboard. My mouth waters and my chest tightens. He's never looked more like a masterpiece. I itch to take his picture.

He pats the bed next to him in invitation. I mimic the process of removing my boots then lay my puffy vest over the arm of the arm chair in the corner, removing my Smith & Wesson and setting it atop his dresser. The heat from his gaze is tangible.

When I climb onto the bed, I briefly see through the open bathroom door to the other room. I'm surprised to find a clawfoot tub in the bathroom beneath a suspended shower head and an enormous, hand-drawn map of Texas on his office wall.

I perch next to him facing the footboard. He wraps an arm around my waist and guides me closer to him. Instinctively, I rest my head against his chest and for a few moments we're silent, his arms wrapped around my midsection, mine laying overtop.

Eventually, his quiet voice fills my ears. "Are you ready to tell me why you've been carrying a gun around?"

I swallow. "We live in Texas. It's perfectly normal for people to carry guns here."

He hums. "That's not what I asked." When I don't respond, he tightens his hold around my waist in an affectionate way and continues. "I've met a lot of women who shoot and plenty who carry. That doesn't tell me why you are."

Ignoring the part of me that wants to know how well he knows said gun-toting women, I shift in his arms, attempting to create space, but his hold remains firm. When I stop shuffling, he moves a hand up to my face and turns my chin toward him gently. "I'm not going to push you. But I hope you know you're safe."

"I don't carry it because of you." He releases my chin, but our eyes stay locked. He's studying me again. I drop my eyes. "In fact, I don't carry it much when I'm with you."

One of his hands moves to toy with the end of my ponytail. I'm beginning to think he has a thing for it.

"I got it as soon as I turned twenty-one. I had Mace before—when I was too young for the license to carry." I fiddle with the buttons of his shirt, tracing the thread and then the outline of each button before moving to the next. Once again, he remains silent, allowing me to continue only when I'm ready.

"When I was a teenager, Stephanie and I were attacked outside of a grocery store here in town." His fingers still in my hair.

Even before the attack, that day had felt incredibly long. All the shopping and arguing Stephanie and I had done was exacerbated by needing to finish with grocery shopping. We both wanted nothing more than to get home and be apart.

"A man in a ski mask got aggressive. It was never really clear what he wanted. He seemed more interested in me than her. He was rough, but I don't think he planned to rape me. For starters, we were in the grocery store parking lot, but it was more like he wanted to scare me. Teach me some unclear lesson." The only thing I learned was that no one else could protect me.

"What happened?"

"After?" I take a deep breath. "A couple saw what was happening. The man ran to help us and the woman called the police. The guy in the mask ran off around the car and no one ever saw him again."

I push up to sitting and Sutton releases me this time. Anger pulses through me as I remember the conversation with my mother recently. "It was because of my step-father." Venom seeps into my voice.

Sutton's eyebrows pull together and he sits upright. "He set it up?"

"No." I shake my head. The next part comes out more for myself. "I can't believe she kept it from me all those years!"

Confusion morphs into frustration on his face. "Who? Your mom knew?"

I nod solemnly. My emotions are erratic. A part of my brain whispers how much has happened in the last few weeks that I've yet to deal with, and another part is telling that part to sit down and shut up. My mouth carries on anyway. "My step-father, Alan, apparently had a gambling problem. It resulted in a huge debt and they threatened us, so he and my mom were discussing moving. She said he managed to pay off the money and they thought all was said and done until the attack. So we moved to Austin. To get away."

Sutton's jaw is the tightest I've ever seen. He's waiting for me to continue, still as can be in his spot against the headboard.

"My mom froze. During the attack. It was panic, I'm sure. I did for a few seconds, too. Afterward, I decided I would never be without an option to protect myself in the future."

He nods his understanding. "You carry it all the time?"

"Not all the time. Obviously, there are some places I can't take it legally, so it stays in my car. But yeah, most of the time I have it." I feel my face flush. "I even bought specific clothing with built-in holsters for women."

His eyes gleam and I detect a little bit of satisfaction coming off him.

"The vest," I gesture to the couch, "a couple pairs of pants, and a few shirts have hidden areas in the waist or around my ribs..."

He reaches out and rubs my thigh with one hand. "My Firecracker. Ready to go off at any time." His mouth tips up and I grin at him. Partially at his comment, but even more so because of his use of *my*.

Later, we grab barbecue takeout and eat on the couch.

"So tell me about life on the ranch."

Sutton chews slowly watching me. "What do you want to know?"

I smirk. "I know you don't like talking about yourself, but what do you do out here?"

He stares.

"You have a horse, I assume."

"Yea. Johnny Walker."

I snicker. "Okay. And what about Strickland Ranch?"

Sutton's lips tip up at the corner.

"Don't. I know what a cattle ranch is. At least, reasonably. I want to know what a day is like for you."

He takes a deep breath. "No day is the same. We have two herds. They aren't very big, but if we get the land I told you about, we'll be expanding the herds. Maybe add another."

"What's 'not very big'?"

He sets his food aside. "Each is about seventy-five pairs. Cow and calf. We rotate the herds as to which group is calving. One is a spring season and one is a fall season."

"That seems like it takes considerable planning." I close my container and leave it in my lap. "Is that your responsibility?"

"Some of it." He runs a hand through his hair, something I don't get a chance to see him do often because it's usually in a hat. I get the impression it's a smidge of discomfort at talking about himself shining through. "I've done just about every job on this ranch at some point. My dad wanted me to understand the importance of each step. I wanted to know all the ins and outs. So I've done most of it. Now I'm on the top end." I smile at him to continue. He clears his throat. "Johnny Walker started as a cutting horse. His role is to help separate animals from the herd."

"Is he good at it?"

Sutton raises an eyebrow at me as if he's offended I would even ask. I throw my hands up. "Fine, he's a rockstar."

He laughs. "Yeah, he enjoys it. I don't help as much anymore. Most of what I do is big-picture. But sometimes big-picture is helping deliver a calf and sometimes it's planning for next season." He frowns in contemplation. "I'll need to find another me once we expand."

"It sounds like it can be really stressful."

He reaches over to play with the end of my ponytail. "Sometimes. But I wouldn't live any other way." His eyes are trained on mine, but in their depths I know he's visualizing his family's ranch and their impending expansion.

My heart tugs. "That's how I feel about photography."

"It sounds like you've done well building from the ground up."

I stack our takeout containers back into the bag and rummage through my duffle to pull out my familiar ribbed pajamas and bathroom bag. "It's taken a lot of work to get where I have steady clients. But I love having a different day all the time, being able to dive into creativity and saving special moments for people."

"You travel a lot?"

"Not much. I could, but I've found a few locations I really like and if I'm not at a family's location, we usually go to those."

He contemplates and it seems like his next question isn't really what he wants to know. "Ever want to get into weddings?"

I laugh. "No way. I did some when I first assisted. They're lovely, but high stakes and way more stress than I care to deal with regularly."

He grins and I slip into the bathroom.

After changing and cleaning up, I pull my hair out of its ponytail. There's no subduing the wave created by the elastic.

A tiny burst of nerves rushes through me. Sutton's seen me dressed down, but not climbing into his bed.

I exit the bathroom and store my things into my duffle bag, trying to ignore Sutton and the bed's existence for a moment. When I finally turn, I'm stunned.

Sutton's eyes rake over me, but that's overshadowed by him being barely dressed. He's removed his shirt and his defined chest and arms are gloriously displayed, the blanket drawn to his waist. I'd love to pull it back.

"I can sleep on the couch if you're more comfortable." His low voice douses my growing heat.

"Don't be ridiculous." I sit on the bed. "I mean, I *should* make you since you forced me here."

He lifts an eyebrow. "Begging is better. Got it."

My core throbs. I clear my throat. "Not what I mean." I lean against the headboard, staring across the room and attempting to slow my racing heart.

"If you behave, you can come closer."

My head whips to him. His right arm is extended to me as he grins playfully. I give an exaggerated eye roll and slide closer. Before I settle against his side, Sutton reaches across with his other hand, tipping my chin to face him.

"I'm gonna kiss you now." He leans his head down and I stretch to meet him.

There's no stopping the moan that rises from my throat when our lips press together. His mouth is warm and tender. A small part of my brain is shouting that I'm already in too deep and I need to back out. I couldn't if I wanted to, though. Which I don't.

"I've needed to do that all day."

"Needed?" I relax into his side and lay my arm across his torso. He's on fire and it does nothing to dampen my desire to climb onto him and explore.

"Oh, it's a need." He brushes his fingers up and down my arm. "Don't worry. I'll behave."

I wish you wouldn't. "You don't scare me."

"And I never want to."

Sutton turns off the lamp on his nightstand. His grip on my waist tightens and his other arm rests along my own. I've never felt so safe.

CHAPTER 30

MACI

In the morning, I wake wrapped in Sutton's arms, pressed firmly against his chest, legs tangled and sweating.

Holy shit this man is a heat rock.

The sun hasn't risen yet. I lie as still as possible, listening to the gentle cadence of Sutton's breathing, his heart beat thrumming a comforting rhythm against my ear. Content doesn't begin to cover my feelings. I don't think there's a place on Earth that could feel more right than right here.

I trail my fingers from Sutton's collarbone down his chest, feeling his hard earned muscles. I don't get far before his warm hand grips my wrist and my eyes dart up to his face. His eyes are still closed, but he grunts at me. "Don't start something you can't finish," he warns.

"I'm not starting anything." As I say the words, I turn my face toward his chest, planting a featherlight kiss on his sternum. His grip on my wrist tightens and a squeak forces itself from my throat.

"Final warning." Even through slitted eyes, the look he gives me is full of warning.

"Very well." I remove my hand coyly from his chest, but when I try to sit up to prove my point, his other arm tightens, forcing me to stay in place. I squash this squeak before it escapes.

"I didn't say move." His grumble warms my insides. I wiggle in his arms, causing his breathing to quiet. Trying to hide the arousal coursing through me, I bite my lip. "I changed my mind. We need to move," he says suddenly.

He releases his hold on me and practically jumps out of the bed, the fastest I've ever seen him move. I sit up, letting the blanket pool around my waist, watching in fascination. I'm about to protest and tell him he needs to get back in this bed, but my eyes follow as he tugs on jeans, making my mouth water. It gives the perfect opportunity to ogle all the muscles of his back and shoulders.

"You know how to use a compound bow?" He looks at me over his shoulder as he buttons his pants and my breath hitches.

I do know how to use a compound bow, but this man is testing the limits of my control. His steely eyes settle on me and, realizing the effect he's had, he turns to fully face me. I think my lips go numb and my hands ache to touch him. He takes two big steps toward the bed that I've yet to move from.

"Maci?" An eyebrow tips up and his voice lowers, intentionally tempting me.

"Mmhmm?" I manage. I'm drenched. Jesus, he's too much.

He places both hands on the bed and leans into my face. I blink like a smitten school girl. My tongue darts out to wet my lip and his eyes clock the action. "Do you plan to leave this bed today?"

I haven't even had him yet and I don't want to leave this bed. What does he expect from me when he looks like he just walked out of a Cattle Ranchers' Sexiest Man Alive feature?

I force my lips together and swallow hard. "Yes."

I finally stand, far less exposed than him in my sleep pants and long-sleeve top, though you wouldn't know it by his perusal of my body.

"So, hunting then?" This time I look at him over my shoulder.

He returns to standing and nods at me, the rest of him frozen.

I let him get his fill, making a show pulling off my shirt, and replacing it with a long-sleeved camo top. Then I slide my pants down my legs, before climbing into my jeans and turning to face him as I button up.

Sutton drops his head back, eyes to the ceiling, and rubs a hand over his face. "Woman, you're gonna be the death of me." I wink at him when he rights his head.

After Sutton packs a cooler in The Big House, we trek to a barn that also has hunting gear. The sky is still dark and a low light is on in the barn. Muffled voices outside let me know the ranch hands are up and moving around.

He grabs two compound bows, handing one to me, and we head off in the direction of one of the blinds on the property. He mentions along the way, his whispering doing evil things to my body, that there are no less than ten on their land. This is the closest to the house. Also doing things to me are the tee stretched taut against his muscles and the ball cap I'm getting to see him wear for the first time. *Does he ever look bad?*

The hunting blind we get to is raised and has built-in windows on each side. There are three small stools against one wall and a pair of binoculars on one of the window ledges.

We tie the window coverings back and deposit what we've carried around the space. The bows are stationed on opposite sides of us and the small cooler and backpack are near our feet. It's barely tall enough for Sutton to stand fully. We could fit one more person, but it would be a squeeze.

We're seated nearly atop each other, watching a grain field blowing gently in the morning breeze, the wind whispering through the blind periodically. The sun is just starting to peek up over the horizon, splitting the sky with gorgeous tangerine and lavender hues. It's breathtaking.

The tension between us continues to grow in the tiny, quiet space. I'm thankful at first that Sutton isn't filling the silence with his whispers. They do things to me that I cannot be held accountable for. But as close as we are, my desire to be nearer deepens.

I gently tap the cooler with my outstretched feet, trying to curb the need to touch the man beside me.

Immediately his head snaps to me. I don't look at him. If I do, I'm liable to start something *I will* finish.

Tap, tap, tap.

"Maci." His warning comes out close to a growl. Nothing is stopping me now. I don't know if he thinks I'll alert the deer to our presence or if he can feel my anticipation, but it doesn't matter.

Tap, tap, tap.

He grips my leg with his large hand and I suck in a breath, fire blasting through me. *Quit*, he mouths, and yet we both know he's not serious. I hold his molten stare.

Tap, tap, tap.

His grip tightens, but there's no anger behind it. Like the magnets we are, he's as drawn to me as I am to him. We both know sitting here in silence with no distractions is impossible.

"You're going to leave a mark," I whisper, resting my head against the wall behind us in feigned nonchalance as I look at him.

His voice is low and clear. "I have no problem marking you."

I've grown to adore his charming, chivalrous side. I tolerate his over-the-top protective side. I also know there's a part of himself he keeps locked away. A part that craves deeply and I'm not letting him hide anything from me. So I push.

"Doubtful. You're such a gentleman."

The words scarcely pass my lips before he leans across me to grab my right leg, hauling me to straddle him. "Are you sure you want to test that theory?" The challenge in his eyes ignites my passion and I grind my hips against his lap once. His nostrils flare.

"It's not a theory. *Sir.*" His eyes flash with intensity.

Pressure releases from my legs as his hands move to grip my cheeks and he slams his lips into mine. I meet his fervor, pressing my palms into his chest to steady myself as he ravages my mouth with his hungry kiss.

One of his hands slides down to my hip while the other comes forward to grip my neck. I'm reminded of the night on the tailgate. I tilt my head up, exposing more of my neck to him, and grind my hips against him in response. He squeezes gently, eliciting a deep moan.

"Fuck, Firecracker," he breathes against my lips. "You're killin' me."

The bulge in his pants against my heat heightens my arousal. His hand on my neck slips back into my hair, gripping it tightly as he kisses and licks along my jaw and down my neck, following the path his hand took. His movements are less controlled than usual. He's barely restrained.

I slide my hands higher, feeling every tight muscle beneath his shirt as they rise. His ball cap is in the way of me gripping his hair the way I want, so I take a moment to reposition it on my own head.

"Fuck, you look good like that, " he says, diving back into my mouth, his grip in my hair tightening, earning him another moan.

My own grip tightens in his hair. It's soft between my fingers.

"You remember me telling you I don't share, right?"

I'm so flooded with wetness that I'm sure it's seeping through my jeans. I bite my lip through a nod.

The hand on my hip slips under my shirt, tracing absently over my stomach. My muscles tighten in response.

His fingers untangle from my hair, his hand slowly sliding down my neck to my chest. A single finger traces over my shirt to my nipple as his eyes bore into mine. There's nothing I can do to stop my back from arching into him. Or the quiet whimper he draws from me. My eyes are glued to his finger as it moves.

I suck a breath in between my teeth as his fingers travel lower, disappearing beneath my shirt with the other at my waist. Teasing along the top of my jeans, inching closer to the button.

My hips rock forward again.

"So responsive," he murmurs, leaning forward and pressing a soft kiss to my collarbone. The shoulder of my shirt has fallen down one arm, exposing more of my chest to him. A warm gust passes through the blind, whispering along my skin.

He's driving me crazy and he knows it. "Quit teasing me, Cowboy."

A chuckle vibrates against my chest. His fingers come together at my button. My lungs seize. When he releases the button from its hold, I exhale in relief.

I use my grip on Sutton's hair to tilt his head back. Fire fills his eyes. My hands slide forward, loving the way his coarse scruff scrapes against my hands, to grab the sides of his face. I press my lips to his, kissing him deeply.

When I release his lips, he studies me before one hand dips into the front of my jeans. My mouth falls open as he grazes my clit with just the wet fabric of my panties as a barrier.

"You're soaked," he breathes against my mouth.

"That's all your fault." My hips are moving, searching for friction. It's all I can do to keep from begging him to fuck me with his hand. My head falls back in frustration and I feel his warm mouth against my neck instantly.

"I will gladly take the blame." His lips are hot against my skin.

I rock again and this time his hand on my stomach pins me in place. His next words are a beautiful command. "Tell me what you need."

I pin him with my stare. Why is asking for what I want terrifying?

"Touch me, Sutton," I plead. He pauses for a beat. "I trust you."

A low groan fills the space right before he presses another hungry kiss to my mouth. My ruined underwear gets pushed aside with his fingers and he teases my clit with his thumb. He swallows the sounds threatening to escape my mouth.

"Do you know what you do to me?"

I open my eyes, studying his face. "Is it anything like what you do to me?"

"Something like that." One finger slips inside me. It's just a taste, but he's winding me tighter and tighter. After a few thrusts of his finger, he pulls back before reentering with two, all the while staring into my eyes. I couldn't look away if I tried.

My hands slide back to his neck, gripping his hair as my hips start rocking again. His touch has the ability to do so many things to me. Soothe, ignite, steady. Right now, I'm not sure if it will send me floating for the clouds or cause me to spontaneously combust. I use my fingers tangled into his hair to ground me.

"Sutton," I breathe. It's all I can manage. My orgasm is building, fueled by the intensity of his gaze and the bliss of his fingers thrusting into me.

Something flickers in his eyes. He sucks my bottom lip into his mouth. "You're so sexy, taking what you need."

I can't respond, can't think. My hips are meeting his fingers on every thrust, my grip tightening in his hair. Storm clouds fill his eyes and I wonder if he's the hurricane to my inferno.

His thumb begins rubbing circles on my clit and I'm positive my brain is going to malfunction. "That's it, Firecracker." Another whimper escapes me. "Explode for me."

And I do. My orgasm rips through me.

My head falls forward, tucked into his neck. I might be gripping his hair strong enough to pull it out, but it's my tether to Earth. "I—" I gasp.

"I know." He kisses the side of my neck. "I've got you." It's then I realize his other arm is around my waist, holding me to him. His thumb rubs soothing circles on my back and he holds me as I come down.

A few blissful seconds later, he withdraws his fingers from my pants. I pull back and study him. He slips both fingers into his mouth, sucking them clean.

"Better than I could've imagined." His voice rumbles through me and I'm heating for him all over again.

"You're telling me. "

He leans forward, planting a slow kiss on my lips before sliding his tongue into my mouth. I taste myself and I can't decide if I'm embarrassed or not.

My past boyfriends have been acceptable in bed, some more teachable than others. Certainly nothing mind-blowing to speak of. Sutton may have only used his fingers, but a part of me is crazed over the fact that it was the best orgasm someone else has ever given me.

My hands fall to his belt and his hand wraps around mine, quickly pinning my wrist in place. I give him a questioning look.

"You do that and I'm liable to bring this whole place down around us." He licks his lips and buttons my pants before looking up at me with a wicked grin. Twisting a piece of my hair around his fingers, he whispers, "Think you can sit still now?"

CHAPTER 31

MACI

Sunday evening after we've made it back and showered, Sutton and I enter through the front door for dinner. He follows me inside and closes the door while I pause at the front of the hallway. I'm met with the scent of a home-cooked meal. It's reminiscent of days at Nana's.

To my right is a sitting room with low couches in front of windows overlooking the south and east sides of the property. I immerse myself in memorizing every detail of this space, with all its books and light, to avoid the heartache rising up. Grief comes and goes. Moments like this fuel reminders of what I've lost.

Sutton reaches for my hand casually as he passes me from closing the door, headed down the hall. I can't bring myself to move. He turns abruptly, standing before me and cupping my face with both hands. "Hey. What's going on?"

My eyes are welling with tears and I'm trying to force them away, but it's no use. His eyes go soft and wide before he pulls me against his chest, wrapping his strong arms around me.

When was the last time I let someone comfort me?

My racing heart calms as I melt into him. A few tears slip down my face, but the threatened flood has receded. I draw in several deep breaths and release my arms from around his torso.

"I'm sorry," I say on an exhale.

His hands move back to my face and he uses his rough thumbs to gently brush the tears from my cheeks. "You have nothing to apologize for. If this is too much, say the word and we'll leave."

I exhale and give him a soft shake of my head. "No. I'm ok."

"Are you sure?" He takes my hands in his.

"Sutton?" A familiar voice comes down the hall.

"One sec," Sutton calls over his shoulder. His features remain soft, waiting for my decision.

"Yes," I tell him confidently, forcing the tears to dry by blinking repeatedly. I take one more breath and squeeze his hand. "Come on. "

I've never worried about impressing someone's mother before. I don't even worry about impressing my own. But the part of me that's honest enough to admit I'm falling for Sutton knows how vital his family is to him. Them liking me is important to him, whether he says so or not. Andi may like me as Ruthie's granddaughter, but will she like me as a partner for her only son? What about his dad?

And why does any of that matter, when my plan is still to be gone for good in a matter of weeks?

At the end of the hallway, the living room spans out to the left. We enter the kitchen on the right. Andi is at the oven, fiddling with something. She smacks a dish towel onto the counter and turns to us in mild frustration at whatever is going on there.

"Maci!" she cries when her eyes meet mine. She crushes me into her arms and I let her squeeze me for as long as she wants. This is a hug like Nana's. A mother's. I cherish every second of it, willing my arms to soak in the love and my eyes to keep the tears at bay.

She pulls back and looks me over at arms' length. "I'm so glad you're here."

Her eyes lift to Sutton behind me. He's leaning against the doorway of the kitchen with his arms and ankles crossed and a smug look plastered on his face. She studies him quietly and looks back at me with glassy eyes. I'm positive I'm missing something. Something important, but I can't bring myself to ask.

My heart flutters. "How can I help?"

She shoots me a look. "You will not. You're a guest. Sutton, get Maci a drink and you two go sit down. Dad will be in soon, I'm sure."

Sutton doesn't balk and leads me into the dining room.

"So, Maci, how did the photos go yesterday? I'm sorry I couldn't stop by and say hi," Andi speaks from the kitchen, dishes clinking against each other. The table we're seated at is beautiful and I run my hands along the grain lines of the wood. Sutton watches my fingers dance along the top.

"They were wonderful. Thank you so much for helping me get in there." I glance at Sutton. "Did Sutton tell you I put him to work, too?" I can't help but put him on the spot. He runs his tongue between his lip and upper teeth, smiling from the corner of his mouth at me.

"He didn't! Only that he brought you something." She looks at him expectantly.

"Maci wanted to borrow a trailer, so I took her one of the white ones." He leans back in his chair, crossing his ankles straight in front of him and his arms over his chest. He has on a fresh tee, and once again, it's stretched over his fabulous body in a too-inviting way.

"Sutton." Andi stands in the doorway between the kitchen and dining room, giving her son a stern look. "You did not take her a dirty cattle trailer." She is appalled.

221

He grins and I know before he speaks that he's about to tease her. "Now Mama, I told her it was full of manure, but she wouldn't listen." His voice is as low and calm as always and it takes everything in me not to smack him in the arm where he sits next to me.

Andi's mouth pops open and her cheeks turn red. She's embarrassed of him for no good reason and he's going to give her an aneurysm.

I open my mouth to interject, but he comes to his senses and comes clean. "I'm just playin'. I cleaned it out before I ran it up there." He leaves his position next to me and strides over to where she's giving him a dirty look. "If you don't have faith in me, at least have faith in yourself. You raised me better than that." He plants a firm kiss on her cheek and pulls some glasses from a cupboard behind her.

Affection fills my chest. So much love fills this space with all its quiet nooks and crannies, all its history. An unfamiliar ease settles over me.

Sutton returns to the table and sets a can of cream soda and a glass of ice in front of me. He takes a sip of his water before setting it on the table, then places his hand atop mine and rubs gentle circles on it.

Everything is so easy with him, and that's scary as hell. I've heard so many people say how hard love is, how much work relationships are. My own experiences lend to that sentiment and yet I never wanted to put in the work. Never wanted to compromise. Maybe because it felt like I was the only one who was going to be losing something. With Sutton, I haven't felt like that at all. Could it always be like this?

The front door opens and closes and heavy footsteps approach.

"Hi, sweetheart." Andi's voice is steady and loving as always. From my spot at the table, the entrance from the hallway into the kitchen is visible. When Mr. Strickland fills the space, it's abundantly clear all the ways Sutton resembles him. Muscular and broad, but not too bulky, tall and tan.

Something tells me there will be plenty of similar personality traits, too, because he doesn't carry Andi's endearing gift of gab. The perfect steely blues and smile are all her, though.

Mr. Strickland kisses Andi on the temple and then looks our way, perking up when he spots me.

"Hi there." His smile is warm like Andi's as he skirts around her to the sink. He washes his hands and grabs a towel hung over the oven door handle. His lips tip up on one side—an expression I've seen on Sutton too many times to count—as he exchanges a look with his son and maneuvers forward into Andi's line of sight. The hand-drying motions are over the top. "So what's for dinner, Mama?"

She's intent on buttering rolls, but the motion of his hands catches her eyes and her face scrunches in annoyance. "If I've told you once, I've told you a thousand times!" All of the aggression is lacking as she snatches the towel from him, smiling broadly. His chuckle is warm and he steps quickly out of her reach into the dining room.

Instinctively, I stand. Mr. Strickland claps Sutton on the shoulder once inside the room. "Dad, this is Maci. Maci, this is my dad—"

"Michael." His large, tan hand extends to me and when I offer my own, he clasps his second over top. Calloused like his son, there's affection in the grip. I swallow hard. "Nice to have you."

"Thank you." Without a doubt, I'm blushing. I will the heat away, but it's no use.

Michael sits across the round table from me, as Sutton retakes his seat. Andi follows shortly with dishes and hot pads. "I'm happy to help," I offer again and she waves me off.

"Not a chance. You just sit right there, honey."

I do as I'm told and Sutton squeezes my leg. My cheeks flame anew as memories from the blind flood my mind's eye. His hands, his mouth. Both glorious and detrimental.

Swiping my drink from the table, I take a huge gulp. Sutton eyes me curiously. I ignore him.

Dinner is amazing. The food is spectacular and sitting and chatting with Sutton's parents is comfortable in a way I couldn't have predicted. It's like being home. Or at least a home filled with unconditional love.

His mother is giddy with excitement that we've hit it off and his father seems so proud of him all the way around. Everyone is pleasant and at ease.

At the conclusion of dinner, Michael excuses himself and Andi starts cleaning up. There's no holding me back. Nana would tan my hide if I didn't help clear the table and clean up the kitchen. Before she can protest, I collect the plates and silverware from the table, following Andi into the kitchen where she's carried her own.

From the corner of my eye, she turns sharply to Sutton who puts his hands up in surrender. The dishwasher is empty, so I begin rinsing and loading without asking.

"Just can't help yourself, can you?" Andi gives me a gentle bump with her hip from my opposite side.

How can something so simple convey so much emotion? Plate in hand, I turn to her. "Thank you again for having me. This has been so incredibly special." My throat constricts and I press my lips together firmly, swallowing.

Her eyes stay locked on mine. "You are welcome here anytime, honey. We're glad to have you." A moment later, she sets the remaining dishes from the table onto the counter.

Sutton's heat permeates my shirt from behind. My body screams for his touch. He's so close and it would be easy to lean back into him, but I refrain because this is new. I'm still not sure what we are and I'm meeting his parents for the first time, as anything other than a grieving granddaughter. Never mind that both of us continue to skirt the issue of me leaving.

His cheek brushes my hair as he draws his mouth near my ear. "You're incredible."

There's that fucking whisper again. I'm undecided if the chill that runs down my spine is from his words or his breath teasing my neck.

My head cocks gently his way, aching to be closer. I'm only slightly disappointed when his gentlemanly nature shines through and he plants a chaste kiss loosely into my hair, backing away.

Leaning against the counter near the refrigerator, he eyes me like dessert. "I'm planning to go see my sister soon. Would you be interested in coming with me for a visit?"

"Oh, Sammi would love that." Andi's voice reminds me of her presence. She goes about finding Tupperware for leftovers before scooting Sutton out of the way and organizing things into the refrigerator.

"I'm surprised I've been given a choice." I dry my hands with the correct towel.

Andi's movements cease and her eyes dart between us. Sutton's gaze goes dark and his mouth tips. "Firecracker." It's a warning.

I want to challenge him. To see what punishment looks like, but again, I refrain due to Andi's presence.

CHAPTER 32

SUTTON

Standing in the kitchen of my parents' house, watching Maci interact with my family easily, I've never been so happy. I'm not an unhappy guy. Some days on the ranch are tougher than others, but I enjoy the hard work and seeing progress at the day's end. Nothing has ever made me as happy as today.

Waking to Maci in my bed, tangled up with me, it didn't matter that we didn't have sex last night. Before her, I never felt like anything was missing and yet now I feel whole. How does one night do that to someone?

I'm walking a fine line between possessive and protective, need and want. I know I don't want to sleep without her curled into me. I don't want to wake up without Maci next to me.

In the blind, I had no intention of touching her. Tasting her. The tension between us was a lit fuse. I'd hoped some release would help her relax.

But *fuck*. Her cries, her body against mine, the way she said my fucking name. I'm never giving that up.

And then with ease, she takes in my family. Granted, she hasn't met Sammi, but it's not a concern. Mama adores her and I can tell Maci is comforted by Mama, too.

Now I want to show her something a little vulnerable. I want her here with me, on the ranch. I have no intention of ever leaving this life. So I want to show her a bit of what the future could look like. I think we can build a beautiful life together. I'm hoping like hell she sees the beauty in it, too. I don't want to imagine doing this without her.

It doesn't matter that the last thirty years of my life didn't contain her or that I've only known her for a matter of weeks. Now that she's here, a part of my life, a part of me, there's no going back.

CHAPTER 33

MACI

Instead of heading back to Sutton's room after dinner, he hauls me into "the Defender". It's basically a golf cart on steroids with a badass motor, but it handles the terrain of the ranch which would destroy something smaller.

"It's just as easy to drive this around the property." He takes a rough trail, running parallel to the driveway, toward the front of the ranch. When he turns on a branch of the road I didn't notice before and goes all the way to the end, I give him a sideways glance.

The wind whips my loose hair around and it's like a wild piece of me I've kept tamed has been released. I've been at the ranch less than twenty-four hours and the entrepreneur from Austin living in a tiny apartment seems so far gone. Can I be both?

Eventually, we come to a gate and Sutton pulls along the fence, jumping out and unlatching it. He doesn't worry about shutting this one.

Tall grass and shrubs create an unruly meadow ahead of us. A mixture of oak and mesquite trees form a natural perimeter on the north side. When he cuts the engine, I don't move. "What is this place?"

"I thought you might like to decompress for a bit." His voice is quiet.

"Are we dancing again?" My head rests against the firm seat and I tip my chin his way with a smile.

He mirrors me, seeming both surprised and pleased. "Do you want to dance?"

"I love dancing with you." My eyes lower to his hand on my knee as I trace his corded arm back up, over his chest. When my eyes return to his face, his lips are pursed gently in thought. It's an uncommon expression for him. My brows furrow.

He gives my leg a squeeze before exiting and rounding the front of the machine. Once I'm out with him, he guides me into the grassy area, placing me in front of him. I relish his warmth as one hand grips each of my hips, pulling me flush to his chest.

For the first time, his silence seems heavy. The setting sun gives the space a mesmerizing glow. A cooler breeze than this morning brushes my hair into my face and brings with it a bubbling sound. My eyes dart around.

Reading my thoughts, Sutton points into the distance to my right. "There's a creek back there." Despite the openness of the meadow, the scattered trees add a feeling of seclusion. There's nothing else as far as the horizon.

He steps out from behind me, turning to walk backward and making his way toward the center of the colorful field. "I'm going to build a house here."

"Oh?"

His face is the Sutton I met in Nana's house. The Sutton from the porch after he saw me chastise flowers. The Sutton from the truck when we arrived yesterday evening. He's studying me, assessing for something. Though unsure, his look doesn't fill me with anxiety.

I've learned during our time getting to know one another that he does nothing without thought. He's quiet, solid, and sexy as hell. And there's a depth to him that he doesn't share openly.

I keep my features soft. "It's a beautiful place for a home." I wonder what kind of dream house he envisions.

Pride washes over his face.

I'm still admiring the space when he walks to the Defender. The engine and lights come on and music pours out. A smile pulls at my lips.

Sutton's fingers slip into my hand and he pulls me against his body, wrapping his other arm around my waist and gliding me through the meadow on our own personal dance floor. My cheeks heat at the idea of it being ours, which is silly because my mind running away with itself is the last thing I need to allow to happen. I tuck my head into his chest to hide the color.

When the song changes to something a little faster, Sutton's pace picks up naturally. Grasshoppers leap out of our path, areas of the grass hip-height for me, as he continues to spin and swing me around. I embrace the tranquility he fills me with. It doesn't matter that his words are few because he easily displays the giant heart hidden inside.

A blue haze overtakes the glow as the sun sets. Sutton shifts suddenly, pulling me tight and looking down into my eyes. "Do you trust me?"

Something giddy lights his features, and despite already telling him yes, I'm convinced he wants me to say it again. His grin is infectious. I'd do anything he asks to keep that light in his eyes. I bite my lip and nod.

On the next spin, he shifts us so my back is flush to his chest again, our arms crossed together around my torso. "Do you like roller coasters?" His warm voice against my ear causes heat to pool between my legs.

"I might be a bit of an adrenaline junkie."

Locking me in place, he sways gently as he gives me instructions. Fairly certain he's going to flip me, I let him guide me through a series of spins before lining me up next to him, where I drop my arms over his as told. My breath catches and he uses both hands on my waist to lift me off the ground and flip me backward over his arm.

Laughter bursts out of me when I land upright on my feet. It's beautiful, and freeing, and I know without a doubt that I'm falling completely and totally in love with this man. And it's not some fancy dance move or giving me an amazing orgasm in a deer blind. It's his heart. The way he cares for me when I'm convinced I don't need it, in a way that I absolutely do.

"There she is." His rugged face glows with pride and elation. He presses me against his body again and doesn't let go, dancing until the song is finished and another one plays. And another. And another.

The sun sets and our bodies move together in the darkness, the song of crickets with the undertones of frog calls performing a concert in tandem. I never want to leave this place.

Coming back from the planned site of Sutton's home, my phone is ringing in the bottom of my purse. An unknown Texas number is listed on the screen. Normally, I screen calls, but decide to answer since I handed out several cards at the festival.

A lone sconce from the hallway offers light to the room, and I have to dig in near darkness to find the tiny electronic. "Hello?"

"May I speak to Maci McCullough?"

Not a potential client then. "This is she."

Sutton is eyeing me intently as he toes off his boots in the hallway. I follow suit, pretending not to notice his attention.

"This is Officer Casey Callahan from the Bull Creek Police Department."

"Oh. Hi, Officer Callahan."

Sutton's posture relaxes and he sits down on the leather couch, spreading his legs wide and keeping his eyes trained on me. His arms spread out along the back. Once again I want to photograph him.

"Casey is fine." It sounds like he's grinning. Casey has such a boyish face. I imagine if he weren't a police officer, he'd be a trouble maker. Maybe both are true. "Sutton's never introduced me to a woman before and I get the impression we'll be seeing more of each other."

"I'm not sure if that's a good thing or a bad thing, Casey." Sutton's eyes pop wide before he narrows in on the phone. My cheesy grin isn't helping matters.

"All good from me."

Tucking the phone between my ear and shoulder, I meander to the closet to pull out my pajamas. My camera bag is tucked next to my duffle and I pull it out as discreetly as possible.

"I don't want to take up too much of your evening. Normally, a detective would call about something like this, but I offered."

"Oh? Well, I'm on the edge of my seat." Sutton's eyes are piercing when I turn to face him. He's unprepared for the shutter and I manage a fabulous candid. I replace the camera and unbutton my jeans, working them down my legs.

"Some young teens got picked up today for vandalism. They were throwing rocks and just overall being destructive. Looks like there's a good chance they were the ones to break your window."

"Really?" Skepticism lines my voice. Sutton stands abruptly, drawing my attention to him and joins me on the opposite side of the bed in no time. A detail is hidden in the shadows of my mind, but I can't give it the attention it needs because Sutton's heat radiates into me as he crowds my space. Intending to treat him as if his proximity doesn't affect me, I turn my head to one side, but promptly tense when one warm hand trails up the inside of my leg.

"Yeah. They were in the area around the right time and didn't keep track of where all their rock throwing occurred."

Anticipation causes my breaths to deepen and I can only hum a response to Casey when Sutton's open mouth presses warm against my neck. The tip of his tongue tickles my skin. My free hand flies up to grip his arm and I tip my head back, granting him easier access.

My mind is in overdrive, trying desperately to focus on Casey's information while also wanting nothing more than to give in to Sutton's touch and the bliss it brings. As if reading my mind, Sutton's fingers dance on my lacey undergarments.

"Wouldn't I have found a rock in my car, if so?" The fact that I can form words is a miracle.

"Sure, unless it wasn't a rock. Maybe it was a skateboard and they don't want to fess up."

A finger sneaks beneath my panty line and I stifle a squeak, squeezing harder on Sutton's bicep. "A skateboard." I'm a parrot now.

"Yep." If Casey has any idea what's going on, he doesn't let on.

Sutton's breath is hot against my ear. "I'm about to light you up, Firecracker." Without further warning, he dips his fingers into my arousal, gathering the wetness and circling my clit. Pain shoots through my lip as I bite down to refrain from making any noise.

"Um, Casey—"

Sutton pulls his head back to pin me with a look. His deep whisper is a warning. "Sounds count as sharing, Firecracker." He kisses my lips. "And you better not say another man's name while my hand is playing with this pussy."

My eyes widen and heat fills my entire body. Sutton holds my gaze.

"Maci?" Casey's voice is quieter, further away, and I realize the phone is slipping.

"Sorry! Was that all?"

"Uhh, yeah." He seems confused by the abrupt change in my tone. "We'll keep you updated if—"

"Sounds great! Thanks so much, Ca-Officer!" My thumb repeatedly taps the end button on the face of the phone until I'm positive the call is disconnected. I hurl it onto the couch without further consideration.

Before I have a chance to ask Sutton what the hell he's thinking, his free hand slides into my hair at the base of my neck, gripping hard. "Why do you insist on teasing me, Firecracker?"

"I don't know what you mean, Cowboy." I'm fully prepared to die on this hill, but he's having no part of it.

"Liar." He kisses me, hard, his hands leaving my hair and my pussy, gripping my waist instead. Right before he throws me.

A constricted squeal leaves my body as I land among the stupid amount of pillows he keeps near the headboard. I've never seen a man with this many pillows.

My legs fall open, exposing my drenched panties, the bottom of my peasant shirt bunched up around my ribs. As Sutton takes me in, his eyes are darker than I've ever seen. He's like a caged animal waiting to pounce.

With one hand, he grabs his shirt behind his head and yanks it off. It lands on the couch. He climbs onto the bed on hands and knees, hovering over me.

The interrupted light from the hallway casts half his face in darkness, while the other half reflects the amber glow. I wish I could frame him this way.

"Cowboy," my hands reach up to touch his chest, "what are you up to?" Every tanned muscle tightens as my fingers lightly trace their outlines. He's on fire and I'm suddenly chilled, wanting to bask in his heat.

He doesn't respond at first. Instead, he's busy studying me while my hands are memorizing him. When they slide up his neck to cup his jaw, his eyes flutter closed briefly. The rough stubble against the smooth skin of my palms has a renewed arousal coursing through me.

Sutton's eyes spring open. A wicked gleam lights his eyes. "Do you trust me?"

Completely. I suck my bottom lip between my teeth and nod.

In one swift movement, he slides back down the bed, each powerful arm wrapping around one of my thighs, yanking me to the middle. Settling between my legs, he kisses the inside of one, staring directly up at me. I lift onto my elbows, unwilling to miss this show.

His mouth moves to the other thigh, placing a mirrored kiss there. Dragging his fingers up the outside of my legs, he grips the lace panties at each hip and lowers them down. He's watching me so intensely he doesn't blink. The panties fly behind him.

Torturously, he kisses and licks at my legs, working his way up to their apex. The thrumming of my heart is so strong, I'm confident he can hear it beating in my chest. My hips rise, begging for him to come higher. His grip on my thighs tightens and I try to contain a whimper.

A chuckle precedes the highest kiss yet and I decide I'm not above begging if that's what it takes. "Please." *That was definitely a whimper.*

Sutton's teeth graze one thigh in response. "What do you need, Firecracker?"

My back arches off the bed and my head falls back. He knows what I need.

"Maci." My head snaps back down at his commanding tone. I hold my breath. "Eyes here." Drier than the Sahara, my mouth falls open. "What do you need?"

"Stop teasing me, Cowboy." The wickedness in his eyes is still there. He doesn't move. "Please."

"Since you asked so nicely." Keeping eye contact, he places one more kiss on my thigh, before shifting forward.

With a flat tongue, he licks me from the base of my entrance to my clit. An appreciative groan vibrates through me, overtaking my own gasp. On the second swipe, my eyes flutter closed. He sucks on my clit, causing them to pop back open, his lips smiling against me proudly as he continues to work me over.

A breathy moan escapes me and he growls into my pussy, causing my hips to buck again. Wanting to increase the friction, again I roll my hips. His eyes shoot up to me and the grip on my thighs loosens long enough for each hand to slip from behind my legs. He presses his palms outward on the inside of my thighs, watching my face as he opens me wider. I'm at his mercy.

His mouth is hot and addictive as he continues to alternate his movements against the entirety of my pussy.

When I press the fabric of my top down to expose my breasts, my nipples are already hard and tight. Sutton's eyes flame as I run my fingers over the sensitive tips, rolling and kneading the flesh. He gives a powerful suck to my clit, popping his mouth off and raising his head. "You trying to kill me?"

"Definitely not. I need you to finish what you're doing."

A hand slides into my wetness, two of his fingers slipping along either side of my clit and rubbing up and down, slow and firm. "You mean my dessert?"

Pausing his mouth's attention to my body is killing me. My grip on my breasts tightens. "Sutton." I don't miss the spark in his eyes. "Please."

"Fuck, Firecracker." Then he devours me. Gone is the gentleman everyone sees. He's gone feral. His arms stretch out to pin my legs wide, gripping a knee in each hand and he laps up my juices like it's his last meal.

One of my hands drops to his head. My fingers thread into the soft, sandy hair with a tight grip. He doesn't need me to guide him. He knows exactly how to work my body. The escalating moans I release are proof.

Like a volcano, my orgasm builds from deep within. Without warning, Sutton shoves two fingers deep inside me, thrusting hard while he continues to circle my clit with his tongue.

"Give it to me, Firecracker. Come for me." The combination of the thrusting, the licking, and his hot breath against my pussy sends me over the edge.

I cry out his name, sure my grip in his hair must be painful now. But there's nothing I can do. He moans into me as he continues to lick up the fruit of his labor, sliding his fingers slowly from me when my orgasm has subsided.

Pressed deep into the pillows, my fingers release his hair, my eyes flutter closed.

His thumb whispers over my clit and my hips jump, earning me a chuckle.

The weight of the bed shifts as Sutton pushes back up to all fours, looking down at me. I don't need to open my eyes to feel his gaze. He kisses my flushed face, my jaw, my neck.

"That's the best thing I've ever tasted." His hot whisper sends a chill down my spine.

With a gentle hand, he guides my face to his and I open my eyes to find him studying me with softness. The wild man is gone.

His hand slides into my hair as he rests on a forearm, kissing me softly. When his tongue traces the seam of my lips, I open willingly for him, tasting myself on his tongue.

This time, passion reignites in my belly.

One lingering kiss precedes him releasing my lips.

"Did you want to get into the pajamas you pulled out?" He makes quick work of removing his pants. I grunt my decline. "Here. Arms up." His hands grasp the hem of my disheveled shirt and I do as I'm told. The shirt comes off with ease and he slides into the bed, shifting to lay on his side. One warm arm pulls me into his chest and draws light designs on my back. Content, my body is quickly succumbing to sleep.

"So, what did Officer Callahan have to say?" I can feel the smirk of his lips against my hair.

"Teenagers," I mumble and drift off.

CHAPTER 34

MACI

I n the morning, my fingertips are greeted by cold sheets on Sutton's side of the bed. I may not know much about ranch life, but I do know his days don't start after sunrise very often.

Muted buzzing fills the room and my eyes flit around, searching for the source. A laugh bursts from me into the open room when I remember tossing my phone onto Sutton's couch last night. I'd love nothing more than to bask in the afterglow of all that took place yesterday, but my window is getting repaired this morning and it's time to return to reality.

With blurry eyes, I slide out of Sutton's heavenly bed and check the time on my phone.

There are two new messages in the group chat.

Izzy:

> **Don't forget the Trunk-or-Treat this week.**

> **Bring the cowboy.**

I grin. I have no idea if that's his thing or he'd want to go, though I doubt the former very seriously.

Me:

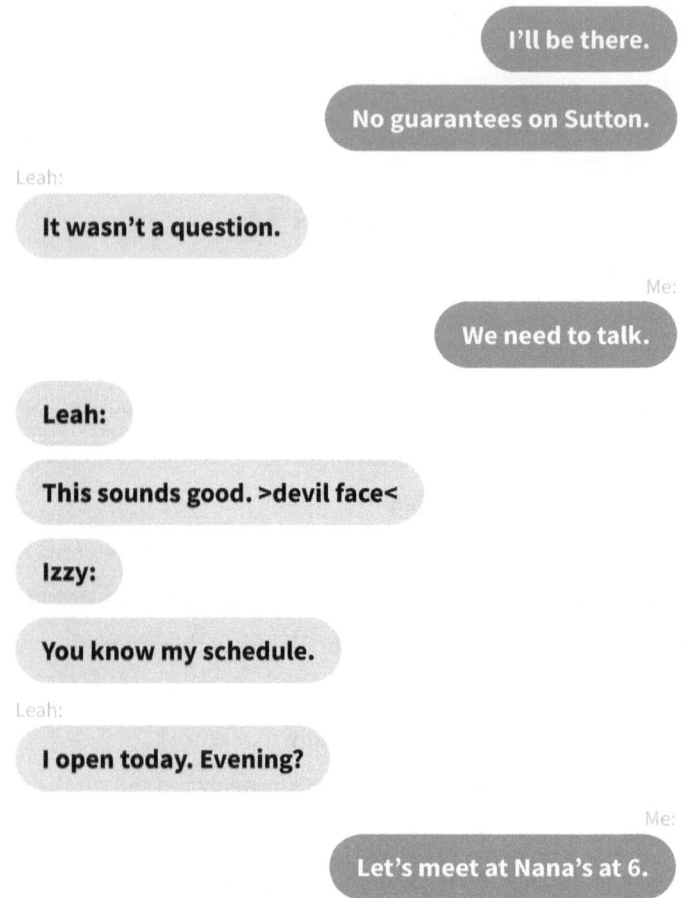

> I'll be there.

> No guarantees on Sutton.

Leah:

> It wasn't a question.

Me:

> We need to talk.

Leah:

> This sounds good. >devil face<

Izzy:

> You know my schedule.

Leah:

> I open today. Evening?

Me:

> Let's meet at Nana's at 6.

After my friends text their agreement to the time, I opt for a quick shower. My wet hair goes into a braid and I don jeans and a soft, plum-colored sweater. Take that, Texas.

Boots on, I throw my camera bag over my shoulder and head outside. The air is dry and crisp, and I send up a silent thank you to Texas for cooperating.

I have no idea where Sutton is and he hasn't given me much of a tour yet, so I wouldn't even begin to know where to find him. The Defender is parked nearby and I wonder if the keys are in it. It's all moot because when I reach the corner of the house, I'm met with a cow who stands as tall as me.

She—I think it's a she?—greets me with a solid moo and a wet boop to my nose.

"Whoa!" My back bounces into the corner of the house. "Well good morning to you, too." I blink.

"Daisy," Sutton chastises, approaching from behind with a coffee cup in hand. The cow's head swings lazily his way and she ambles over to nose his chest in greeting. He pats her gently on the head. "You big oaf." She gives him one more solid nudge in the stomach before sauntering off around the house.

Her rear swings a sassy walk as she goes.

"I didn't realize you had cattle around the house," I say in greeting. Sutton's in his usual dirty boots, jeans, brown button-up, and hat. I look my fill of him.

Waking to him in bed with me is the most exquisite feeling, but taking him in here in his element stokes an ember that remains burning deep inside. I'm immediately heated and wanting.

"Just Daisy." He extends the mug to me. "For you."

"Me?" I don't wait to take the mug from him, enlivened by its cozy heat. I take a whiff, squeezing the porcelain in my hands, surprised by its creamy color.

"I know you need coffee in the mornings. It's hazelnut creamer. I don't think that's your favorite, but I figured it was better than black." His hands land on his hips.

Stupid fiery butterflies. It's only coffee. It's not that serious.

Without taking my eyes off his, I lift the mug to my lips for a deep drink. "Thank you."

He responds with his usual dip of his chin. "You look ready to go."

I wince. "I'm sorry. I didn't think about your timeline today. I should have asked you. I need to get back for the appointment on my window."

In the shadow of his hat, his brows furrow. "Why are you apologizing?"

"I know you have a large operation to run and now you're running around trying to be my protector." My hand waves around in the air, gesturing at the entirety of the ranch.

He steps closer to me and I clutch the mug tighter, looking up at him. "We have employees for a reason. And nothing is more important than your safety." He arches one brow, daring me to argue, and I purse my lips in response. That perfect mouth tips into a smirk. I'm ruined.

"Come on." He hitches his head toward the front of the house and I fall in step with him. Gravel crunches under our feet, soon interrupted by mooing cows and a whinnying horse.

Daisy is making her way down the grassy shoulder of the driveway on a solo mission I can't figure out. Her auburn body waddles side to side on her way.

Sutton stands silently with the passenger door open, his intense gaze on me. I'm not sure I'll ever get used to that.

He reaches for my mug and I relinquish it slowly. Once I'm seated, he says, "I'll be right back," and closes the truck door.

Taking the stairs two at a time up the front steps, he disappears into the house and reappears shortly with an insulated mug. He rounds the truck and climbs in, extending the new mug to me. This man.

We make it back to Nana's with a few minutes to spare before the appointment. Sutton sets to work removing the makeshift cover he put in place of the glass.

My phone rings as I unlock the door. Stephanie's name shows on the screen threatening my good mood.

"Good morning." I walk straight through the house to the back porch.

"Maci."

"Yes." Who else does she think she called?

"Randi received the death certificate." Well that was abrupt. Predictable enough.

"Ok. I'll reach out to Ha-Mr.Campbell and let him know so he can get started on the probate process."

"I've already left a message with his secretary." Of course, she has.

"Well, thank you for letting me know."

"You're welcome." A prolonged silence drags.

"Alright, well I have an appointment. If I hear anything else, I'll keep you updated." I don't wait for her to respond before ending the call.

Heading back to the front porch to offer Sutton breakfast, I drop my things onto the table in the foyer. I'm sure he has a long day, but he's driven me all the way here and I'm starved. The technician is already working on my window as I make my way outside, but my eyes are trained on Sutton, standing beneath the largest oak tree in the front yard, fastening a tire swing to it. The tire swing of my childhood. I stop in my tracks.

Momentarily, I can't decide if I'm mesmerized by the swing dangling beneath my favorite tree as it once did, or him tying a knot into the rope in an erotically aggressive manner.

It's smaller than I remember. Or I just thought it was bigger at the time because of how small I was. Where the hell did he find it?

Forcing my feet to move, I head down the steps and approach him under the tree. His head snaps my way and a sheepish look covers his usually sure face. "I hope this is okay." He grips the rope tightly, waiting.

"It's—" My voice catches. "—it's more than okay."

"I found it when I was grabbing things for the window the other day. I meant to ask. I didn't mean to upset you." He releases the rope.

"No. I had been wondering where it went. I didn't even think to look in the garage."

A grin tugs at his mouth. "Do you trust me?"

His hands find mine and he squeezes. Excited energy radiates off of him in waves. He's doing his best to keep it contained, but it's infectious and I grin back at him. For the first time, he appears youthful and carefree.

"Yes, Sutton, I trust you."

"Good." He looks back to the tire and then to me suggestively, an indication of his plan. I lift a foot to step forward, but he moves in a flash, swiping my legs out from under me and cradling my back with his other arm.

I squeal and he beams, swinging me in a wide circle while I exert a death grip on his shirt. Then he guides my legs through the hole of the tire and I reach my arms over the top, grabbing the thick rope with both hands. I wonder why the swing was down if the rope and tire are both still intact, when Sutton whispers, "Hold on," against my ear and my skin chills.

Together, the tire and I shift further into the air, way higher than anticipated, before we plummet. The drop is deep and fast, and I let out what I hope is a tiny scream, but it quickly turns to laughter as the tire returns the way it came.

Lacking any form of control, the tire rotates as it swings so I'm facing Sutton. His wide smile will live on in my memory for eternity. I want it framed on our wall for our children to see. The thought causes my heart to ache, knowing this will be over before it really gets started.

We need to have a serious discussion about what we're doing because we're both playing around like there's no end in sight. Or maybe that's all it is to him.

My thoughts are cut short when Sutton pushes the tire with force again and it twirls gently from the impact. Like a slow twirling top, the tire and I spin back and forth across the lawn as one. Tears from laughter stream down my cheeks, and every few rotations I catch sight of Sutton's beautifully rugged features.

The laughing becomes so consuming, and I'm so far out of breath, that I lean back deeply, knowing I'm not going to be able to hold on much longer. With perfect timing, Sutton reaches around my midsection and hauls me off the swing, pulling us both down to sit on the cool grass. I flop backward, my sides cramping as I right my breathing.

He follows, setting his hat on its crown and resting his head on his arm, watching me in humored silence. I roll my head to the side to look at him. So much affection seeps from his eyes. Gingerly, he rolls onto his side, propping his head on a hand, and reaches over with the other to press a piece of errant hair behind my ear.

"I love listening to you laugh."

I'm caught off guard by his admission. Though he's affectionate with me frequently, and I can feel the growing bond between us, I'm unprepared for his honesty, even if it's in reference to a quality or action, versus me as a whole.

"I haven't laughed that hard in a long time. Thank you." I slide my hand through the grass to tangle my fingers with his.

"All set!" comes a shout from the driveway and I startle.

Sutton and I sit up in unison. "Be right there," I call back, jumping up to grab my wallet, but the guy is already walking to his van and I'm not sure if he heard me.

"I already took care of it," Sutton says, still seated in the grass. He replaces his hat.

My head snaps his way. "What? Why?"

He stands and looks into my eyes. "Because I wanted to."

"You didn't have to do that." Needing something to do with my hands, I fiddle with the end of my braid.

His eyes turn hard and he drops his chin. "You don't have to do everything on your own, Maci."

Maci.

In some ways it feels so foreign for him to use my given name. And yet there's an importance to it. He's not being playful, or coy, or seductive, or even dismissive.

Things are just getting more and more complicated, and this is further proof that I need to finalize things here at the house and get back to Austin. It's making it harder for everyone for me to drag things out.

"Are you hungry?" I can't entertain this conversation so I change the subject, eyeing the ground.

"I am." *Now* his tone is seductive and he takes a step closer.

Just like that, I'm on fire. It's impossible to be frustrated with him, and even more unlikely that I can be in his general vicinity without being completely and utterly turned on. Thankfully, I know he isn't free today and I'm determined to set things back on their proper course. "French toast or pancakes?"

His grin only drops minutely.

Izzy and Leah barrel through the front door five minutes before six. I'm coming out of the hallway into the foyer and jump at the welcome intrusion.

Leah calls, "What's up, sweet cheeks," as she nearly sprints past me into the kitchen and I hear her rummaging through cabinets when Izzy wraps me in her arms.

"How are you?" It's a loaded question at this point.

"I'm getting better." She eyes me speculatively, scanning my face and body, and then wraps me up again.

"It looks like you are." As if I need her agreement. I breathe a laugh. She leads the way to the kitchen. "Come on, I need food and all the details on your sexy cowboy."

"He's not mine." She throws a look over her shoulder, brows furrowed and lips pursed. Ok, so we both know I'm lying. A smile tugs at my lips.

In the kitchen, Leah is mixing margaritas in a pitcher, snacks sprawled all over the counter. She fills three plastic margarita glasses, all of which read, 'But first, Tequila!' Always the creative, she spent a month hand-lettering vinyl onto everything. "I propose Margarita Mondays become a permanent thing."

"As in, mutual Happy Hour on the phone?" I smirk.

Leah's smile falters. "No. I mean you keep your ass here permanently." She perks up. "Then we can test different flavor combinations each week. Lemon Lavender, Pina Margarita, Prickly Pear..."

I blink. "Prickly Pear?"

She shrugs.

"Are you on another Pinterest kick?" Izzy asks, swiping the first glass. Leah flips her hair over one shoulder and grins. I move around to stand by

Leah on the other side of the island, picking up my own drink. "Saw the tire swing out front. When did you put that up?"

I take a big drink before responding, giving myself brain freeze. "Sutton found it and put it up today."

"Today?" they parrot in unison.

Leah smirks next to me. "Come on. Let's take this shindig outside. It's gorgeous." We gather the snacks into dishes, each of us grabbing one in one hand and our drinks in the other, following Leah out the backdoor to the porch.

"Today?" Izzy prompts again, once we're seated.

I grin. "Yes." Izzy pops a cube of cheese in her mouth as I start talking. "He went all caveman on me after the window incident I texted you about, so I spent the rest of the weekend with him and he brought me back this morning."

Izzy's chewing slows and Leah's mouth falls open. They both stare at me without responding. I keep talking to fill the heavy silence. "He found it in the garage and put it up while my window was getting repaired."

"Like a surprise?" Leah sips her margarita. I shrug.

Izzy looks between us and settles her gaze on me. "Any *other* surprises? Staying over that long seems serious." She has always been the most cautious of the three of us and I can tell by her tone and the way she's eyeing me that she's concerned. No doubt because whatever is going on with Sutton and me is developing quickly, especially for me, and I'm set to leave any day now.

"I know what you're thinking. I don't know how to explain it. Everything is just so easy with him." I shake my head at myself and chew my lip. How do I convey what's going on without sounding cliche?

They continue to watch expectantly. I take a deep breath. "Ok. The night we met at the bar, he only came over because Colt was making me tense—"

"Only?" Leah sips her drink as if she didn't interrupt. I ignore her despite giving her a dirty look.

"—*and* he saw that I was happy on the dance floor, so he danced with me." Izzy's face softens, spurring me on. "When I asked to use one of his trailers for the Fall Festival photos, he didn't even balk. He cleaned it and drove up there, ready to go before I arrived. This morning, he let me sleep when he got up, and then he brought me coffee. With a reasonably appropriate creamer. Even though we've never discussed it."

"You do have a bit of a caffeine addiction," Leah says, margarita glass pressed to her lips.

I smile. "When he took me out for our only official date, he brought me a cactus."

Both of them seem confused, and they exchange a look of questioning my sanity. "A prickly pear," I say with a pointed look at Leah, "because he heard me yelling at flowers one day and remembered that I don't like them and the prickly pear grows at the ranch."

Leah is gaping at me now.

"He took the time to propagate one?" Izzy crosses her legs on the bench. "Where's the caveman part?"

"He didn't want me out of his sight until we found whoever broke my window," I rush the words. It still seems so ridiculous. "But Casey called and it was just teenagers."

"Casey?"

"Office Callahan. He's a friend of Sutton's. He was the responding officer when we called."

"Does he know you're packing?" Leah asks, as if that's the only relevant consideration. I know she's referring to Sutton.

"Yes." I realize I never mentioned the Trunk-or-Treat at the clinic to Sutton. Also not the most pressing matter, but the one that comes to mind.

"Are you guys coming Thursday?" Izzy directs her question at me as if reading my mind.

"I didn't get a chance to ask this morning."

"Ask now." She jerks her head toward my phone.

"Yes ma'am." I salute her and snatch my phone up, sending a text to Sutton. I follow up that he's not obligated to go.

CHAPTER 35

SUTTON

Leaving Maci this morning was torture. Our weekend together could never be enough. Despite the very consensual play, I'm convinced she still feels at least halfway forced into staying with me given the circumstances. I need her to want to be with me.

Her response to the build site was understated and I'm not sure if she understood why I was asking, or if she was being intentionally vague.

We left so much unsaid this morning. I don't know what her plans are for the rest of the week. Hell, the rest of the year. She hasn't mentioned Ruthie's house or the will in a while.

It's obvious we're made for each other. I'm trying really damn hard to let her get to that decision on her own. But I also can't fucking stand the thought of being away from her.

Dad and I head over to Terrence's midday to discuss the sale and get a lay of the land. It's good timing because it will give my mind plenty of other information to mull over.

Because of the size of the property and nature of the land, we ride over, me on Johnny Walker and Dad on Dusty. Dusty was bred next door and seems happy to be here again.

"Mornin'," Terrence greets us near the front corral atop his own black horse. "Why don't I give you a general tour and we can head in for some lunch."

"Sounds good." Dad tips his hat in agreement.

The sheer size of the place means hours riding around. The majority of the buildings are toward the front of the property, with some trails and open pasture further back. I consider some of Maci's ideas as we ride.

My head is swimming with information when we're done. Terrence's ranch isn't currently a cattle ranch. They raise quarter horses. Dad and I haven't discussed changing directions, but we'll need to plan everything out whether we do or not.

"Thanks for your time, Terrence." Dad shakes his hand. "We'll have an answer next week. Assuming that's not drawing things out for you. Want to give this the thought it's due."

Terrence ducks his head politely at my dad before shaking both our hands. "I can wait a bit longer."

Back at Strickland Ranch, we hand the horses off to Kelly at the stables. I pull my phone from my pocket to check messages. It buzzed against my heart during the meeting and it took way more self-control than usual not to look at it then.

Firecracker:

> **Izzy wants us to come to a Trunk-or-Treat thing at the dental practice this week.**

> **You are not obligated to go.**

> **Pretty sure that sentiment doesn't apply to me.**

Us. Tiny word, big meaning. I doubt she even realizes she looped us together that way, but I like it. I can't figure out if I want her to know it's not possible for me to tell her *no* on anything or not.

CHAPTER 36

MACI

Jeeps and rubber ducks are kind of a thing. Over the eighteen months I've owned mine, I've gotten so many different ducks of all sizes. Sometimes they come with notes, other times a duck waits alone on my handle when I return to my parked car. It seems only fitting that as part of the items I put together for Izzy's Trunk-or-Treat bash, I would have a thousand costumed duckies. A thousand ducks is an exaggeration. Probably.

Given this event is at the dentist's office and Izzy is a hygienist, someone is bound to be giving out toothbrushes. Who wants a toothbrush on Halloween? So it's my duckies and me to the rescue.

I arrive an hour and a half before the start of the event, as instructed. It's dusk and my Jeep is only the third car in attendance. Izzy's is, unsurprisingly, the first, and I can't decide if I'm impressed or pissed that Leah's is the second. Our cars are butted up to make an Izzy trunk sandwich and my best friends have already popped their trunks and started decorating.

Izzy is dressed as Tooth Fairy, complete with a white bodice, tutu, and sturdy wings. Her ice-blonde hair is styled in fat ringlets down her back and she wears a crown atop her head.

I slide my handmade costume on and stand in the driver's seat.

"Don't tell me you don't have a wand."

Izzy's head pops out of the trunk when I yell out to her. Whatever she was going to say dies on her lips and her smile turns into a perfect O as Leah draws out, "Ho-ly shit," from the other side of her.

Thanks to Sutton's help with the Jeep top earlier, and entirely too many balloons, my Jeep is about to resemble a full-on bubble bath. I stand, grinning down at my friends, my head and torso above the roof of my seat. Once all is said and done, I'll be a rubber ducky raining down mini ducks and chocolate on the trunk-or-treaters. I couldn't hide my cheek-splitting smile if I tried.

"That's fucking amazing!" Leah cries, finally gathering herself. She's bouncing up and down, the tail of her leopard costume swaying behind her. Where she found a one-piece bodysuit in leopard print is beyond me, but she's gone all out on her big-cat makeup and paired it with ears on a headband. Her wild tresses hang down in beautiful chaos as usual and she's every bit the wild animal she's portraying.

Izzy's bright smile hasn't left her face. "You've outdone yourself this time, Maci Grace."

I bow as much as my ballooned costume will let me and swing my hand around with a flourish. I'm not always one for theatrics, but when I do, I do it right. I spent entirely too long sewing too many half-inflated yellow balloons onto a body suit for this. I may have permanent hearing damage from all of the accidental popping.

I climb down from my seat, opening the driver door so I can attach the last of the cardboard which will give the Jeep its bathtub feel. My bucket of ducks and candy is riding shotgun, waiting to make its debut.

"Where's Sutton?" Izzy peeks into the passenger seat like he may be hiding there.

"He's coming. They ended up with two cows calving today so he was sticking around in case there was any trouble. I think it's just precaution."

"Look at you, picking up ranch lingo." Izzy bumps me with her shoulder before attaching the final piece of her car's costume. Paper teeth larger than my head dangle from her open hatch. The storage area is lined with black trash bags and a red, plastic tablecloth sticks out the back, folded to look like a tongue. Green and purple goody bags line the faux mouth, ready for little hands to grab. "Look! Bacteria." She cackles.

"This is really cute." I wrap both arms around her, admiring her hard work.

"Thanks, friend." A tiny bit of pink colors her cheeks. "I'm glad we're all together."

I squeeze her tighter, about to tell her I wouldn't miss it for the world, but the pressure causes one of the balloons on my costume to pop and we all jolt and scream together, bursting into laughter as one.

"Jesus, Maci. Leave it to you to give us a heart attack," Leah chides once we've calmed ourselves. The three of us lean against the back of Izzy's car, staring out to Main Street. The sun begins to lower behind the tree line across the street.

I turn to them suddenly. "Ok!" In unison, their eyes widen. "A leopard, a duck, and a tooth fairy walk into a bar." And with that, we're a mess of laughter all over again.

Like clockwork, families start strolling in at seven o'clock. Sutton hasn't arrived yet, but I'm not worried. He's yet to let me down.

I'm perched in the Jeep, Izzy and Leah at their respective trunks, along with about fifteen other people who agreed to pass out candy and goodies. A plethora of costumed children, and some parents, file through below me. Spider-Man, princesses of all kinds, a toddler dressed as Chucky who totally gives me the creeps, and babies in fluffy lion and pig costumes. Their squeals over the ducks raining from the sky, and a boat-load of candy, fill me with joy.

Everything is going off without a hitch up until a motorcycle revs. Judging by the volume, I assume it pulls into the parking lot next door which is also the home of the only Italian restaurant in town. A few of the kids startle at the loud noise, but the parents are quick to shush them and candy makes everything better at this point, so they're all happily on their way. Crisis averted.

"What time is it?" Leah calls up to me.

I eye the glow of the dash below me. "Seven-thirty."

"Still no word from Sutton?"

I shake my head. "It's fine. I'm sure something came up at the ranch."

Izzy and Leah exchange a look, but I ignore them.

A low voice comes from the front of my Jeep. "Would've pegged you for a princess." A chill runs down my spine and I drop the ducks in my hand just off the side of the car, whipping around to see who's there.

Colt.

"Nope, no princess here." I turn back around, ignoring his remark. "Hi, Belle!" It's an effort to kick my excited voice into overdrive, greeting children with a broad smile. Especially because I know he isn't leaving.

Out of my peripheral, Colt moves closer, fitting himself between Izzy's passenger door and my driver door. He leans against Izzy's car, not taking his eyes off me. I continue to ignore him.

Izzy and Leah are giving me questioning glances. Chewing my lip, I shake my head tightly at Izzy.

If I ignore him, he'll go away.

It's a lie. For the life of me, I can't figure out what Colt wants, but the pit in my stomach is warning that this is going to be more than a menacing wink over his shoulder.

"No cow-fucker tonight?"

My head snaps in his direction, my eyes darting to Izzy briefly. She's eyeing the families walking by the backs of our cars, who are now eyeing the biker clearly up to no good. Her voice is getting louder to compensate for the added distraction. "You are such a cute Cinderella! Happy Halloween!" Leah follows suit.

With both hands on the roof of the Jeep, I lean over to whisper-yell at Colt. "What is your problem!"

It's not a question. I know there isn't a logical answer at this point. I also know drawing attention to it won't make him go away.

He brings a cigarette to his mouth, taking a long drag, and eyes me from head to toe. "Usually you're hot. But tonight you look fucking ridiculous." The cigarette returns to his lips.

"Ouch, that hurts," I deadpan.

Night is descending quickly, the sky darkening to an indigo color, and there are no lights in this parking lot. A massive oversight. Only the cherry of Colt's cigarette lights the space between the cars.

"I'd still fuck you if you asked nicely." Smoke leaves his mouth in a cone. "Well, I would." He snickers the second part as if someone's with him.

My climb out of the truck is far less graceful than the last time I did it. I shove the bucket of ducks and candy at Izzy, who now stands between our two cars attempting to block the view. Her ability to put her back to Colt is either really brave or really stupid, but I don't have time to deal with that right now.

When I turn on Colt, he stands fully again, flicking the cigarette under Izzy's car.

"Get out of here!" Without thought, I move toward him. He grins at me, backing up slowly. Too slowly. Taunting me.

"That what you want, princess?" Every time he calls me *princess*, a cold chill runs down my back. Nausea coils in my stomach.

Continuing forward, I move to shove him, but he's ready and he grabs my wrists, pulling me into his chest. My feet falter at the change from pavement to grass as he pulls me around the front of the Jeep. "What's wrong, *princess*?"

His emphasis on the last word lets me know he's doing it on purpose. I'm fighting against his hold, simultaneously trying to push him away and pull my arms free, but neither thing is happening.

In front of the Jeep, I can no longer tell what people can and can't see. My senses zero in on what's happening right here, in this moment, and everything else is distant. A sense of familiarity washes over me as I struggle against him.

"You seem a little worked up." His eyes gleam and his grin grows, and I'm two seconds from throwing up on him. "Need a little release?"

"You couldn't give me release if you had a map where X marks the spot," I spit at him.

His grin never falters. "Maybe if you expected more than to be treated like a common whore in an alley—"

I explode. I bounce up on the balls of my feet and slam my head into his nose with all my force. There's a satisfying crunch and he releases my wrists.

"FUCK YOU!" I scream. I no longer care if there are families with children.

"Motherfucker!" He's holding his nose which is pouring blood. When he pulls his hand back, his eyes shoot up to my face. I've never seen a look contain so much fury.

Pounding footsteps and skidding tires mesh with the whooshing of my own blood in my ears as Colt launches at me. I'm fully prepared to grab two handfuls of hair and give him a knee straight to the dick, but his gaze shoots over my shoulder and he missteps.

"We're not done, bitch," he says under his breath, the pounding in my head getting louder.

Movement from my peripheral catches my attention as Colt darts into the darkness. Sutton's truck is parked on a side street, driver door open, lights on, as he runs straight for me.

"Maci!" A male's voice yells behind me. I whip around.

"Jesus!" Nick stops short, hands up. "Sorry, I didn't mean to scare you. What the fuck happened?"

Before I can respond, Sutton shoves between Nick and I, gripping my face with both hands. He looks between my eyes for a moment before holding me at arm's length and looking me over. "Are you ok?"

Heaving breaths cause my chest to rise and fall. I close my eyes and tilt my head to the sky, sucking in air and willing my heartbeat to slow. My chest burns. The pounding is painful and my eardrums throb.

Izzy's and Leah's voices infiltrate the other sounds. Everything is starting to meld together into noise.

I suck in a breath and hold it for a four count before blowing it out.

Nick's low voice breaks through the flurry. "I'm gonna go move your truck." A soft thudding on the grass follows and I finally open my eyes to see him jogging to the truck.

"Oh my God!" My hands fly up to my face. "Izzy, I'm so sorry!" I still can't see between the cars to the other side and now the space around me is mostly filled with bodies anyway.

"Shh, Maci, it's fine." Izzy's brows furrow. "Most everyone had moved on and your safety is more important."

"Maci, what the hell happened?" I face forward to Sutton again. His warm hands still hold my shoulders, steadying me. A tornado is building beneath his surface. The energy contained is practically vibrating out of him.

My brain chooses now to catalog his attire. His usual look is replaced by an all-white uniform with pinstripes and a dark ball cap. "What are you wearing?"

He's stunned. "My old baseball uniform."

I can't stop my grin.

"Not the time," he says sternly.

The past few minutes wash over me again. Tears threaten, a combination of coming down from my adrenaline high and knowing that he made a point to dress up for this event.

I slip my arms around his waist and lean into his chest, seeking his comfort, but inadvertently popping another yellow balloon and causing yelps to sound from Izzy, Leah, and I. We break into laughter, an accidental comedic relief in this moment of tension, but my face is pressed against Sutton's firm chest and I can't bring myself to let go as I bounce softly with laughter. His strong arms encircle me, squeezing me against his body.

Peace washes over me.

I've missed him. I want him. I never want him to let me go.

CHAPTER 37

SUTTON

I 've never been more prepared to end someone's life than I was tonight.

The dentist's office is visible at the turn onto Main Street from the county road. Even in the dark, Maci's yellow ballooned costume caught my attention.

The night Sammi was admitted to the hospital was the hardest night of my life. My baby sister was in danger and there wasn't a single thing I could do to help her or my sweet niece. I had to standby and trust the doctors and team assembled to help them. I had to lie to Mama, telling her everything was going to be okay, even though I had no idea if that was true. I saw Dad cry for the first time in my life. It gutted me.

Following that, I assumed I could handle anything. Losing a parent is expected. It's going to hurt like hell when it happens. But the fear of losing my baby sister unlocked a different set of emotions in me, and once all was well, I was convinced they were locked right back up again.

Pulling up on Maci fighting with Colt tonight exposed an entirely different set of emotions.

After seeing her at lunch, helping with the Jeep, everything that could have gone wrong this afternoon did. The culmination of which was two springing heifers calving today. Unfortunately, this resulted in having to help deliver one after the heifer became stressed. So heading into town, I was already on edge with the events of the afternoon coupled with running late.

I'm pissed I let Maci down. In multiple ways. I'm livid Colt had his hands on her. And I'm worried.

Colt approached Maci with a group around. He's clearly off his rocker. That fucker is lucky he got away before I got my hands on him.

Despite the short time we've known each other, Maci is incredibly important to me. I can't imagine life without her in it. The idea of some scumbag doing something to jeopardize that causes too many things to swirl around inside me.

So I don't loosen my grip on her as her body shakes with laughter pressed against my chest. The balloons of her costume squeak in protest between us, but her grip on me is snug and I'm not budging.

Two days without her was unbearable. Even worse than previous weeks. The possibility of more is killing me bit by bit.

I tell Maci none of what's going on in my head. I wait for her to calm and release me willingly.

"I called dispatch. County's on the way." Nick returns from moving the truck.

"County?" Maci leans back to look up at him.

"Sheriff's office. City limit's there." He points to a parking lot up the road.

"You need to file a restraining order, Maci." Izzy squeezes closer.

I agree with the sentiment, keeping the idea that it may do nothing to deter him to myself. Tonight, she's coming home with me, and I'm going to keep her at the ranch as long and often as possible. Still, I know she'll have to be away and out of my sight at some point. For starters, when she heads back to Austin.

Any time away from her is too long at this point. Having her out of my sight if Colt is on the loose sets me on edge.

CHAPTER 38

MACI

Falling asleep in Sutton's arms with him running his fingers through my hair and holding me tightly against his body was everything. Waking up still cocooned in his warmth is pure bliss. I don't think we've moved the entire night.

Curtained darkness blankets the room when my eyes flutter open. I have no idea what time it is. It doesn't matter. I'll stay here all day given the opportunity.

I suck in a giant breath of his leather and hay scent, basking in the peace of the moment. Undecided if I want to wake him or not, I press a tender kiss to his sternum. Something about the heat of his skin on my lips does things to me and wetness gathers between my legs. I press another kiss to Sutton's chest, this one longer with my lips parted. I ache to taste him.

Sutton sucks in a deep breath and stirs. "Morning, Firecracker," he mumbles into my hair. A delicious tingle snakes down my spine.

"Hi, Cowboy." Kiss. "Want to make it a good morning?" Kiss.

His lips press into my hair and his arms squeeze tighter. "It's always a good morning waking up with you in my arms."

To hide my heating cheeks, I tuck my face deeper into the soft sheets. My heartbeat has kicked up and those stupid butterflies are threatening to take flight.

"How are you feeling?" He shifts us in the bed so he can take in my face. My forehead is beginning to ache and I suspect there's a bruise.

"Mm. My head hurts a little." Sutton places a soft kiss on my forehead and begins to untangle himself from me. My protest comes out as a whine. "Where are you going?"

His low chuckle causes more wetness between my legs as he pads to the bathroom in boxer briefs. "I'm going to get you some Tylenol."

Groaning, I roll onto my stomach and place my chin on my folded hands, eyes trained on the doorway. "I hate for you to leave, but I love to watch you go," I call after him.

Another chuckle floats into the bedroom. "Yeah, you caused yourself some damage last night."

"Nope," I say, popping the P. He returns, holding out a glass of water and two pills.

My phone begins vibrating atop his dresser as I swallow them. With an annoyed grunt, I slide off the bed, finishing the rest of the water as I check the caller ID. *Stephanie.* "Well, this should help my headache." Next to me, Sutton's eyebrows raise.

Cringing, I swipe to accept the call and press the phone to my ear. "Yes?"

"Maci," she huffs. No doubt because of my less-than-appropriate greeting. "I'm planning to be in town Saturday to discuss Mother's house with Randi—"

"You mean Randi's house?" I begin searching through the clothes I left previously for something to wear. Normally, the annoyed tone Stephanie has adopted wouldn't bother me, but I'm emotionally tapped out from last night.

"If you'd let me finish. That's not why I called. If you will be in town, I'd like to have lunch."

I plop onto the bed. I can't remember the last time my mother and I had lunch together as an event. Our relationship was already so strained when I was in high school, it had to have been prior.

Sutton sits with his back resting on the headboard. Even in my peripheral, the intensity of his eyes isn't lost on me.

"Alone?" My voice betrays the kernel of hope buried deep within.

"Yes." I half expect her to tack on that Alan has an engagement which will prevent him from coming, as if her preference would be for him to be there, but she adds nothing else.

I slide my eyes to Sutton before pushing off the bed. "Yes, that will be fine." My voice is mechanical. "I had planned to be back in Austin, but I can extend my trip."

Following my conversation with Stephanie, Sutton and I take turns in the shower. He lets me go first and when I'm dressed in my mauve babydoll dress with hair blow dried, I come out to find a steaming mug of coffee waiting for me.

Warmth floods my system. He always knows just the right way to care for me. "Thank you."

He winks from his place against the woven headboard.

"I'm keeping you from work again."

"Not at all. I checked in earlier with Dad. Everyone seems fine so far. I'll get out there in a bit." He rises, running his hands down my arms. "I wanted to be with you when you woke up in case you had any complications with your head from being a badass last night." He grins.

I throw my head back and laugh. "Not exactly how I planned on showing off my skills."

His lips press tenderly against my hairline. "I hate that you had to defend yourself, but I'm glad you could."

For the second time this morning, my phone vibrates along the dresser. Upon inspection, it's an Austin number I don't have saved.

"Take that. I'm going to check in with Shane and jump in the shower."

Making a mental note to find out who the hell Shane is, I answer the phone.

"Hi, Maci? It's Jessica at the front office." A pleasant, professional voice greets me on the other side.

My brain stalls, trying to process how I should know a Jessica who seems to know me. *The front office?* "Oh! Hi, Jessica!" My voice comes out too loud when I realize it's the property manager at my apartment complex.

"I'm calling because we haven't received your notice to vacate or request for a lease renewal."

Shit. "I'm sorry. I've been in and out of town and I meant to stop by with the form for you."

"I know you've had a family emergency...So, that's why I'm calling. You're required to provide a 60-day notice to vacate. That's today. Or we can renew for twelve or eighteen months."

"Today?" I stand from the couch. "I'm not in town today."

"You don't have to be here to file. I can upload your preference to the Resident Portal."

Speech evades me. Since the first notice I received, I had planned to renew my lease. Standing here in Sutton's bedroom, I think of all the reasons that have trickled in, or become clearer lately, as to why I haven't completed the form.

My life is in Austin. Right? My business is there.

My friends' and family's subtle comments over the last few weeks run through my head. My business is easy enough to move. In fact, there's nothing saying I can't still schedule shoots in and around Austin while building clientele here.

What makes a life anyway? My friends and closest relatives are here.

A man I think I'm falling in love with is here.

Does he feel the same? Or has he been comfortable knowing I planned to be here short term?

When I don't answer right away, Jessica speaks again. "Which document would you like me to upload?" Her professional tone holds a bit of uncertainty herself.

"Um." My eyes are flying around the room. What do I want?

I want Sutton. I want more time with my friends. More time with my loved ones.

"I can give you until the 3rd. Sunday." Authority has taken over Jessica's voice. "I'll upload both documents. But I need one completed by Monday morning or we'll assume you intend to renew and prepare the lease for your signature. If you decide not to after that point, you'll be responsible for an additional month's rent."

"Thank you, Jessica," I say, finally finding my voice. "I'll make sure to have everything completed by Sunday. I appreciate your understanding."

"You bet. Have a good day, Maci." She doesn't wait for me to respond before hanging up.

I busy myself, folding and packing all of my belongings. The zipper of my duffle spears the room as Sutton steps back in with a towel wrapped around his waist and wet hair.

My breath catches.

I'm torn between wanting to jump him and confessing everything going on in my head.

With a composed face, he studies me. "Everything ok?"

"Yep."

His eyes narrow. I swallow. The bed separates us, but he steps forward anyway. "Was that your mom again?"

"Hmm? Oh, no. It was my apartment complex." Snatching the phone from the dresser at the end of the bed, I round the foot to tuck it into my purse which sits on the couch. Behind Sutton.

"Firecracker?" He knows.

I lean around him, shoving the phone in my bag before standing fully and facing him head-on. "Cowboy?" The usual coy tone that accompanies his nickname is gone. Instead it comes out unsteady.

He presses my chin between his thumb and forefinger and lifts my face, drawing my gaze up. His voice is tender. "Tell me what's going on."

How does he expect me to talk when he does things like that? "There's a form I need to fill out by this weekend. I forgot with everything going on."

A slight purse of his lips and narrowed eyes betray his suspicion, but he releases my chin.

"What did Shane say? And who is Shane?" I need to move on to another conversation for now.

He looks me over once more before turning and pulling a white tee from a drawer. "Shane is the sheriff." He pulls the shirt over his head.

It fits entirely too perfectly and my mouth begins to water. I press my thighs together. He catalogs my fidgeting legs with a smirk. "I was calling to check on the status of finding Colt."

Cold floods my system. "Oh."

His jaw tightens. "They haven't found him yet. I made sure they had the MC information to check in."

"Ok." The look he gives me says *ok* is not an acceptable response, that I should be more upset. "What's on your agenda today?"

"You keeping tabs on me, Firecracker?" His grin is edible.

I chew my lip. "It turns out I'm going to be in town a few more days."

Mischief gleams in his eyes and he takes a step back toward me, still clad in a towel and his white tee. I put a hand up quickly and he halts, his eyes widening and face going slack.

"If you plan to dress and get work done today, I suggest you not come any closer."

He snorts before a full-body laugh bursts from him. "Otherwise, what? You'll have your way with me, Firecracker?" Not heeding my warning, he comes close enough for his warmth to seep through my linen dress.

"I will."

"I'm not sure you're in a position to threaten me." Two fingers dance along my thigh near the hem of my dress and wickedness fills his eyes again.

That's all it takes for my body to light up and wetness to renew between my thighs. So I trace two fingers along his waist, above where the towel is tucked into itself. "It seems to me you're in a very precarious situation yourself."

I press up on my toes, leaning into him as if for a kiss. His head drops to meet me and his eyes darken. Just as our lips brush I whisper, "You're playing with fire, Cowboy, and I'm not sure if you're prepared for the fallout."

The hand playing with my dress presses firmly against my thigh and he crashes his mouth into mine. Threading my hands into his still-wet hair, our tongues battle and dance together.

"I have a thing for pyrotechnics," he says on a breath and kisses me again.

I flick my hand to his waist, tugging the fabric apart and dismissing his towel. "We'll see about that." I sink to my knees.

As far as cocks go, his is pretty and impressive. I don't think he wants to hear the first part and I'm not going to stroke his ego by telling him the second. Instead, I grip the base of his shaft in one hand and stroke him up and down twice. His erection pulses.

Fingers grip my hair and Sutton uses his hold to pull my head back, forcing me to look up at him. "What are you doing, Maci?"

Maci.

Wetting my lips with my tongue, I watch his chest rise and fall with deep breaths. "If you aren't familiar with this, then you're in for quite a show." I tighten my grip on his shaft and circle my tongue around the head of his cock, maintaining eye contact.

A groan rumbles out of his body, urging me on. His hand in my hair squeezes tight and the other comes to cup my cheeks. "You don't have to do this." His voice is strained.

Not releasing his eyes, I lick him from base to tip. Pure lust overtakes his features. "I want to." I don't give him a chance to respond before I take him into my mouth.

His hips jerk forward, shoving his cock deeper and I hum around him. "Fuck, you're going to be the death of me."

His thumb rubs my cheek as I continue to suck and lick. He lets me set the pace even as his grip in my hair tightens, gloriously painful at this point.

I'm on fire underneath his gaze, soaked from his attention and his pleasure. The room fills with sucking and quiet moans from me, heavy breaths, and occasional grunts from him.

Simultaneously, I open wider, taking him deeper, while slipping my free hand beneath my dress and plunging two fingers inside myself. His hips jerk again and a quiet grunt slips from his mouth.

"Are you playing with yourself?" His heated words shoot straight through me and I moan my response, full of him. He thrusts deeper. "I don't know what I'm enjoying more. Your perfect mouth that was fucking made for me, or the fact that you're enjoying my cock in your mouth so much that you wanna come."

His dirty talk is adding to the rising tide within me. I suck my cheeks in and release him with a resounding pop. Pupils so wide there's hardly any color left, his voice is deep and husky. "Let me taste."

I offer my hand to him from my position on my knees and he ducks his head, sucking my wet fingers into his mouth. Renewed wetness drips from me. I imagine my face mimics his own. Lustful, hungry.

"Fucking delicious," he says with a final suck.

"My turn." Without warning, I retake him in my mouth, sucking stronger and faster than before. His head drops back momentarily, groaning loudly. When he returns his eyes to me, I pull back to his tip, licking delicately around the head. "Let go, Cowboy."

Finally, *finally*, he pushes back into my mouth forcefully. I let him set the pace now, eager for every thrust and jerk of his hips as he claims my mouth.

"Fuck, Firecracker. You've ruined me."

I whimper around him and am rewarded with his release filling my throat. Neither of us breaks eye contact as I swallow every drop.

He helps me to stand before grasping my face with both hands and kissing me possessively.

His hands reach down to the hem of my dress and the tips of his fingers whisper along my thighs as he begins to lift. "Do you trust me?" he asks against my mouth and I can't help but grin against him and moan assent. "If you don't want this to continue, tell me now."

"Don't stop."

He leans back from me, peering deep into my eyes, and lifts my dress over my head slowly. The time it takes is excruciating, while the tickle against my skin as it lifts away is exquisite. All of my nerve receptors are at heightened awareness.

With eyes darkened like the sky before a Texas thunderstorm, Sutton studies my body. He grips my face in his hands, both possessive and gentle. "You're fucking gorgeous." His hot lips press against mine and I drink in his kiss before he pulls away to remove his fresh shirt.

One of his hands dips into my hair, grabbing the base of my neck, while the other slips around my back to unclasp my bra. The bra falls to the floor unceremoniously, but still his eyes roam over me. Power courses through my body at the hunger reflected there.

My nipples tighten and peak under his gaze. I'm about to step toward him when he reaches both hands down to slide off the scrap of fabric left over my aching core.

When we're both fully nude, Sutton takes one last look over my form before sitting back onto the couch and pulling me to straddle him. His thick erection presses against my pussy and I moan low and needy.

He draws me close enough to whisper into my ear. "I fucking love the sounds you make."

I rock against him in response. "I hope you plan on putting this to good use."

He chuckles against my ear, vibrations shoot through my chest and down to my pussy. "Oh, you wanna use me, huh?"

"Not any more than you want to use me."

He grips my shoulders and presses me back. "Not a single thing I have done or will do is about using you. But my cock is certainly not done with your greedy pussy today."

My eyes widen at his admission and I grin. This is what I've been waiting for.

With one hand on my hip, he reaches to a small table beside the couch, opening a drawer I never noticed before, and retrieving a condom. My eyebrow quirks. He sheathes himself quickly and I raise up for him to guide the tip of his cock to my entrance before he guides me down slowly.

Fully seated, I let out a half-moan, half-gasp at the sensation. I've never felt this full and didn't anticipate it could feel so fucking good. "Sutton." My head falls forward in amazement and we haven't even started.

He pulls me in for a deep kiss.

My hands on his chest soak in his warmth and steady me. I raise up until only the tip of his cock remains inside of me before sliding back down again. Sutton lets out a hiss and trails hot kisses down my neck toward my chest. His teeth sink into the sensitive skin as I repeat the action again.

"I never gave you that mark," he growls against me.

I move slower, sliding my hands up his neck and into his wild hair. It's hardly damp now. My skin lights up as he nips in a chaotic pattern, interspersed with kisses. One more stinging bite and I slam down hard onto his lap.

"Fuck. You want it, don't you? Always enticing me to lose control." His mouth hovers over my nipple as he finishes speaking, his dark eyes trained on me.

My words come out quietly. "Yes. You're always so chivalrous and charming. Let your wild side out. I can take it."

His hips thrust into me and a pleasured gasp breaks from my mouth. Without warning, he lifts us both off the couch, wrapping his arms around me and taking the few steps to the bed where he drops me onto it.

Anticipation floods me as he hovers over me. One hand rests next to my head while the other slides under my back. He grabs a handful of my hair and tugs hard, pulling my head back and exposing my neck. His hot tongue traces a line up the side to my ear where he whispers, "I hope you know what you're doing."

"Ravage me."

He bites onto my skin and I groan at the pressure. The hand next to my face moves between us, where he repositions himself and thrusts into me in one swift motion, forcing a loud moan from me. It's followed quickly by another deep thrust. "This what you want?"

My eyes fly to his. "Yes."

His movements increase and I wrap my arms around him, digging my nails into his shoulders. He leans his head forward, biting my breast deeply, right above the nipple.

His eyes return to mine. "You're not just going to bear one mark. Every piece of you is going to hold something of me." He kisses me hungrily before biting my bottom lip between his teeth. Not enough to draw blood, but enough for a delicious sting.

His mouth continues to roam over me, kissing and licking here and there, nipping occasionally, and biting down in equal parts pain and pleasure over my neck and breasts. I don't bruise easily, and despite the pleasurable pain he's creating, I know I won't be covered with visible marks. But the truth remains: everything will be different after this.

He draws back again, sitting on his heels and pulling me to straddle his lap. The thrusts deepen and become more insistent as my orgasm builds. I've never climaxed with penetration only and I'm surprised at the sensations that he's ripping from my body. I cling to him, wrapping my arms around him and tucking my head into his neck to return the biting and sucking.

Pleasure fills every piece of me and I whimper into his neck. He keeps one arm wrapped securely around me, the other cradling my head as he leans his head back to look in my eyes.

"Don't take your eyes off me. I want to watch you come apart completely."

I'm not sure if I can actually do what he's asking, but I nod vigorously anyway and grip him tighter.

"You were made to take me." His words tip me over the edge and my orgasm rips through me. I cry out his name as my body spasms around him.

A few thrusts later, he swallows my cries in a searing kiss, his own moans mingling with mine. His next kiss is softer, before our foreheads meet and we work to right our breathing. "You're stunning all the time, but watching you succumb to pleasure while I'm inside you is devastating. Nothing else will ever compare to that sight."

I don't know if I should tell him that was the best experience of my life.

His nose brushes against mine as he composes himself, eyes closed. "I want the fallout."

"What?" I smirk at him. When he opens his eyes, they're filled with something different. Something deep and powerful. My throat constricts.

"I think you're on the edge of a big decision. I feel it, even if you don't want to tell me everything. And that is entirely up to you." His heart is shining right through his eyes at me.

"Whatever you decide, I couldn't live with myself if I didn't tell you this. I want every part of you, Maci. The good, the bad, the ugly. I want to go to sleep with you every night and wake with you in my arms. I want to be the only one lucky enough to see you come apart in pleasure and to share mine with you alone."

"Sutton—" Tears blur my vision.

"You don't have to say anything." He kisses me tenderly. "And this isn't about what just happened. There are no words for that. Either way, you need to know that I'm all in. You're it for me."

CHAPTER 39

MACI

Ahead of lunch with Stephanie, my anxiety is through the roof. Our mother-daughter connection was damaged long ago. There has been so little attempt on her part, or desire on mine, to rectify the situation. It's hard to want a relationship with someone who insists all of your emotions are too big, too bold, too rash. As if emotion is unwarranted and I'm here to appease other people.

I can't imagine what we have to talk about. Certainly nothing that truly matters.

The air is finally beginning to cool, though it's not an overly crisp day. The wind gusts casually and the sun has stayed low, a large amber orb in the sky.

We never discussed where lunch would take place, but it will be a cold day in Hell before my mother is caught underdressed. I choose a green, long-sleeve smocked dress and knee high suede boots. It's a young, sophisticated look and dressier than usual for me, especially with my hair pinned up on one side, so she shouldn't have much to comment on.

I'm past the point of caring whether or not Stephanie has an opinion, but sometimes I pick my battles. Especially going in blind, like today.

She arrives with a flourish, sweeping through the door grandly and calling loudly for me despite my location in the living room. Something she would know if she'd take a beat to observe. "Maci Grace!"

Her stilettos tap on the entry floor. She looks lovely in her pink, organza blouse and sleek, black pants. "I'm right here, Stephanie." It's an effort to keep my tone pleasant, but an effort I make because I'd at least like to try and start on the right foot.

The deep sigh she expels tells me it doesn't work. "Let's get going. I'm meeting Randi here in two hours and I don't want to keep her waiting."

"Are we taking your car?" I slip my leather crossbody on and lock the door as I follow her onto the porch.

"Yes. I'm not driving around in your death trap."

She's not even trying.

"It's not a death trap. That model is one of the most dependable years, too."

"The point remains."

At the restaurant, a German establishment on the river, she requests a patio table. As soon as we're seated she begins her usual.

"I'm surprised you chose that dress."

The laminated menu snaps against the table as I set it down firmly and force a pleasant smile. I can't convince my eyes to soften yet. "You look lovely, Mother." Again, I choose the high road. My tone is genuine because the sentiment is.

Stephanie blinks. Her menu drops softly before her. Momentarily, she purses her lips in contemplation.

When she says nothing after a moment, I allow my gaze to wander, taking in the residents and tourists milling along the street. Though River Road is a main entrance to town, only a few locales have storefronts here. The majority of people are feeding ducks, against the warning of the posted signs, and walking, running, or biking along the riverfront trail.

"Alan wants to contest the will." Her voice is matter-of-fact, but it wouldn't make a difference how she said it, I'm not even a little surprised.

The server approaches with our drinks, offering to take our order. When she's gone again, I finally respond.

"I'm not surprised. All he's ever concerned with is status or assets." She pins me with a long, hard stare.

"I'm not going to do it."

My eyebrows jump. "I'm surprised you aren't moving forward with it, since Alan wants you to. But like you said while you were here for the funeral, you took what was sentimental to you. Your life isn't here."

"Your life isn't here, either." She folds her hands in her lap, minute movements jostling her arms. My gaze narrows. Have I always missed her fidgeting this frequently? Certainly not. She's always impeccably composed.

"You're right. I started building a life in Austin. But I'm young, it's a lot easier for me to move. Nothing is truly tying me there." Her eyes widen slowly. "My best friends are here. Liv is here, and I would love to have a stronger relationship with her."

I don't mention Sutton. Not because he doesn't matter, he matters more than I care to admit, but Stephanie will assume my entire choice is based on a man. I don't care if she thinks I'm foolish, but a part of me wants to protect Sutton because I love him.

I love him.

"Friends come and go."

"Not these friends."

A huff. She leans forward and places her hand atop mine. Ice flows into my veins. "This isn't the right place for you." Her eyes are insistent, still wide, and there's a level of anxiety in her voice.

What the hell is going on with her?

I place my other hand on top of hers and lean forward, holding her gaze purposefully. "I *wish* we had a relationship where I could come to you and you could advise me on my life. But that's not us. You don't ask about my work, you've never seen my apartment, you don't care to know my friends, and you've repressed anything emotional I've ever tried to share with you. You chose your husband over me time and again. Even when it was dangerous. Something you clearly knew.

"So please don't sit here and act like you care what I do. I wish you did. I always will. Because I *do not* understand what I could have ever done as a child for you to always find me so inferior. But I have come to terms with our relationship." My voice is barely a whisper when I finish. Tears line her lower lids, but she blinks them away. And I do not feel sorry for her. She drove us to this cliff.

Abruptly, she pulls back and places her hands back into her lap. Her stoic facade has returned.

"I've never found you inferior. I told you, everything I've done was to protect you. To provide stability for you."

I stare at her for a long moment. "So having emotions would put me in danger? Showing me love would make my life unstable?"

She shakes her head and looks up at the sky like I'm being ridiculous. "It's not that simple."

"Of course not." I don't know what the point of this lunch was. "So what now? Randi sells the house and you never have to come back? You're done raising me. Apparently I'm safe enough because you never reach out. You don't want to know me." My questions hang between us.

Stephanie swallows thickly. Her voice comes out quieter than I've ever heard. "I didn't know how hard it was going to be." Her eyes fall to the brick patio and I suspect she's trying to hide more tears forming. When she looks at me again, it's like she's finally looking *at* me. Seeing me. "You look just like your father. Every day was more unbearable."

My brows scrunch. "You...you don't like me because I look like my dad?" Pain radiates through me and my eyes burn.

"That's not what I'm saying." A tear rolls down her cheek. She's never cried in front of me and my eyes track the lone escapee down her face until it plummets into her lap. "I love you immensely. So much it hurts. Every day was a reminder of losing the life I had planned. But I had to be strong for us."

The server sets our food on the table and scurries off, knowing she's interrupting something.

"I don't like being in Bull Creek because it's too painful."

I return my gaze to the people along the river. I have nothing else to say.

A group of motorcycles turns onto River Road from Main Street. The leather cuts all stand out. Instinctively, I scan the riders for Colt, but don't find him.

Two riders lead the group, side by side. As they pass the restaurant, the one closest to us slides his gaze over the patio. James, the President.

As he did before, he does a double take, this one harder than the last. My brows furrow as he rides past. He wasn't looking at me.

When we return from lunch, having said little else, I say a cordial goodbye to Stephanie and retreat to my room.

I've thrown myself onto the plush bed, staring at the unmoving ceiling fan when a thought occurs to me. Swiping my phone from the bedside table, I send Randi a quick message.

Me:

> I know you're meeting with Stephanie. Let's talk before you make a decision.

Randi:

> Anything for my favorite niece.

A smile crosses my lips. I don't reiterate that I'm her only niece.

A short time later, she arrives, her sweet chatter filling the foyer, followed by my mother's clipped words.

Unsurprisingly, no more than half an hour passes before their voices fill the entry again. The front door snicks shut at the same time that I rush out.

Randi turns, prepared to see me judging by the smug look on her face. "Why were you hiding?" She opens her arms to me and I let her squeeze me tightly.

"I wasn't. We went to lunch and I had nothing left to say." My aunt holds me at arm's length, taking me in as I do her. Color has returned to her face, her eyes are no longer red-rimmed and puffy, and her hair is styled in beachy waves, all evidence of her healing. "You look good."

"Thank you, sweetheart. I love this dress." Momentarily, she drops her eyes to the dress, but when they return to my face, one eyebrow lifts. "What's going on?"

I frown. "Sorry?"

A mischievous smile takes over, scrunching her eyes at the corners. "Well, first, you feel different. Alive in a way you haven't in a long time. There's a spark." My cheeks heat, but I say nothing. "And secondly, you don't usually call meetings with me, especially where your mother is concerned."

Randi is the easy-going one, so it's easy to lose track of how much she takes in. I gesture to the couches with one arm. "Let's talk?"

Her loving smile renews my confidence.

When we're seated, she waits patiently for me to begin. At first, I'm not sure where to start. Are the house and Sutton two different scenarios? Did the possibility of one shift my view of the other? Would I have ended up here if one was missing?

Yes. Because Nana was the catalyst. Not the house for Sutton, or Sutton for the house.

Randi continues to study me quietly.

"Are you going to sell the house?" Given that I messaged her, her lack of surprise is anticipated.

She continues to study me openly. "I told you, I have fond memories here, but I have no need for this house." As suspected. "Are you going to buy the house?"

I shouldn't be surprised by her question. She's hinted at something like this. "Even with my business being steady, I'm not confident I could make a loan happen right now. My savings is tiny." I don't feel weak admitting my current situation to her. "I think this house has the potential to share its beauty and love with many more people, though. And I have some ideas on how to do that. If it's something you might be interested in."

"I'm listening."

"I want to be closer to you guys." For years, I've kept most of my emotions surface level, conditioned not to show them. It feels important to be open. My life is at a crossroads and I want to be active in it. Including taking risks for reward.

"We would love to see more of you. We miss you, too." She squeezes my knee where ours touch on the sofa.

I place my hand on top of hers. "I'd like to move here. Move my business here. There are so many special places on the property that would be perfect for photo shoots." Randi's head leans to one side. She knows there's more. "I don't need a house this big, though, and even if I could secure a loan, my business will need time to grow here. I think we should consider turning the house into a bed and breakfast." At last, I suck in a large breath and hold it, chewing my lip.

Randi has been focused on me, listening carefully. Now, she studies the floor absently and the wheels in her brain are turning. "Do you know what your mom asked me for?"

I shake my head. "We didn't discuss it. Only that Alan wants her to contest the will."

She nods. "She won't." A smile passes her lips. "She asked that if you decide to move back I keep an eye on you. Though, I got the impression she's really hoping you don't."

"She tried to persuade me against moving at lunch."

"Maci, if you want Nana's house, I'm happy to sign it over to you." She pauses, chewing her bottom lip. "I never would've kept the house from Steph if it wasn't Mom's wishes. I'm not surprised over the stipulation, given her feelings toward Alan, though. Anyway, it's a family house. Hopefully there's a way to maintain that."

"Liv already told me she's never wanted to live here, but I didn't tell her about business ideas. I'd love to share it with her if she wants. Thank you."

Randi leans forward and we wrap each other in a long hug. Something about the new plan for Nana's house is therapeutic. Knowing it won't be lost from our family or fall into disrepair. If anything, this house has so much more life coming into it.

"I'll let you know as soon as the documents are taken care of." She stands and together we walk to the front door. "You better be coming around a lot more often."

"Of course."

Randi pushes through the storm door, waving behind her. As she crests the top stair, a motorcycle rumbles down the street toward the driveway.

Randi slips into the driver's seat with another wave as the motorcycle pulls onto the drive and my heartbeat accelerates, expecting to see Colt. The man atop the bike isn't him, though.

It's James.

He parks near the base of the porch steps and slides off the bike. He doesn't have a helmet and somehow his hair is impeccably styled despite the wind. Vibrant, green eyes never leave mine as he makes his way up the steps, no cut in sight.

He doesn't seem hesitant and yet I still have no idea why he's here. The top button is open on his black dress shirt and a hint of ink and hair peek out. Even coupled with dark jeans and riding boots, he's far from the quintessential biker look.

The wood planks of the porch thud softly beneath my boots and I let the storm door close with a snap behind me.

"James." My greeting is formal. *Is he here for Colt?* My brows are growing sore with how tightly I've pulled them in and it's an effort to soften my expression. Nothing can be done about my heart.

287

"Maci." He remembers my name? "Is she here?" His green eyes flit over my shoulder to the open front door.

I cock my head. "My grandmother? She passed recently."

Returning his eyes to me, he swallows. "I'm sorry to hear that." His accent filters through again. "I was asking after your mother."

"Stephanie?" Now, I'm thoroughly confused.

"Aye." Irish then. He remains silent.

I blink. My heart hurts. Anticipation crashes through my body.

"She's not. She doesn't live here. In fact, you just missed her." I press my lips together before adding, "We had lunch together." I'm fishing. I know he saw us.

James rubs a hand over his mouth. "I can see now she hasn't told you."

What don't I know? Is Stephanie having an affair? I'm going to be sick. My throat is thick and my voice comes out hardly above a whisper. "Pardon?"

He takes a half-step forward. "Maci, I'm your father."

CHAPTER 40

MACI

For an undetermined amount of time, I don't respond to James. My brain is doing damage control and the best it can come up with right now is to keep me upright and breathing. Anything else is system overload.

James allows for a long silence to linger between us. Finally, he continues, softer than before. "So she didn't tell you then." His eyes soften. "I suspected as much at the bar."

"You knew then?" I finally find my voice.

"Aye."

"Can we—" I gesture to the porch swing, "—can we sit?"

He tips his chin in affirmation, reaching out subtly as I walk by. No doubt to catch me if I decide to take a tumble off the front of the porch. Thankfully, I don't. Despite my offer, James leans against the railing of the porch after I'm seated on the swing.

I study his face, taking in features which initially felt familiar, and realize it's because I saw a bit of me reflected in him. "I have your eyes."

"Aye, lass, you do." He looks proud for the first time. Coupled with his affectionate term, it causes the little girl of my childhood to peek out.

"I have so many questions." I twist my hands in my lap. Did he miss me? What's his side of the story? Does he know where Colt is?

Finally choosing a direction with my thoughts, I pin him with a look. "Did you hear what happened with Colt on Halloween?"

The proud look in his eyes deepens for a moment before it's replaced with the composed demeanor I recognize. "I do. He came by the clubhouse going on and on about you." The pleasing Irish lilt of his voice is more noticeable the more he speaks and I wonder if that's why he was quiet at the bar. "Had half a mind to re-break his nose for you, but you did a good job. The VP told him to scram before I had to step in. Took his cut. We don't take to that nonsense."

My mother's words about my father being dangerous resurface. "Have you been seeing Stephanie? Why did you come here?"

James crosses his ankles and locks both arms over his chest. "I have not seen your mother in over twenty years. Not since she stole you away in the night." My eyes widen. This isn't the story she's told. "Had half a mind to come looking for you both, but she left a note asking me to stay away. Said it was safer that way. She was right."

Softly rocking the porch swing, I listen as he continues. "She tell you we ran away to Vegas?" He grins at me.

My eyes bug and my mouth falls open in half awe and half humor, as I shake my head.

"Stephanie was wild and free. We dated for three weeks before we eloped to Vegas. Hid away in my house after and a few weeks later we found out you were on the way." He winks.

"That doesn't sound like my mother at all." Stephanie doesn't have a wild bone in her body. Randi's description of her resurfaces in my mind.

"Don't know much about her now, but she was then." He straightens and places both hands in his pockets, dropping his eyes to the floor. "We had three perfect years together. Then word came about my brother in Ireland." His green eyes look vacant for a few quiet moments.

"What happened?" Unable to sit still any longer, I stand and move to lean against the railing near James.

"Murdered." He blinks before meeting my eyes. "Like I said, your mam was right. My family has a dangerous history. Ties to the Irish mafia." There's no change in his tone to indicate this seems odd to him or that he's joking.

"Irish mafia?" My voice on the other hand is almost a screech.

A hint of amusement dances in his eyes, though I think it's directed at me and not at the topic of discussion. "Yes. Suffice it to say, there was concern after his murder that others would come for me. And my kin." He holds my stare, his green eyes full of seriousness. "So when Stephanie ran off in the night to protect you, it broke my heart, but it was the right thing to do. And though I'd never betray your whereabouts, it was better I didn't know."

"Have you been here the whole time?"

He dips his chin in affirmation. "Your mother kept a low profile and I tried not to interfere. She never sent cards or photos, and it killed me not to see you grow up." His eyes take in my face. "But I knew it was you when I saw you."

"Why didn't you say anything? Oh my God, does Colt know?"

"Most of the club doesn't know much of my history. Adds to the mystery." A devilish grin brings a youthfulness to his face. He's incredibly handsome and I can guess when he was younger he was heartbreaking. "I didn't tell you that night because it didn't seem like the right time."

"And today did?" My arms cross on their own. Never mind all the questions swirling in my head about if the rest of my family knew he was still around and never mentioned him to me. Or how we never ran into each other until now. There's so many years missed between us, and I know we won't get through it all in one conversation.

"Saw you both at lunch. I figured if there was a good time, it'd be now, when we could all clear the air." He says nothing else, letting his intention hang in the air. Letting me process. "I don't expect you to trust me. Especially if your mom has shared only the scary things."

"She didn't share much." I interrupt his follow-up. "Stephanie has never been forthcoming with me." My hands rub a non-existent chill from my crossed arms. "We aren't very close."

"No?" His full lips purse.

I smirk. "Enough family stories for one day."

For a time we're quiet. James surveys the land and I contemplate all I've heard. When he speaks again, it's an unasked question. "Colt said you don't live here."

"I didn't." I smile. "Looks like I'm going to be sticking around."

"The cowboy?" He eyes me carefully, like depending on my answer, he might have more to say.

"He's a rancher. I'm staying because I'm going to buy Nana's house, though. This house." I chew my lip for a moment.

His eyes twinkle. "Lovely woman. Think she liked me, too." He exhales a long breath. "Don't know what she thought once your mam ran off with you, though."

"She never said anything to me about you," I tell him honestly, taking him in again. "Maybe we can see each other again."

He smiles. "We can. You stop by the clubhouse whenever you want. It's out past Walnut Grove. There's a gravel road about three miles back on the right, easy to miss. Follow that to the end."

James shifts to go and so many things rush through my mind. "The police are still looking for Colt. Do you know how they can find him?"

He pauses and looks over my face, then shakes his head. "Not sure what he wanted from the club, but don't think it was brotherhood. He never got close with anyone."

His statement fits with what I observed the night at the bar. Colt only talked with Pete, but even that seemed sparse.

Having never done it before, I'm not sure how to say goodbye to a man who has just disclosed he's my father and has ties to the Irish mob. Silently, I watch as he heads down the porch stairs, before stopping at the bottom and turning to face me.

"Oh, and Gracie?"

His use of my middle name as a nickname causes my breath to catch. The best I can do is try to filter my emotions and listen to what he's about to say.

"For his sake, I do hope you picked better in the rancher than you did in the prospect. You probably got your fighting side from me, so it may not turn out well for him if you didn't." He winks and then climbs onto his bike and starts it up. Revving it once, he turns to go and I offer a small wave from the top of the steps.

This day keeps getting wilder and wilder. Did he just threaten Sutton?

Determined to shut down my brain for a while, I message Izzy and Leah with a plan to celebrate.

Me:

> **You two available to dress up Nana's backyard?**

Leah:

> **Fuck yeah!**

Izzy:

> **Anything for Nana.**

Me:

> **Meet me as soon as you can!**

I can't wait to tell my friends the news.

Knowing what's coming, I trade out my dress for jeans and a light sweater, securing my handgun into the hidden holster. After the events of Halloween, I won't be unprotected again.

Bouncing on the balls of my feet at the top of the porch stairs, I'm thankful when Izzy and Leah pull in at the same time, a few minutes later. Izzy's blue Nissan Armada goes next to my Jeep, and Leah's red Acura sedan falls in line after her.

Unable to contain myself any longer, I rush down the stairs, sweeping them both into my arms in a much-needed group hug. The three of us stand there squeezing each other happily, even if they have no idea why.

"Spill it," Leah says when we release each other.

My grin rivals the Cheshire Cat. "We're going shopping!" I'm burying the lead and they can tell.

"Why?" Izzy's hands go to her hips.

"Because I'm moving here!" Energy rushes from me and it's all I can do to refrain from jumping up and down. It's like making the decision to stay has lifted a giant weight from my chest.

Leah is squealing before Izzy has a chance to process. "So Margarita Mondays *are* going to be a thing?"

I laugh. "How about monthly?"

"Oh my God! We get to see you whenever we want?" Izzy wraps me in her arms again.

Closing my eyes, I relish the feel of her embrace. Weeks ago, touch was foreign to me. Something that caused overstimulation. And maybe in some ways, it always will. But right now, with my best friends, celebrating big changes in my life, I feel home.

"So what now?" Back is the analytical Izzy when she releases me.

"Now," I say, looking between them, "we dress up Nana's backyard. I want to celebrate. Later, I'll tell Sutton and see where he stands with things."

Izzy frowns.

Leah laughs. "What does that even mean? He's in love with you."

My heart skips a beat. Over the weeks, Sutton and I have started building something. I know I'm in love with him, and after his declaration yesterday I think we're on the same page. I'll feel better once we have an open conversation.

"We'll see."

My friends exchange a look.

"Well, let's go spend your money!" At Izzy's insistence, we pile into my Jeep and head to the only lawn and garden store in town.

Two hours and several hundred dollars later, the three of us return to Nana's with a firepit and a million boxes of string lights in tow.

Leah is giddy with excitement. "This is going to be gorgeous!"

Her energy is infectious as if I wasn't thrilled already. "I'm going to check Nana's garage for a ladder. Will you two start unloading?"

"You just don't want to help with the fire pit," Izzy jests. She flicks one eyebrow at me.

"You aren't entirely off base there." I laugh, heading in the opposite direction of the house.

With the ladder, we make our way around the vast yard, stringing Edison-style bulbs from tree to tree. For tonight, the rectangular fire pit is stationed in the middle of the yard. I already have a plan to situate it somewhere else with new chairs, once the transition for the bed and breakfast happens. We set out lawn chairs from Leah's that we picked up on the way back and call it done.

I'm not even sure if Sutton will be able to come by. So caught up in the emotions of the day and preparing everything for a celebration, I haven't reached out yet.

Sweaty and satisfied, the three of us hang our arms around each other's shoulders, taking in the made-over space. "This turned out really cute," Izzy admires.

"It's not the end goal, but it'll do for now."

"Of course, it's not." Leah shakes her head, playfully. "You're such a perfectionist."

"It's not even that," I argue. "I have a picture in mind."

"Ohhh, a *picture* in mind." Izzy snickers next to me.

"Both of you can shut up." Snaking my arms off their shoulders on either side of me, I twist quickly and start tickling them both instead. We become a wild tangle of arms and twisting bodies, laughing and sucking in air when we can before we crash to the ground together in a heap. Our laughter continues until our faces are tear-streaked and we can't breathe.

When our breathing has evened out, I squeeze their hands where they lie on either side of me. "Thank you for your help."

"No thanks necessary." Izzy squeezes back.

"Ride or die." Leah's voice is quiet and serious.

"What happened with your sister?" I look at Leah.

She sighs. "She's mad, but I can't have her and three kids in my one bedroom place."

"I'm sorry. I know it's hard."

"It's just Lily." She shrugs dismissively.

"Guess you need to see about a cowboy." Izzy sits up and brushes off her shirt. "Tell us all about it."

Heat rushes to my face. This is really happening. Giving each of my best friends one more tight hug, we say our goodbyes and they leave. When the yard is silent again, minus the occasional whisper of the wind, I pull out my phone and text Sutton.

Me:

> Hey, Cowboy. I know you're busy this week. If you can get away tonight, I'll be hanging out in the backyard at Nana's. Just come on back.

A few minutes goes by and no bubbles appear. I'm sure he's busy, so I pocket my phone and set to starting the fire.

I think the assumption is I'll be back at his place tonight since he's feeling protective again. Even if he can't get away, I want to enjoy this yard and the new things on the horizon for a bit.

CHAPTER 41

COLT

My fucking nose is throbbing when I wake up. I'm going to repay that bitch in kind.

It's late in the day. I've been sleeping them away since Maci went all GI Jane on my ass. She's lucky her dick squad showed up or I would've shown her what happens to chicks who want to fight like men.

I still intend to.

The last two days I've laid low. My supposed *brothers* who I could count on threw me out on the streets like I'm nothing.

I served this country. Took down a shit ton of extremists. I'm not nothing.

I rub at my temple trying to quiet my head.

I don't care if those pussies at the MC don't have my back. I'm going to show that princess she won't always get her way. I should've made it clearer before. That's not how life works.

CHAPTER 42

MACI

It's the perfect night for a fire. The air is chilling quickly and the breeze from earlier has picked up, forcing the smoke away.

With a mug of coffee and a blanket, I settle into one of the chairs we placed around the new structure. Aside from being pressed against Sutton in his bed, this is the most serene I've been since Nana passed.

Pride fills my chest as I take in the change that's already come to this beautiful space. I'm eager to share it with others. Mostly, I'd love to share it with Sutton, and I'd be lying if I said I'm not disappointed I haven't heard from him yet. I know deciding to run my business from here and pivot the purpose of Nana's house will breathe new life into the space. New life into me.

Despite not hearing its chime or feeling a vibration since Izzy and Leah left, I pull my phone from my back pocket and check the screen for notifications. Nothing.

I tell myself the worry I have is over the ranch and something happening to one of the animals. Sutton explained some of the risks when cows are delivering. Calves getting stuck, the uterus being delivered, and more. There are still several more who need to deliver over the weekend and into next week.

Truthfully though, I hope he's not rethinking his admission. It felt genuine and he shows his love well, so I work to curb my insecurity.

Unfortunately, he hurried out after his admission yesterday and both he and his dad were out late and up early, so we haven't had a chance to talk.

My phone falls into my blanketed lap and my mind drifts off to what else I'll change around the house, to distract myself. I'm excited to turn the loft area into a proper reading nook and explore the idea of the garage transforming into a photography studio.

An unidentified rumble in the distance catches my attention. It's far enough away that I can't decipher what it is, but that doesn't stop me from narrowing my gaze and looking through the fire to aid my brain.

Maybe thunder. I wouldn't know because I rarely, if ever, check the weather. Thunderstorms aren't really a November thing in Texas, but maybe.

Maybe a motorcycle. It did seem to move.

To slow my accelerated heart, I remind myself that plenty of people ride. It doesn't stop my brain from conjuring Colt's image.

The sound has ceased and I continue to stare through the fire toward the street on the other side of the house. The backyard has a gentle downward slope, so from here the street is elevated and, thanks to the many trees in the front and lack of street lamps, completely cast in shadow.

When a quiet minute passes, I release a long breath and chastise myself for panicking.

You're carrying, anyway.

One hand rubs gingerly across my stomach to confirm my gun is still in the hidden holster.

My phone ringing causes me to jump and I laugh at myself. *Sutton.*

"Hi, Cowboy." Excitement floods my chest.

"Hey, Firecracker." His warm voice is a balm to my soul. Comfort washes over me. "Still got time for a dirty rancher?"

"What kind of dirty are we talking?"

His chuckle warms other parts of my body. "I'm up for anything."

This time, I'm the one to chuckle. "Oh really?" He hums a response. "How far out are you?"

"Fifteen minutes." Sutton's response is met with crunching. I hold a breath. The two sounds don't make sense together.

Movement catches my eye in the fire and that's when several things become clear at once.

One. The crunching wasn't coming from Sutton's end of the line, but rather my gravel driveway.

Two. It was, in fact, a motorcycle previously.

Three. Colt is at my house.

Colt's eyes hold pure malice. Looking solid black in the night, he moves toward me, quick and confident. This isn't like Halloween. He isn't toying with me this time.

I jump up from my seat, inadvertently flinging my mug into the side of the fire pit and my chair in the distance behind me. My fingers hurt from the grip I place on the phone. "Sutton."

"Maci?" Thankfully, his use of my given name indicates that he understands we're no longer playing.

"Colt is here." I swallow hard.

"What the fuck? What does he—never mind." The truck revving echoes through the line. "I'm on my way—"

"There's no time for that." Colt is almost to the firepit and certainly within hearing range. "Sutton, I'm not letting him take me. No matter what." I hope he knows my intentions. "I love you."

I disconnect the call and stand.

"No one's here to help you, princess." Colt's tone is acidic. He stops moving a few feet on the side of the fire. The flames lick up the air between us.

I toss my phone onto my blanket at my feet. "I didn't need help last time. What makes you think I'll need help tonight?"

"You stupid bitch," he spits. "You have no idea what you're up against."

Colt flips open a knife in one hand. The handle has a black and white depiction of the American flag. Markings cover the blade, but from my position it's unclear what they are. "I should've killed you when I first had the chance." His voice is low, loosely masked by the crackling of the logs between us.

"You forgot the part when I broke your nose."

"Not Halloween." His expression has gone smug and he shakes his head the tiniest bit. "Ten years ago."

The blood in my veins turns to ice. My breathing stops and my lunch, however digested it may be, is threatening to come up. *There's no way.*

"What did you say?" As they pass my lips, the words are barely a whisper. He may not even hear them.

"Not so smug now, are you, princess?" The tip of his knife meets his thigh and he twists the handle, spinning the tip.

Even though I told Sutton I would do whatever it takes, the idea of actually shooting Colt was a smoke screen. Some part of me still hoped that he'd realize he's out of his element and tuck tail and leave again. Maybe in cuffs, but not in a body bag.

However, the way he's spinning the knife with a large serrated blade, tells me the only way out at this point is with one or both of us being injured.

"Colt, I have no idea what you hoped to achieve ten years ago and I don't know what you want now. But I need you to know I'm armed and I will shoot you if I have to."

His laugh is dark. Wide eyes and skin taut around his mouth, his expression is somewhat manic. "*What I hoped to achieve.*" His repetition of my words is mocking. "You were being a spoiled brat. Someone needed to show you that you don't get everything you want. Instead, you stole my dad away." The last part is the loudest, but it makes the least amount of sense.

"Stole your dad?" *What the hell is he talking about?* My eyes trace over the blades of grass surrounding my blanket and phone as I try to make sense of what he's saying. "James?"

I'm fairly confident that's not who he means, but nothing else is registering.

His eyes widen before a slimy grin takes over his face. "James is your dad?" He huffs a laugh. "Oh, that's rich. I should've seen that coming."

Now I'm even more confused. "If you're not talking about James, then who are you talking about?"

Taking a step to one side of the fire pit, something I suspect he's trying to camouflage, he inches closer to me. His gaze is lowered. Contrary to what he may believe, I'm not falling for his machinations. Countering, I lean my weight onto the opposite foot. Two can play this game.

"My dad. Alan."

Bile floods my stomach. "Alan is your dad?"

Disgust and horror roil inside me and I'm doing nothing to hide it.

I had sex with my step-brother.

That may be a trope in some taboo romance book, but it's not what I'm about. A new level of revulsion covers my skin and I want nothing more than to douse myself in bleach.

He laughs. "Yep. You're a little slut who fucked her step-brother." Pausing in movement, he adds, "If it makes you feel any better, I didn't know who you were until much later." His eyes gleam and he resumes his prowl around the pit. "But if I'd known, I would've gutted you in that alley instead."

Tipping his head to one side, as if considering further, he adds, "After I fucked you raw."

"Maybe if you had a blue pill in your pocket," I spit. Many would argue that I shouldn't be provoking him right now, but he makes it so hard to maintain my composure.

He pins me with a darkened look. "Care to test that theory?"

Side-stepping again, but not keeping as much space between us as I'd like, I slip my left hand under the hem of my shirt. It's further from him, as he approaches on my right, but I want to limit movement in hopes of getting my gun out before he lunges. "No, thanks. Been there, done that. Don't need the shirt."

With a clenched jaw, he continues moving. "My dad told me not to fuck with you, but I couldn't help myself." *Step.* "He was furious when your bitch of a mother ran home telling him all about the crazy person in the parking lot. Granted, she thought it was that stupid gambling ring, but nope. It was me." He smirks, proud of himself.

"To be fair," *step,* "he wasn't a great father even before your mom came around. Guess he thought I was a lost cause." A step and a shrug. "But you were enough to cause him to cut me off. After he chewed my ass that night, I never heard from him again."

I gape, still shuffling in the opposite direction. My fingers tease the handle of my gun, warmed from proximity to my skin. "I had no idea." Once again, I'm trying to piece together bits of information with what I lived, myself. It still seems off somehow.

"You had no idea that while you were playing happy family with my dad, my mom and I were living in a shitty ass trailer park?" He smirks in disbelief. "Yeah, his gambling ruined my life, too."

I shake my head, gripping the gun handle firmly. "No. It's not what you think. He didn't leave you for me. He hates me."

Colt pauses in motion and I wonder for a moment if I've gotten through to him. For a split second, something wars in his eyes, but it's gone as quick as it came.

"It doesn't matter now. You're still a stuck-up princess bitch." He's wielding the knife in wide, abstract circles. "I had hoped to have your cow-fucking rancher here to see me end you. Take him out after. He was so pissed after he saw your window." He grins proudly. "But my patience has run out."

I release the gun from the holster, holding it in front of me with one hand. "I warned you."

He smiles wickedly, shifting his weight side-to-side, but so far not moving forward any further.

"Do not come any closer."

"I hope you know how to use that thing, because if you don't kill me with the first shot, I'll make sure your death is slow and painful for my trouble."

"You'd be surprised what I can do with either of our weapons."

"Doubtful." His weight shifts forward and back this time. "Don't forget to take the safety off."

Then he lunges.

THANK YOU FOR READING!

Maci and Sutton are so incredibly dear to me, and I hope you loved the start to their story! If you're ready to jump back into the action, *When the Smoke Clears*, book two of The Fallout Duet, is available now!

If you enjoyed this book, would you consider taking a minute to post a review on your favorite site? A few words and a star rating go a long way!

Also by Amanda Marquardt

The Fallout Duet

When Sparks Fly

When the Smoke Clears

Bull Creek Series

A Penny For Your Thoughts

Book Two – Coming 2026

Falcons MC

Untamed – Coming 2026

ACKNOWLEDGEMENTS

This book would not be a reality if it weren't for some very special people. People whose talents and support allowed me to create my first novel and achieve a dream I wasn't sure would ever come true.

First and foremost, my family. My husband, who is always so incredibly supportive, even in all the ways I don't want to hear. My kids, who are so loving and understanding every time one more minute ends twenty minutes later. R, your excitement and belief kept this project going more than you'll ever know. Thank you for being my constant hype girl. My mom, who endlessly brainstormed with me on those tiny details that I was particular about but couldn't get on my own, while also being mostly in the dark on the actual plot!

My editor, Megan. I so appreciate your ability to give me the good, bad, and ugly. Your insight and delivery are invaluable. These characters are greater for having you in their corner, and I am better for having you in mine.

My cover designer, KBG Designs. You took my ramble of messages and thoughts and turned them into a beautiful cover. Then you did it all over again with swag. Thank you for dealing with my inability to make a decision! I'm not sure if I could put into words the ways in which you helped me to grow. Working with you was a gift.

My beta team! Tabitha, Elise, and Stacey, your feedback was so helpful in fine-tuning what I was trying to achieve in this book. You were able to identify those little things that I couldn't place my finger on that needed working out. Thank you for dedicating your love and attention to this story. It's so much better because of you.

To all the readers, thank you for taking a chance on a debut author! I truly hope you enjoyed the ride. I'm so excited to continue on this journey with you.

ABOUT THE AUTHOR

Amanda Marquardt is a native Texan, wife, and mother of four. She considers herself a chaos coordinator, taking on more tasks than she can manage and setting nearly impossible deadlines for herself. Her days consist of lots of caffeine, sometimes equal amounts of wine, and minimal sleep. When not homeschooling or writing, she can be found spending time with her family or reading.

To stay updated on upcoming releases and access exclusive content, visit amandamarquardt.beehiiv.com or subscribe to Amanda's newsletter.